INSPECTOR CHEN AND THE PRIVATE KITCHEN MURDER

INSPECTOR CHEN AND THE PRIVATE KITCHEN MURDER

Qiu Xiaolong

**SEVERN
HOUSE**

First world edition published in Great Britain and the USA in 2021
by Severn House, an imprint of Canongate Books Ltd,
14 High Street, Edinburgh EH1 1TE.

Trade paperback edition first published in Great Britain and the USA in 2022
by Severn House, an imprint of Canongate Books Ltd.

severnhouse.com

British Library Cataloguing-in-Publication Data
A CIP catalogue record for this title is available from the British Library.

ISBN-13: 978-0-7278-5071-3 (cased)
ISBN-13: 978-1-78029-816-0 (trade paper)
ISBN-13: 978-1-4483-0554-4 (e-book)

All Severn House titles are printed on acid-free paper.

Typeset by Palimpsest Book Production Ltd.,
Falkirk, Stirlingshire, Scotland.
Printed and bound in Great Britain by
TJ Books, Padstow, Cornwall.

To Xiaohui, whose friendship encourages Inspector Chen to go on during the increasingly difficult days in China.

DAY ONE

Chen Cao, the ex-chief inspector of the Shanghai Police Bureau, now the director of the Shanghai Judicial System Reform Office – though currently on 'convalescent leave' – woke with a start.

It was just one of the weird dreams he had been having of late. He had found himself in a magnificent imperial court with gigantic dragon-embossed pillars, but the people groveling in front of the glittering throne were dressed in contemporary style – mostly in suits or Mao jackets rather than any ancient costumes. Unsure about the identity of the one perching majestically on the throne, he was debating with himself whether to kneel down like the others when, all of a sudden, a golden dragon tore itself violently from a vermilion-painted pillar, spitting fire, soaring over the court in the midst of the screaming and stampeding people. With the entire palace shaking, the dragon shot straight up through the roof—

Breaking into a cold sweat, Chen tried to reassure himself that it was simply a nightmare, but an elusive feeling of unease lingered on in spite of himself.

Yet why should he care anymore?

'*You do not hope to turn again . . .*' Chen murmured a half-forgotten line, yawning with the knowledge that there was nothing urgent for him to do, and glancing up at the lazy sunlight streaming in through the checked curtains, which cast dubious shadows at the beginning of another day.

For once he was in no hurry to get up. On the contrary, he was supposed to stay relaxed in the dramatically changed circumstances.

Nominally he was the director of the new office, though it was a position of no real power after he had been removed from the police bureau and put on convalescent leave. A role specially designed for a Party cadre regarded by the higher authorities as unfit for the position, yet whom it was unwise to fire right away. After a leave of uncertain length, however, it could be a different story and he would sink into oblivion.

With the term 'convalescent leave' an unmistakable signal that something was politically wrong with the ex-inspector, speculation spread online like uncontrollable wild weeds, in spite of the frantic governmental Internet control.

According to one blog post, it was not necessarily without a silver lining, however, since the term might also be read as an indication that 'Chief Inspector Chen was not yet totally finished, not without the possibility of staging a comeback in the changed circumstances'.

Turning in his bed, Chen thought he knew better. He reached for his cellphone on the nightstand. Sure enough, there was a short online article from *Wenhui Daily* about the Chinese writers meeting with the French writers' delegation in the Shanghai Writers' Association. Among the Chinese names, Chen's appeared as well as his new title, with 'convalescent leave' added in brackets. Underneath the news, several netizens had simply copied the phrase 'convalescent leave' along with a variety of emojis such as 'grimace' or 'rage'. One had actually chosen that of 'burial', showing a white-faced clown vigorously digging a grave, as in a Shakespearian play.

Chen had ruffled feathers in one of his recent anti-corruption investigations, so his 'burial' was seen as only a matter of time. The news about his appearance on an irrelevant occasion was, more likely than not, nothing but a reassuring gesture to the people who still wanted him to stay on as one of the few good, honest cops.

He took a pack of cigarettes out of the drawer – *Red Generation*, another of the 'Red' products suddenly popular again in China – but he put it back without lighting one.

The change in China's political landscape could not have appeared more ominous. One of the 'Red princes' was now sitting on the throne, and Chen's investigations had involved some other related Red princes. Those investigations, while hailed as 'our great, glorious Party's determination to fight corruption at whatever level' in the official media, could not but have been seen as acceptable to those in power.

Politics aside, a short leave might not be too bad an idea

for him. He needed a break, having worked for years under the unrelenting stress of so many 'special cases'. He was becoming easily tired, constantly highly strung, and restless.

Rather than get up for a cup of coffee, he decided to stay in his bed.

His hand reached out to the nightstand again. This time he picked up a copy of a Judge Dee novel in English. It might be just as well for him to read throughout a day like this. With his head propped against a couple of pillows, he started reading in leisure – truly like one on leave.

The novel had been given to him by a French writer named Bertrand at the meeting mentioned in the *Wenhui Daily*. In the conference room of the Shanghai Writers' Association, Bertrand had said to him with a grin, 'I finished reading it on the plane. An excellent book. I'm leaving it to you, Chief Inspector Chen. You may be a better reader for the Judge Dee novel, what with your knowledge of classical Tang dynasty poetry and your expertise in police investigation in China.'

Chen thanked him profusely, took over the book, and said in earnest, 'In my college years, one of my roommates discovered the series by Van Gulik and raved about it for weeks, yet without ever lending me a copy. Thanks to you, I'm going to read it.'

'Judge Dee is so popular among Western readers. Quite a number of French writers have been writing and rewriting the Judge Dee stories. But this is an original one by Van Gulik. *Poets and Murder*. Let me know what you think of it – the opinions of an ace inspector in the city of Shanghai, a modernist poet, and a Judge Dee of the twenty-first century.'

'Come on. I'm no judge nor . . .' He did not finish the sentence by saying the word 'inspector', which he was not anymore; but he was not yet used to *not* being an inspector, either. And he saw no point elaborating on the complicated Chinese politics to a visiting French writer.

In the morning light, Chen immediately noted something intriguing in the title of the book: the *Poets*, plural – so more than one involved in a Tang murder case?

The Tang dynasty, the peak of classical Chinese poetry, had produced a number of outstanding poets, but surely not that many poet murderers.

So how come a Chinese poetry-loving sinologist like Gulik would have chosen to write a murder investigation set among the Tang dynasty poets?

Leafing through the pages, he found several poets in the novel, among them a young, beautiful poetess who appeared to be a likely suspect in a bizarre murder case.

If she alone had been involved, then why the plural *Poets*? There seemed to be two or three cases going on in parallel, along with a mysterious fox spirit prowling in the background. How could all of them have been related to one another?

Resisting the temptation to fast-forward to the story's ending, he began to read from the beginning in earnest.

The opening of the novel proved to be far more riveting than he had expected. It was surprisingly relevant to him for at least three reasons: it was about poets, it was about murders, and it was about a legendary Chinese investigator in the Tang dynasty. Although regarding the last aspect, the ex-chief inspector was not that sure.

So why not spend the day in bed, reading all the way to the last page of the mystery?

Before Chen could make too much headway with the book, a phone call came in. It was Detective Yu, his long-time partner in the bureau. With Chen assigned to the job in the new office, Yu was serving as acting head of the 'special case squad', in which the two had worked closely together for years.

'What's up, Yu?'

'My father called me asking for your special cellphone number, but he would not tell me why.'

It was like an alarm clock beginning to ring in the back of his mind. The retired cop nicknamed Old Hunter must have called for a reason, which he did not even want to reveal to his son, not merely a long-time partner in the police bureau, but a good friend of Chen's. The request for his special phone number sounded anything but reassuring.

'Well, Old Hunter must be up to one of his tricks, sounding

mysterious like a Suzhou opera. Don't worry about that. How are things in the bureau, Yu?'

'Nothing special. Party Secretary Li has asked about you several times, but it's just like a skunk greeting a rooster, we both know what he's really after. Why should I tell him anything about you? In fact, I haven't seen you for days.'

'I'm doing fine, you know.'

'So you're going to work in your new office soon?'

'Well, it's not up to the doctor to say whether I'm well enough for the job, but up to the Party authorities, ultimately, to tell the doctor what he is supposed to tell me.'

'I'll be damned.'

'It's a leave I need anyway. At least I have time to do some good reading in leisure. And I like it.'

Putting down the phone, Chen picked up the book again.

He was beginning to feel a bit curious about Judge Dee for a different reason.

As far as he knew, Dee in real life was not exactly a judge, nor an inspector. In his long official career, Dee might have worked as a judge on occasions, showing his extraordinary talents in ruling over difficult cases. But first and foremost, Dee was a successful politician. At one time he was as high ranked as the prime minister, playing a pivotal role in the complicated politics of the Tang dynasty.

The little Chen knew of Dee's official career came from his translation of the Tang dynasty poetry, during his research into this period of history, thus coming across the name of Dee Renjie in the background. Dee was highly thought of as a capable, honest official at a critical moment when the ambitious Empress Wu was seeking to turn the Tang dynasty of the Li family into the Zhou dynasty of the Wu family. A realistic Confucianist, Dee managed to serve under her, knowing better than to rise in futile rebellion, but at the same time trying his best to keep the line of the Li family unbroken. His perseverance led to the eventual restoration of the Tang dynasty under the Lis, which happened shortly after Dee's death.

With his limited historical knowledge, however, the

ex-inspector knew he was not in a position to tell what Dee really was.

For that matter, Chen was barely in a position to tell what he really was himself?

He made an effort to pull himself out of self-pity and went on with the reading.

Then he became fascinated not just by the legendary Tang figure, or the double or triple murders under Dee's investigation in the novel. There was something else pleasantly surprising. In those crime novels he had read, no main characters ever wrote poems, not even Inspector Adam Dalgliesh in the series penned by P.D. James, who portrays Dalgliesh as a published poet without ever producing a single line throughout the series.

Not so with this Judge Dee novel. Some of the poems in it struck Chen as authentic. It was not unimaginable for a renowned sinologist like Gulik, with all the background research he must have done for the book.

It did not take long for Chen to come across a poem seemingly so familiar to him, though he failed to recollect any clue as to its authorship.

> *Bitterly I search for right words*
> *for this poem, written under my lamp,*
> *I cannot sleep the long night,*
> *fearing the lonely coverlets.*
> *In the garden,*
> *in the soft rustling of the autumn leaves.*
> *The moon shines forlornly*
> *through the gauze window panes.*

Nor was he sure whether the lines quoted in the murder story comprised the entire poem. The question turned into an annoying puzzle for Chen, like an insistent fly buzzing around his ears.

Shaking his head, he resumed his reading, but he was not meant to read on any longer that morning.

His special cellphone rang. It was a new, silver-colored one, with a chip purchased just a week earlier, and its number known only to three or four people he trusted. He picked it up in haste.

'Long time no see, Chief Inspector Chen. How about having a cup of Dragon Well tea with me?'

It was Old Hunter, a retired cop turned part-time private investigator. It was probably a well-meant invitation from the old man who had learned about his trouble.

'That will be great, Old Hunter. Where?'

'Let's go to People's Park. You remember the "birds' corner", don't you? Not far from it there's another one called the "matching corner". People have different names for it. "Love corner", "mating corner" or "marriage-arranging corner". Just to name a few I can think of. Whatever the names, the corner is listed as one of the must-see hot spots in the latest Shanghai tourist guidebook. Of course, I'm not interested in it for myself. But you have heard of my daughter's problem, haven't you? She is in her late thirties, a single mother, staying with us in the back room of the old *shikumen* house. I want to take a look at the corner for her, and you may give me some suggestions there. Indeed, like the blue ocean having turned into the green mulberry field, the world has changed too much for an old, old-fashioned man like me.'

True to his other nickname of Suzhou Opera Singer, Old Hunter could keep gushing on and on, rambling with continuous digressions and quoting proverbs and fables like a chef generously adding peppers. Chen listened with a touch of amusement. He had heard about this matching corner and about the problems of Old Hunter's daughter, too. After her divorce, the old man had had no objection to her moving back in with her little boy, but what worried him was her wallowing in self-pity all day long in the dark, damp back room, instead of trying to turn over a new leaf for herself.

But was Old Hunter really that anxious to find someone in the park for her? Or for the ex-inspector too, who remained a bachelor? The old man had talked to him about it a couple of times before. Holding the phone, Chen knew that his plan to lie in bed reading for the day was finished.

'We'll take a good walk in the park,' Old Hunter was going on, 'and a cup of excellent tea afterwards. Guess what? I know the owner of a hot water house on Xinchang Road, just across Nanjing Road. I'll bring in the genuine Dragon Well tea with me. The place also serves earthen oven cakes, salty and sweet, still hand-baked in a traditional way.'

'I'll be there, Old Hunter, in about half an hour.'

'Great. It's close to the number five entrance of the park, you know.'

Getting up, Chen put a bookmark reluctantly among the pages of *Poets and Murder*.

Old Hunter was waiting for Chen in front of the park, standing by the side entrance close to the ex-Shanghai Library, which had become something similar to an exhibition center for the ever-changing city.

Still, Chen registered something recognizable about the ex-library, despite the dramatic changes in the area. On top of the umber-colored building, the black hands of the big clock kept moving in an undisturbed circle, with its beginning invariably coming to its ending, like a metaphor he had read in his college days.

On that early May morning, Old Hunter appeared to be over-dressed for the occasion, wearing a black blazer of light material, khaki pants, black loafers, and holding a bright red umbrella in his right hand.

It was a fine, cloudless day, but it seemed to be understandable, Chen reflected, for an old man in his brand-new clothes to carry an umbrella.

'Well, you'll soon learn the true reason for such a bright-colored umbrella,' Old Hunter said with a mysterious smile, much like a Suzhou opera singer about to reveal an astonishing secret in an exciting drama.

Once they entered the park, they turned immediately right to a tree-shaded trail with green-painted benches scattered at intervals. The park, though smaller thanks to the nearby skyscrapers and subway stations continuously encroaching on its original size, appeared to be touching an equivocal cord in Chen's memory.

Old Hunter raised his hand, pointing to a sizable crowd at a turn in the trail. Most of the people gathering there were old, gray- or white-haired, sitting on stools or squatting, talking loudly to one another like in a morning food market.

Chen noticed something else. Almost every one of them had an umbrella set out in front of them, unfolded on the ground. It made an amazing scene, eerily reminiscent of colorful mushrooms popping up in the sunlight after a spring drizzle.

'You see,' Old Hunter said, moving closer to one of the umbrellas. 'The umbrellas function like stands, with information sheets scotch-taped to them along with the color pictures of young men or women. So detailed and vivid, their parents are therefore capable of matching them for all sorts of arrangements.'

'And umbrellas can be handy for a rainy day too, I see,' Chen said, nodding. 'A clever idea indeed! So the practice at the corner is just like a first step in the tradition of arranged marriage in ancient China, isn't it?'

'For those steps in ancient China, you should have listened to more Suzhou opera, through which you will learn all the details about the routine practice of professional match-makers in the old days, such as the consultation of the fortune teller by examining the Chinese horoscope and the birth date for matching of the young people in question,' Old Hunter said with greater gusto. 'For the matching corner here, the arrangements are done by the parents, and based on nothing but commercial or materialistic considerations and calculations in today's society.'

'Yes, totally materialistic. It's some progress for China in the twenty-first century!'

'Tremendous progress, you may say,' Old Hunter said, shaking his head like an angry rattle drum. 'But you have to be realistic. In the present-day China, how can young people afford to be romantic without an apartment under their own name? A medium-sized one near the park is worth seven or eight million yuan. For an ordinary couple, that amount means more than they could possibly make by working hard all their lives without spending a single penny.

'The housing market is soaring out of control like crazy, but few are worried about the enormous bubble, thanks to the wonderful myth that the Party authorities can always keep the bubble from bursting, so everything is all right with China.

'Take a close look,' Old Hunter went on, leaning down to the information sheet posted on a yellow umbrella before an elderly woman.

> *Attractive, tall, slender in her early thirties, and looking younger for her age. Never married. Good job in the state-run bank with excellent pay – more than ten thousand per month along with numerous benefits. The shikumen unit she stays in with her parents is already under her name, and under the government planning for demolishing . . .*

That meant she was eventually entitled to the unit, Chen supposed, which could be worth more in the event of its being pulled down in accordance with the city planning, as people living there would then be able to claim sizable compensation.

Bemused, he moved over to a purple umbrella next to the yellow one.

> *New apartment in Luwan District along with a car spot in front of the building. All the mortgage paid. With another wing room for rent in Huangpu District . . .*

'That beats me, Old Hunter. How come a car spot is listed here?'

'Your luxurious apartment with a garage spot was state-assigned to you before the beginning of China's housing reform. At the time, you did not pay a single penny for it, did you? And certainly not for the garage spot. That's why our Party officials are supposed to be loyal to the Party – in return for all the benefits. But it's just human nature for them to want more. Hence all the corruption cases under our one-Party system,' Old Hunter said, almost in one breath. 'Back to the garage spot for your apartment – it's a matter of course for a Party official like you, whether you need it or not. You have a bureau car and a designated driver anyway. But for the ordinary people, a designated car spot can make all the difference. Otherwise, you may have to drive around for hours without finding a parking place. Guess how much for a car spot?'

'How much?'

'Two hundred thousand yuan. For the young people listed in the matching corner, they lose their social status without a car spot and a car.'

'That's absurd. The air quality is getting so horrible with more and more cars in the city.'

'Who cares? Incidentally, you may also see how much the second income at the agency means to me. For my poor daughter, she has not even a spot for her bike in the common courtyard of our *shikumen* house. Nothing whatsoever worth showing off for her in the matching corner here.'

'I'm on leave, you know, but I may be able to speak to some people about a job—'

Chen cut himself short, choosing not to elaborate further. A number of his connections were beginning to avoid him, he recalled, since the news of his being on convalescent leave had come out.

'Your situation is totally different, Chief. You don't have to worry about things on the info sheet on an umbrella. A three-bedroom apartment for yourself at the upper end of the city. Not to mention your Party cadre rank with numerous perks. And a real celebrity as the published poet to boot.'

'Come on, Old Hunter. You are looking for someone for your daughter, not for me. I'm here today only as a consultant for you.'

'Have a piece, sir,' a woman in her mid- or late-fifties stood up and handed a sheet over the umbrella to Chen. 'Take a good look at the picture, and you may call me any time at the number listed. Absolutely a beauty, my daughter, only twenty-two, and so sweet too. All she needs is to have a good, successful man like you with a large apartment. And a bureau car too under your disposal, right?'

Chen took the info sheet without answering the question. She must have overheard his talk with Old Hunter. He cast a glance at the color picture above the description: a sweet girl with almond-shaped eyes and cherry lips, smiling up at him like in a dream.

'It's too noisy. We can hardly talk,' Old Hunter said. 'Let's move to the bench over there.'

It would make a natural scene, Chen observed, the two of them discussing the information gathered at the matching corner. After all, the visit to the corner might have functioned like a prelude in a Suzhou opera, which would then lead to what Old Hunter had not yet disclosed.

But Chen was uncomfortable at the idea of sitting there with those colorful umbrellas incessantly twirling in view. He looked up to see something like an antique bamboo tea pavilion at the end of the park trail.

'Let's have a cup of tea there, Old Hunter. Years ago, I used to go to Bund Park for my English studies, but for a change, occasionally to this park too, sitting on a bench possibly just in that area. But I don't think there was a tea pavilion standing there at the time.'

'That's fine with me, wherever you prefer, our nostalgic chief inspector. We can go to the hot water house next time.'

For the time of the day, the business at the tea pavilion appeared practically non-existent. It was too expensive for the old, and too old-fashioned for the young. Nor was it a traditional teahouse; in addition to tea, it also sold soft drinks, coffee and a variety of snacks.

They turned out to be the only customers, sitting at a bamboo table outside, yet close enough to the pavilion window where they were able to have hot water added easily.

The tea waiter brought out a teapot along with several small dishes of sugar-covered yang berries, roasted peanuts and fried sunflower seeds, and placed all of them on the table before withdrawing into the pavilion without further ado.

'The tea is not too bad,' Old Hunter said wistfully, taking a sip from the dainty cup. 'Alas, if only I could come here every morning with my birds, sipping at the tea, humming a Suzhou opera tune, carefree just like other retirees.'

'Yes, after three sips at the tea,' Chen said with a knowing smile, mimicking the old man's way of talking, 'it's time to come down to business, just like in one of your favorite old proverbs. But retirees or not, who can afford to be really carefree in today's society?'

'Exactly, like in another old proverb, people don't go to the temple without having to pray for some special favor from the Buddha image. And I have to talk to you, Chief, about a proposal made by my boss Zhangzhang.'

'Sure, it's something to talk about over the tea.'

'I was told about your taking sick leave from that new office of yours. It was a young secretary named Jin who picked up my phone call, but she hummed and hawed about what's wrong with you. You're fine, aren't you?'

'Well, it's up to the people above to tell the doctor to say whether I'm fine or not, but it's an enjoyable break for me, I have to admit that.'

'But you're not a man who would enjoy such a leave, that much I know.' Old Hunter was spitting out a much-chewed tea leaf. 'So how about joining our agency? As a special consultant, as Zhangzhang has just discussed with me this morning. You may keep the position at that new office of yours, whether still on convalescent leave or not.'

Chen was taken aback by the retired cop's suggestion, but he saw where it was coming from. One of the questions he had to answer for himself, however, was how long such a leave would last, and for that matter, how much worse his trouble could turn out to be?

Besides, it could give his enemies another handle in the event of his being caught moonlighting for the agency. Not to mention the fact that private investigation was not officially allowed in 'the socialism with China's characteristics', with it practicable only in a sort of gray area.

'Remember the consultant job you gave me at the Traffic Control Office years ago, Chief? I mentioned it to Zhangzhang, and he thought it's a good idea for you to serve as an honorary consultant for our agency – with a six-figure pay annually. For a man of your caliber and connections, it's nothing. But you don't have to come to our agency regularly. No more than four or five times a year. And we'll talk just like today, drinking tea in a park or listening to Suzhou opera at a teahouse.'

'What a generous offer! Your agency must have been expanding and making a huge profit.'

'We started by catching those cheating husbands and making not much, you know that. But then we had some more lucrative cases, doing what some of our Big Buck clients do not want police to do. Of course, we make risk control management our top priority, and you don't have to worry about it.'

'But I cannot get paid for doing nothing – simply drinking tea or enjoying Suzhou opera in the name of a special consultant. You have to tell me what I am supposed to do.'

'Well, as a matter of fact, there's something you may be able to help us with at this moment. Not as an active investigator, of course, but believe it or not, your name has been brought up by our client, a mysterious man named Sima. In fact, he could have come to us with you in mind.'

'That's strange.'

'It's a long story,' Old Hunter said, clearing his throat. 'To begin with, as an experienced gourmet, you must have heard about those most expensive dining places in the city.'

'I know a thing or two about those expensive restaurants, but I don't know exactly what you're talking about.'

'The most expensive one in the city today is not a restaurant. Rather, it's something called a "private kitchen".'

'That's more and more interesting! Go on and tell me about it.'

Chen was not unfamiliar with the trend of the so-called private kitchen dining, but he was amused at the ironic reversal of roles between the two men. Old Hunter was anything but a gourmet, and it was fun to have him deliver a culinary lecture in a Suzhou opera fashion.

'You know what? The real art of cooking is the last thing people care about in the restaurant business today. First and foremost for them, the profit. For instance, the chickens marked as free-range, natural-food-fed could be just a joke of imagination. Likewise, the shrimp not fresh, the fish long dead, the meat frozen for months, the vegetables rotten, you can go on and on. So imagine the quality there. But for a private family dinner, the host doesn't have a fixed menu, nor an expense spreadsheet to calculate for profit. That's why the private kitchen came into fashion for the wealthy.'

'Yes, I've heard something about private kitchens or "private recipes", but they're like other restaurants in the end. They still have to open for business seven days a week, so there's nothing that private except for the self-claimed private recipes.'

'But this one is truly different. It's in a private *shikumen* house. Residential, not for business, with dinner served only for selective guests, once a week, at a traditional round table for no more than eight people, and the menu depending on the food supply of the day. People have to make a reservation long beforehand. What's more, they have to prove their qualifications.'

'What qualifications?'

'Wealth, social status, and so on. The minimum expense per person is at least ten thousand yuan, sometimes much more. The chef as well as the host there is a young woman named Min Lihua. A courtesan, or a *mingyuan* – a recently rediscovered word for a celebrated courtesan in the high society before 1949 – since our official newspaper today will not admit the existence of courtesans in the socialism with China's characteristics.' Old Hunter resumed, stroking his chin energetically after taking another gulp of tea, 'Not too long ago, I went to an *ernai* – second concubine – café for one of your investigations, you remember? Min is different. She is not kept by a man. Still single, but with a number of rich and powerful men dancing around her. They spend money like water in her company. At first, she just entertained those really close to her, but the word about her private kitchen dinner spread around, making it increasingly difficult to book, even at such an exorbitant price. And an invitation to the dinner meant people gained a lot of face, almost like an acknowledgment of their social status.'

Chen nodded without making an immediate response, thinking he had heard about the new trend, but of late, his own trouble left him with little mood for such a private kitchen dinner, let alone one of dubious reputation.

'According to our client Sima, Min is not just a consummate

chef, but a knockout with incredibly charming grace and sophistication. She's from a "good family" in the Republican period before 1949, with her great-grandfather being a scholar/ official and a culinary connoisseur, and her grandfather being a wealthy banker, both of them spared no cost to develop the Min specials at the dinner table. She is said to have inherited the family recipes. That's how she got the Internet nickname, Republican Lady.'

'The nickname does not sound politically correct,' Chen said reflectively. 'Ours is "People's Republic of China" under the Communist Party after 1949, not "Republic of China" under the Nationalist or Kuomintang. The "Republican" seems to refer to the pre-1949 period exclusively.'

'As Sima has told us, the nickname was given to Min online because of someone named Lin Weiyin. A beautiful, talented poetess who shone in the Republican period. No one like her has emerged since the Communist Party took power—'

'Lin Weiyin. Yes, she's a gifted poetess who hosted a renowned literature salon with an elite circle of men competing for her attention. But she did not cook – or, at least, she wasn't known for her culinary skill.' Chen decided to change the subject before digressing too far. 'But what about Min's trouble?'

'She's in custody for a murder case after a private dinner party last Friday.'

'A murder case!'

'As private investigators, we make a point of keeping away from a case already under official investigation. As you know, some of those cases could have conclusions reached for political reasons even before the beginning of the investigations. We know better than to get ourselves into trouble. But Sima turned out to be one with numerous connections, as he assured us, and the retaining fee he offered was too high for our agency to say a downright no to.'

'How much?'

'Two hundred thousand to start with and another two hundred thousand at the end of the job. Plus all the expenses covered.'

'Unbelievable. But what does Sima want you to do for such an amount?'

'To prove she is innocent and get her out as quick as possible.' Old Hunter paused theatrically again. 'But there're some odd things about the case. Min is celebrated, but she's not involved in politics, and for that matter she's not even a Party member. But she's *shuangguied* like a corrupt Party official in an undisclosed location.'

Literally, *shuanggui* meant detention at a specific location and for a specific duration. It was not part of officially established legal procedure, but was supposedly justified in that, for some high-ranking Party officials, once out of custody after the detention time limit, they could destroy evidence and conspire with their accomplices. In reality, *shuanggui* was adopted mainly for damage control, through which the authorities made sure that any dirty details of corruption scandals would not come out; by the end of *shuanggui*, it would be a matter of course for those involved to plead guilty to the pre-written script, leaving the Party's great, glorious image untarnished.

'That's weird,' Chen said, tapping first one finger, then two, on the table. 'What else have you learned about the case, in addition to the information from your client?'

'With Min locked up in an unknown location, there's no way for us to contact her. I've talked to Yu, but he has hardly heard anything about it in the bureau. The case did not come under the special case squad, but under Detective Xiong of the homicide squad. And then Internal Security took over.'

'Internal Security took over a murder investigation!'

'Astonishing, isn't it? I don't know any details yet. There's one possibility Sima discussed with us. Her trouble may come – partially at least – from her nickname of Republican Lady. Her popularity on social media spooked some orthodox Party officials, who saw it as an endorsement of the Republican era values at the expense of the value system today.'

'Hold on, Old Hunter. How old is she?'

'In her early thirties. But she grew up listening to those family stories of hers, about dinners and parties and cultivations and decorum in the Republican period.'

'In that very *shikumen* house?'

'Her family was driven out of it during the Cultural

Revolution, but several years ago, she managed to get the house back. And she made herself known with the online posts and blogs and pictures about the gracefulness of the Republican era. In short, her punishment could be seen as a public denouncement of the Republican myth. Politically—'

'I see, but even so, *shuanggui*—' Chen cut himself short again.

Several elderly people were walking over, dragging their feet toward the tea pavilion, carrying folded umbrellas in their hands, and worn-out smiles on their faces. Having done their daily work at the matching corner, they were casting curious glances in the direction of the two men.

Chen and Old Hunter kept on drinking their tea, cracking the sunflower seeds, which broke the silence.

'Now go on with the murder case itself,' Chen said, after the elderly people moved out of sight.

'We're getting there, Chief. Her dinner parties, originally a means to entertain her guests, then became something like an end in themselves. A profitable business, it brought her extra income and extra connections, too. No way could she have afforded not to continue, but she found it hard to manage all the preparation and cooking by herself.

'For a dinner in the *shikumen* house, with no less than twelve courses, most of which had to be served fresh and hot, the chef-hostess really had a hectic time, stir-frying the first special in the kitchen, rushing out to serve it at the table, saying a few polite words to the guests, explaining the beauty of the delicacy, before hurrying back into the kitchen for the next course. For an ordinary family dinner, that would prob-ably be no big deal. A self-centered husband might go so far as to take pride in his wife's toiling and moiling around like that. But not so with Min. She's the one and only hostess – and the chef, too.

'Besides, some of the guests at her table came not just for the culinary delights. An online article about her dinner was titled "She Is So Delicious, She Could Be Devoured". It's a paraphrased quote from Confucius. And it's understandable that the men were not too pleased with her being constantly away from the table.

'So she hired people for help. One of them was named Qing, a clever, fast-learning apprentice, who was soon able to cook in a fashion like her. It gave Min a much-needed break. She did not have to run to the kitchen and back so many times during a meal. Unexpectedly, trouble came.'

'That sounds like an exciting Suzhou opera, Old Hunter. So it's finally coming to a climax?'

'Yes, after such a dinner party about a week ago, the Friday of the week before last, having had a cup too much, Min retreated to her bedroom earlier than usual, so the guests had to leave. Qing stayed on to take care of things in the kitchen. The next morning, Qing was found killed in the kitchen, the back of her head fractured with a heavy object. Min claimed that she had slept like a log throughout the night. As the one and only possible suspect – with no sign of forced entry to the *shikumen* house, and with a plausible motive as Min was said to be very upset with Qing for quitting for another job – she was put into custody.'

'Just because of a maid quitting?'

'It's unbelievable, and that's why Sima wants us to check into it. He does not believe she would have committed the crime because of it.'

'So your rich and romantic client offered you almost half a million yuan for the job.'

'The autopsy has excluded the possibility of Qing having stumbled and hit her head on something. It could not have been an accident.'

'Has Sima offered you any different scenario about the case? Something he happened to have known.'

'No. He has not. In fact, I don't think Sima is his real name either. But we have promised to keep his background info confidential – except that he is one with connections high up. As for her background info, I've gathered something for you in a folder.'

'What would happen to her,' Chen said, without taking the folder, 'without your looking into the case?'

'When she's out of *shuanggui*, there'll be an open trial with a judge – Judge Liu Xiaohua – already assigned to the case. Most likely with a foregone verdict. "You just need to think about her celebrity status as a Republican Lady in today's politics" – that's one thing Sima said to us. And there are wild stories and speculations about the case on the Internet. Some are describing the murder case as a setup. Some are digging into her relations with the wealthy and powerful. Some are even pointing their fingers at the assignment of the judge, who is said to have been on the waiting list of her dinner parties for a long time, yet without success, and who would consequently revenge himself—'

'Did your client give any specific instructions for the job?' Chen had to cut the Suzhou opera singer short again. Some details he could check online himself.

'With no alibi for her, and with her locked up in an unknown location, there's little we could possibly do for her.' Old Hunter paused again, draining the tea. 'It was then that Sima mentioned you as the trump card.'

'How?'

'Sima said that you could help. Apparently, he has done his homework about you, saying that with Detective Yu as your longtime partner, it makes sense for you to talk over a cup of tea with me.'

That was shrewd of Sima. With Chen on leave, it might not be a good idea to drag the ex-inspector into the investigation in the open, but it was a different story for him to have a cup of tea with Old Hunter.

'But what the convalescent leave means, you know only too well, Old Hunter. I may be watched. Any misstep on my part could easily get you into trouble too. In your phone call, you talked about the matching corner without saying anything about the case. It's because you knew my phone could have been tapped, isn't it?'

'It won't hurt to be cautious, but you don't have to do anything in the open, Chief. You can be a special consultant to us without it being known to others. As for Min's case, it would not raise any alarm for you to have an occasional talk with a chatty retiree like me – at the matching corner in the park, or at a teahouse.'

'You really have everything figured out,' he said, thinking he owed the old man too much to say a downright no. 'But let me say this again. Given my own trouble, I'm not supposed to put my finger into any investigation, nor to serve as a consultant to your agency. That should be understandable to your boss Zhangzhang, and to your mysterious client, too.'

'I know, Chief, but it's so—'

'Having said that, I don't see any harm for us to occasionally have tea together.'

'Right, we will have our tea, genuine Dragon Well tea. I've made a point of going to a small village not far from Hangzhou, where I have a trusted old tea farmer friend. No fake teas.' Old Hunter then added in a loud voice, breaking into a broad smile as he once again pushed the folder over to Chen, 'Take a look into it. All the possibilities for you in the matching corner.'

'Not for your daughter, but for me, you scheming old man,' Chen also said in a raised voice, at the sight of several more people moving in their direction.

But it might have been true. As Old Hunter had mentioned a couple of times, it was the order of the day for the ex-inspector to settle down, particularly with his having nothing else better to do for the moment.

'Well, it may be the time for me to settle down. I'll take a good look at the pictures. Call me if you have anything new, Old Hunter.'

'I will. And we'll have good tea next time. I'll contact the tea farmer tonight. I met him thirty years ago—'

'You've told me about it,' Chen said in haste, being too familiar with the other's digression.

A lone yellow-feathered bird came flying overhead, flashing its wings through the suddenly glaring light.

Back in his apartment, the first thing Chen did was to open the folder Old Hunter had handed him in the park.

As suspected, it had nothing to do with the possibilities at the matching corner, but with the Min case discussed at the tea pavilion. The ex-inspector did not think he had explicitly promised to help, but it would not hurt for him to take a look – with a cup of tea afterward, or not.

A bright color picture fell out of the folder. A young woman of striking beauty in a custom-tailored white damask mandarin dress was looking up at him, smiling, reclining against the mahogany headboard in a *shikumen* house, with her bare legs and feet reaching out of the dress. He leaned over to pick it up when a vague image – a different woman in a red mandarin dress lying on a thin layer of dust that covered the floor of another *shikumen* house – flashed through his memory.

The folder contained several other pictures of Min, and he was particularly impressed with one of her in a sleeveless red phoenix-embroidered mandarin dress, serving a willow-patterned platter to her guests at a red-painted round table. The picture was used in an online article, with a line underneath: '*Nothing is harder than to pay back the favor from a beauty.*' The line, possibly from a half-forgotten Chinese poem, made a clever quote in the context.

Then he moved on to a description of the crime scene, which was penned by Old Hunter and read more like a detailed case report. He got a lot of kicks out of beginning a tale from the very beginning, like an impossible Suzhou opera addict.

'The murder happened Friday night the week before last. But to have a full picture of the case, we have to tell it from the beginning . . .'

Chen made a cup of strong black coffee without any sugar. He added a small spoonful of non-dairy cream lest it would upset his stomach, before he resumed reading in earnest.

Min came from one of the most prominent families in the late Qing dynasty, and quite prominent during the Republican era too until 1949. The tide of luck then turned in China. During the Cultural Revolution, her family was driven out of their *shikumen* house in the former French concession. Seven or eight years ago, however, Min managed to get the house back in accordance with the new government policy, but the feat was commonly attributed to her 'personal connections'. After having purchased apartments elsewhere for her parents, she lived by herself in the *shikumen* house, sporting an extravagant lifestyle characteristic of the Republican era. With her celebrated beauty and established status, she attracted the rich and powerful like moths to a flame.

Whatever the interpretations about her success, she became

an Internet icon. An embodiment of the values of the Republican era, she was versed in the zither, *go* chess, calligraphy and painting, in addition to her legendary culinary talents. What with pictures and stories about her continuously popping up online, and with her own posts about those so-called private recipes, the specials on her dining table held the whole city spell-bound.

The popularity of her private kitchen dinners necessitated her hiring Qing, a maid or 'kitchen assistant' from Sichuan Province. In addition to the *shikumen* house, Min still had the *tingzhijian* room in another old house in the lane. Apparently, it was a practical arrangement for Qing to work for Min in the *shikumen* house during the day, and go back to the *tingzhijian* room for the night.

On a day with a dinner scheduled, Min would send Qing to the food market early in the morning with a shopping list, and then Min herself would prepare the food without sharing any details of her recipes. In the not-too-large kitchen, Qing turned out to be a quick learner, glancing over Min's shoulder to the sizzling wok, and learning a trick or two with or without Min's knowledge.

So it did not take long for Qing to assume a more pronounced role in the kitchen, with Min only needing to visit it a couple of times during a dinner, adding the secret ingredients at the crucial moments. Her guests were naturally pleased with the change as they got to see more of Min. That Friday night, Qing helped not only in the kitchen, but also saw the guests off later with Min already gone to bed feeling unwell. Qing was supposed to be the last one to leave the *shikumen* house.

In addition to Qing, Min employed another part-time helper named Feng for the household chores. With her own family in Yangpu District, Feng came over just two or three times a week. As a rule, for those days after late dinner parties, she was the one preparing breakfast for Min in the morning.

On that Saturday morning, Feng arrived shortly after nine. She knew that the party the previous day could have lasted late into the night, so she let herself in quietly with the key to the front door, moved light-footedly across the courtyard, then upstairs to Min's bedroom. From the bedroom door, which was slightly ajar, she thought she heard Min snoring lightly in bed.

Feng made her way down to the kitchen, where she was surprised to see a chair knocked over in the corner. It was unusual, but perhaps not too unusual after a wild party. Stepping over, she was startled at the sight of a body – that of Qing lying on the kitchen floor, close to the marble counter. She leaned down to touch Qing's hand, which felt cold, stiff – no pulse. A tiny streak of blood had already dried at the corner of Qing's mouth.

She turned, stumbled, and shot upstairs, screaming for help all the way up. Through the opening of the bedroom door, she caught a glimpse of Min scrambling up, naked, and pulling on a white silk robe in a hurry.

The two of them ran down to the kitchen. According to Feng, Min looked absolutely horrified, with a dazed look in her eyes. Pulling herself together with a visible effort, Min lost no time calling for the police, and she also instructed that nothing at the scene should be touched before their arrival.

The police team led by Detective Xiong arrived. They examined the scene, took pictures, and got the testimonies from the two women. After the body was sent to the mortuary in another car, they left about two hours later.

In the crime scene report submitted by Detective Xiong – which Old Hunter had acquired through the help of Detective Yu – it stated that there was no sign of forced entry through the front or back doors of the *shikumen* house. No sign of breaking in through any of the windows, either. As a traditional *shikumen* house, an advanced double spring lock had been installed on the door above the original wooden latch still kept there for the sake of decoration, and that morning, Feng turned the door key twice before she got in, so she was positive about it being properly locked up.

Apart from the upturned chair in the kitchen, nothing Detective Xiong could find at the scene seemed to suggest any violent struggle there. No apparent bruises were visible on Qing's body, either.

The cause of death was later concluded as a brain hemorrhage, with the skull fractured by a heavy object. The time of death was estimated to be shortly after twelve.

Min's testimony was longer, but with no relevant details. She had drunk too much the night before, she claimed, so she was helped into the bedroom. There she sank into stoned sleep. She had no idea how and when the guests left. Unaware of any disturbance during the night, she slept on until Feng came screaming up from downstairs.

'That's about all for the moment.' Old Hunter had added a line in red pencil. 'I'll keep you posted.'

Putting down the report, Chen stood up to pace about for several minutes before he turned to make a phone call to Lu, an old friend of his once nicknamed Overseas Chinese Lu, who was now a Big Buck in the city of Shanghai with more than a dozen restaurants under his name. In spite of his success in business, Lu remained a friend of Chen's, like in their middle school days.

'Now I'm not that busy, Lu, I may have more time to come and enjoy the wonderful borscht in your Moscow Suburb.'

'So you are finally thinking of me, my old partner. That's really the spirit. For all the restaurants under my name, you have half of the shares, you know that. So come any time.' Lu insisted on calling Chen his partner because of a loan from Chen at the beginning of his restaurant business. 'Time really flies. Those days, your generous help came like a cart of charcoal in the snow.'

'Come on. I happened to have just received the advance for the translation of a crime novel. Don't bring that up again.'

'But you're no longer a cop, and on convalescent leave too, it's time for you to join me. Whichever restaurant you choose to run, you'll do a great job, what with your extraordinary gastronomic taste, your fame, your business acumen, and your connections.'

'Here you go again, Lu. I'm no partner of yours. I know nothing about the restaurant business. Besides, I'm too old-fashioned. Nowadays fashionable people are talking about private kitchen dinners.'

'What are you talking about?'

'I've just read several blog posts about a private kitchen run by a lady named Min, nicknamed Republican Lady, in a *shikumen* house.'

'Oh, that Republican Lady. She won't have an impact on our business. Few could have afforded hers,' Lu said with a chuckle. 'But you only call me, I'm afraid, when you start doing some investigation. What do you want to know?'

'I'm not doing any investigation, but she's an interesting character, and it's an intriguing new trend. Tell me what you know about her. And about the people who attend her private kitchen dinners as well.'

'Well, I think I've heard something—'

But a call was coming into Chen's phone. It showed Old Hunter's number.

'I've got an urgent call,' he spoke to Lu. 'Can I talk to you later, Lu?'

'No problem.'

He picked up the call from Old Hunter. 'What's up?'

'Sima has just contacted us again. He was so excited that we had tea today. He's offered to cover all the expenses – for cafés or teahouses or restaurants or whatever you like. Special allowance of up to ten thousand yuan per day.'

'Wow, your agency has hit the jackpot. Tea or coffee aside, I've been reading the folder about the possibilities of the matching corner.'

'Not too much in it, I know,' Old Hunter said, 'so another report is on the way to your place. Special delivery by Little Cha, a part-time assistant at our agency. A very reliable young man, but of course you don't have to say anything to him.'

In less than fifteen minutes, Chen had a large envelope delivered to his home by Little Cha, a tallish young man of very few words, who left almost immediately.

Inside the envelope was a briefing on the latest development of the investigation. Again, it could have been gathered with the help of Detective Yu, who was on friendly terms with Detective Xiong of the homicide squad in the bureau.

After the initial visit to the crime scene at the *shikumen* house, Detective Xiong had followed it by re-interviewing

Feng at her home in Yangpu District. Among other things, Feng was positive that she saw Min sleeping naked – alone – in the bedroom that morning. She did not know much about how upset Min had been about Qing quitting the job, but Qing had only mentioned her plan the day before the dinner party. So it could have come at annoyingly short notice to Min.

The same evening, Xiong interviewed Min again and questioned her about what he had just learned from Feng. Min failed to explain why she was sleeping naked that morning – with nothing but silk panties pulled down to her ankles. There was a lot she had not remembered about that night, being too drunk, but there had been no one with her that night, she was adamant. It was possible that after she had vomited and fallen asleep, Qing had helped to remove her clothing, she reasoned with Detective Xiong.

But it did not appear that likely to Xiong. Removing her shoes made sense, but it was not an easy job to peel off a curve-hugging mandarin dress from an unresponsive body. Besides, what was the point in pulling down her panties?

As for Qing's quitting, Min said she had not been pleased with the short notice, but that was no big deal. She could have easily secured another kitchen helper.

Detective Xiong then interviewed over the phone some of the dinner party guests. According to them, the private dinner was not the usual weekly arrangement, but one made for a special reason, though they seemed not to be too clear about it.

There was nothing strange or suspicious about the arrangement – except for one small thing which occurred during the dinner.

Halfway through it, Min called out Qing from the kitchen in order to make a toast to her, with the announcement of Qing's plan to quit for a more promising future in another household. It seemed to be a toast made on the spur of the moment. Kong Jie, the chief editor of *Wenhui Daily*, one of the regular guests at the dining table, happened to have mentioned Qing's progress in culinary skills under the guidance of Min, when Min stood up and dragged Qing out of the kitchen.

'A phoenix chooses a higher tree branch to perch, it's totally understandable,' Min said, with a cup raised high, 'so as to soar up for thousands and thousands of miles against the skies of unlimited possibilities.'

Min's sarcastic toast made no secret of her frustration, to which neither Qing nor the guests knew how to properly respond.

With Qing hurrying back into the kitchen, Min drained two or three cups in a row. That was quite unlike her usual self, a polished and sophisticated Republican Lady.

Soon she was drunk, hardly capable of sitting still at the table. And she had to be helped by Qing and Zheng, one of the guests, into her bedroom.

The guests were all nonplussed. They were aware that Qing had been doing more and more in the kitchen, but none of them believed Qing's leaving could have turned out to be such a big deal. After all, with most of the cooking done under Min's specific instruction and supervision, she could easily find another assistant for the private kitchen dinner.

Perhaps it was like an old Chinese fable: once the tiger student has learned from the cat master about how to jump, the former will try to be independent. Min must have taken it hard, an act of unforgivable betrayal on Qing's part. And Kong's compliment about Qing's cooking skills sent Min over the edge.

Whatever the interpretations, the guests had to leave with the dinner unfinished. It was just about eleven.

Kong, Peng and Shang all stated that they left together. Qing saw them out on behalf of her mistress. As Kong was waiting out on the curb for his car, he saw Zheng come out too, after having helped Min into the bedroom. Zheng waved at him, heading to the garage of the Pacific Shopping Mall across the next street, and then Kong's *Wenhui* car came.

In other words, those guests practically provided an alibi for one another. They were all out of the *shikumen* house around eleven to eleven fifteen that night, several minutes earlier or later.

With no sign of forced entry, and with only Min and Qing there afterward, the murder could have been committed only by someone inside, or with the key to the *shikumen* house. According to Min, only three people – Qing, Feng and she herself – had the key, no one else.

But Feng had played Mahjong at home that night until around one, with three Mahjong mates confirming her alibi. There was no way for her to have come to the *shikumen* house around twelve.

So Min alone appeared as a possible suspect, and not one without a motive. She could have been so upset with Qing that unimaginable things had happened in an uncontrollable rage.

In the bureau, Detective Xiong made a rudimentary report to Party Secretary Li, who reiterated that people above were concerned by the case. Given Min's celebrity status, it would only be a matter of time before the news spread around, which would not be helpful to the 'positive energy' of the society. Detective Xiong and his team had to go all out for a speedy conclusion.

Detective Xiong then went to interview Feng for the third time. This time, Feng revealed something else not mentioned before. About the possible relationship between Min and Mr Rong, a once regular guest at her dining table. A successful businessman, and a 'diamond bachelor' to boot, Rong had spared no money to gain her attention, but Feng had overheard Min calling him a 'country bumpkin', which must have hurt him badly. Anyway, one early morning three or four weeks ago, as Feng came into the lane, she happened to see Rong sneaking out of Qing's *tingzhijian* room. She suspected a possible rendezvous between the two, especially after she learned that Qing was going to work for Rong.

But why should Rong have chosen the maid rather than the master? It was understandable for him to give up the hopeless effort of going after Min, but what was the point of bringing Qing into the picture?

For a sense of revenge, possibly.

Qing was not exactly a beauty, but young, with a slim, youthful figure, eager to serve Rong at the table, and in bed too. To Rong, she could have appeared more than a clever and cute girl in the kitchen.

To Min, Rong had initially been a country bumpkin who paid to sit at her dinner table, but it would have been a totally different story once he chose Qing over her. That would have thrown Min into a murderous fury. The double betrayal on Qing's part provided Min with a motive to kill.

If so, her getting drunk in front of the other guests at the dinner table that night could have been a smokescreen.

So Detective Xiong wanted to put her into custody lest she turned to her high-up connections to attempt obstruction of the investigation. He had another talk with Party Secretary Li, who agreed that they ought to move quickly, and that he himself would talk to some people in the city government first.

And then an unexpected turn occurred. After the phone call made by Li to the city government, Detective Xiong was told that Internal Security was taking over the investigation, and putting Min into an undisclosed place, pretty much like in a *shuanggui* case for a Party official.

According to Party Secretary Li, the intervention of Internal Security came for the very reason they had discussed. They had to cut Min off from her connections.

'Besides, an open investigation will not be in the Party's interests. We have to take into consideration things she may spill out to journalists and netizens. In desperation, she's capable of babbling irresponsibly and dragging others down with her. And Internal Security is more experienced in dealing with such a sensitive situation. If Min proves to be innocent, the secret investigation of her would have caused her less harm.'

It was just like Party Secretary Li, capable of justifying any political maneuvering. *Shuanggui* was done for damage control, Detective Xiong knew. It made sense for Internal Security to take over.

But the news of her being put in secret custody started leaking out online, along with a lot of wild speculations and theories, particularly about Min being punished as a Republican Lady who challenged the value system of the socialism with China's characteristics.

Chen put down the latest report from Old Hunter, underlining the part about the *shuanggui*, and about the noise on the

Internet. It was natural for netizens to see it as a setup to suppress the Republican era values as represented by Min. And as if to add fuel to fire, one of the Party newspapers had come out with an editorial the day before, declaring that the values embodied by Min were nothing but a myth with an ulterior motive, and that people should keep themselves alert about the insidious ideological erosion.

Heaving a sigh, he started re-reading the section about the dinner that night. Min's toast to Qing was conceivably an attempt to embarrass her. Min had an evident grudge against the maid. But was that enough for her to commit murder? Feng's scenario about Qing's possible relationship with Rong failed to add up.

Chen pulled out one cigarette from another pack, yet without lighting it. He had to cut down his nicotine intake, though he felt his energy ebbing helplessly. He had skipped breakfast, having nothing but the tea with Old Hunter in the park.

With no mood to make a meal for himself, he decided to order food for delivery, which had become so fashionable in the city. Young people practically ordered everything by tapping on their cellphones.

Checking in his 'ordinary' phone, he found the number of a ramshackle yet popular eatery just around the corner. The place was known for its two inexpensive yet savory specials: fried cabbage rice and fried mini soup buns. He remembered the nickname of the owner and chef as Big Zhou. There was usually a long line of customers waiting outside.

For that day, Chen did not want to wait outside for an hour for the fried soup buns.

'Big Zhou, this is Chen Cao, your old customer. Remember me?'

'Of course I do, Chief Inspector Chen.'

'Can you do me a favor and have two portions of fried soup buns delivered to me?'

'No problem. It's an honor for us to have you as our old customer,' Big Zhou said with a sizzling sound from the large flat pan in the back. 'I'll have it specially delivered to you. Guaranteed with the buns fresh and hot from the pan, and the soup inside ready to burst out.'

'Fantastic! Thank you so much.'

'Yours is in that high-ranking Party cadre building, I remember, but which apartment number?'

'It's 3C.'

'Great. But with so many customers inside our place right now, you may have to wait for about an hour.'

'That's fine. The fried soup buns are so popular, I know. Of course the customers waiting at the restaurant have to be served first. It's no problem for me.'

Putting down the phone, he found a text message in his special phone: 'Check your email.' It was Old Hunter again, who was moving so fast.

He opened the mail. It was a list of the people who'd attended the dinner party that Friday night. Old Hunter had lost no time doing his homework, though he had not approached any of them yet. After all, those at Min's dinner table were not that easily approachable. The list included the names of the attendees with basic biographical info about each of them.

Huang Zhongluo, a semi-retired Big Buck, 'Shanghai number-one antique collector' with several galleries under his name, also known for his impossible epicurean passion.

Kong Jie, the editor-in-chief of Wenhui Daily, *as well as the Party Secretary of the Wenxin Group, influential but going to retire soon. A regular at Min's because of his book titled* Old Tastes of Shanghai, *which includes pictures of recipes from her private kitchen.*

Peng Jianjun, a successful venture capitalist with millions of followers for his financial Weibo blogging posts, in extraordinary relationship with top Party officials in spite of his 'capitalist practice'.

Shang Guanhua, one of the largest real estate developers in the city, also nicknamed 'Shanghai number-one developer', with his personal wealth estimated to be as high as five or six billion yuan.

Zheng Keqiang, with just a small print shop under his name, also serving as a special assistant to Huang, apparently the lightweight of the five.

The preliminary check into the background of the five people yielded nothing suspicious. Nothing to give any of them a motive for the murder. In fact, they would not have seen Qing that night had Min not unexpectedly called her out of the kitchen for a toast.

There was a footnote added by Old Hunter under the name of Zheng Keqiang: 'Huang's the one on the original invitation list, but he failed to make it there for some undisclosed reason. He sent his "nephew" Zheng over for the dinner party that night.'

That meant there were only four people with Min. Chen printed the email out, studied it more closely, and drew a line under Huang's name. It would not have been strange for Zheng to jump at the unexpected opening at the dinner table, but for a well-known gourmet like Huang, how could he have chosen not to be there?

Chen made a question mark on the list before taking a look at his watch.

It was more than half an hour after his phone call to the eatery. With a long line there for the fried soup buns, he was still only halfway through his wait to receive them. He turned back to the report again and noted down a couple more points.

Who was the mysterious client named Sima?

For one thing, Sima must have been aware of all the possible complications in the background, but he was committed, ready to spend an incredible amount of money to clear Min's name.

Was it because Sima, rich and well connected as he was, had fallen helplessly for a courtesan like her?

'What is love in this world? / People live or die because of it.'

It was a couplet from a Yuan dynasty poet, but Chen pulled himself from the waves of sentimentality.

On a moment of impulse, he picked up the Judge Dee novel again, recalling something that had elusively flashed across his mind earlier in the morning.

This time, it took only a couple of minutes for him to find it as he skipped through the pages to the postscript penned by Gulik:

> *The adventures related in the present novel are entirely imaginary, with the exception of the poetess Yoolan. For her I took as model the famous poetess Yu Hsuanchi [Yu Xuanji in the present-day pinyin phonetics system], who lived from ca. 844 to ca. 871. She was indeed a courtesan, who after a checkered career ended her life on the scaffold, accused of having beaten a maidservant to death, but the question of whether she was guilty or not has never been resolved. For more details about her career and her work, the reader is referred to my book* Sexual Life in Ancient China *(E. J. Brill, Leyden, 1961), pp. 170–175. The poem quoted on p. 155 of the present novel was actually written by her.*

That was why he had had a feeling of déjà vu. He had translated a poem of Xuanji's for a Tang dynasty poetry collection, along with some research done about her for a short biographical note.

With his interest roused, Chen put down the novel and turned on the computer for a search about Xuanji's life. Surfing the web, he bookmarked some of the sources so he could come back to them later. After checking through several websites, and experimenting by cutting and pasting, he managed to gather enough for a biographical file of Xuanji no less than seven pages long. He printed it out.

The street outside was covered in the gathering dusk as he picked up the printout. Highlighting sentences and paragraphs, he began to note a lot of differences from what he had read in Gulik's novel.

But he found his mind wandering away, as if being pulled by an invisible hand back to the Min case.

What intrigued him, he realized, were a number of similarities between the two 'suspects' – Xuanji and Min – and the two murder cases.

Both were well-known courtesans or social flowers, and

both became involved in murder, with similar implausible motives.

Whatever the scenario, he had a hard time bringing himself to see Xuanji as a cold-blooded murderer, having read those wonderful poems of hers.

And what about Min?

He produced a piece of paper and started listing the similarities between the two.

Perhaps all these years of working as a cop had shaped him into one, irrecoverably, even at a moment when he was no longer a cop and trying hard to change.

Still, he hesitated about committing himself fully to the Min case. And not just because he felt too tired.

But it was not a day meant for him to read on, uninterrupted, while enjoying his convalescent leave.

A light, tentative knocking came on the door. The delivery of the fried soup buns, he supposed, and he rose to open the door in haste.

He was surprised to see that it was Jin, the young secretary of the Judicial System Reform Office, standing tall, slender, with her right hand raised, ready to knock on the door again.

He knew little about her, though the two of them were supposed to be working at the same office. With Chen put on leave before the new office sign was even put up, it was Jin who had been taking care of things there from day one. He had only paid a short, symbolic visit – no more than ten minutes – to the office, where she was kept busy with a pile of paperwork like a competent secretary. They had since talked only on the phone, in a strictly business-like way, with something like a tacit understanding between the two: he might never come to work at the office, but for the moment she made a point of reporting to him dutifully, and asking for his specific instruction on a number of occasions.

'Oh, it's you, Jin.'

'Sorry to come to your home without proper notice, Director Chen. I have tried to reach you several times today, but without success.'

At the matching corner in the park, he recalled, he had taken out his ordinary phone and turned it off. Back home, he was too intent on the Min case report, and then on the Xuanji case in the Judge Dee novel. He had forgotten all about the phone.

But why should she have made such an unannounced visit to him at home, a dutiful secretary as she was?

'Come on in. There's nothing for you to say sorry about, Jin. I was out this morning. Drinking tea and talking with an old friend. I turned off the phone and then forgot all about it. What's up at the office?'

'The city government called, insisting on an official statement made in the name of our office. Something urgent,' she said, reading the surprise in his eyes as she seated herself opposite on a chair pulled out for her. 'It's supposed to come out in the government newsletter tomorrow.'

'About what?'

'About the scandal of Judge Jiao. The sex video is turning into a huge storm on the Internet.'

He took in a deep breath. Judge Jiao scandal? He knew nothing about it. Surely too many judges for him to keep track of in one single day.

For a statement in the name of the office, Jin could have done it by herself. Nothing but a heap of political clichés in accordance with the instruction from above, cutting and pasting from the official newspapers like *People's Daily* or *Wenhui Daily*. How could the fall of a corrupt judge have turned out to be such a big deal?

No one would have been bothered as to whether the statement was composed by the ex-inspector, who was known to be on convalescent leave and not well enough even to go to the office.

'Really! Judge Jiao scandal. I've hardly heard anything about it. I'm not a chief inspector any more, you know, and I've been seeing doctors, reading and sleeping most of the time. But please, go ahead and tell me about it. Then we'll discuss it.'

He rose to pour a cup of green tea for her.

'It's a long story, but I'll try to give you a short version,' she said, taking a small sip at the tea, a tender green tea leaf between her lips.

'It's about the revenge of Pang Xinguo, a sensational drama

like that of *The Count of Monte Cristo* in China. Pang was a fairly successful businessman, having started his business early in China's economic reform. About two years ago, he started to convert an old property into a boutique hotel in the center of the city. For the project, he signed a contract with an interior designer named Ren, agreeing on a sum of two million yuan, which covered all the material and labor. He paid it there and then, as Ren said that he needed the money for all the material. At the end of the project, however, Ren charged Pang eight million more in addition to the two million. Pang refused, citing the clause in their contract: "Pang pays Ren the total sum of two million yuan for the project at the beginning of it." So Ren sued Pang, claiming the first two million yuan as nothing but the down payment. When the ruling came down, Ren won. Judge Jiao of the District Court too read the sum paid as the down payment, which was said to be "conventional in the business". Pang appealed, but he lost again.

'Pang then found out that Judge Jiao was the First Party Secretary of the District Court – untouchable because of his position in the Party system, and what's more, Judge Jiao was married to Ren's cousin, and the two families were really close. With the case irrecoverably lost, Pang had to sell his other properties to pay the amount, knowing he was in no position to fight back. Definitely not in the normal way. So he decided to do it his own way.

'He began shadowing Judge Jiao around in secret, like a PI. It did not take long for him to establish a pattern of Jiao's daily routine. Despite the façade of an honorable Party-member judge, Jiao frequented a club-like hotel run by the local government in Qingpu County, with all sorts of dubious services in the hourly rooms there. It was no secret about what happened in those rooms. Of course, no police would take the trouble to check into a government-run place. As those Party officials made up only part of the business for the hotel, it was also open to other non-official customers at a higher price. For them, going there was symbolic of their social status, not to mention the fact that they did not have to worry about any police raid. So the higher price was well worth it.

'Pang kept on wandering around the hotel for days before

checking himself in as a customer. A doorman named Xiahou took him as just one of those Big Bucks seeking fun in the hotel, where Pang did a comprehensive reconnaissance like a pro. Then one afternoon, Pang spotted Judge Jiao and his colleagues entering the hotel, and he followed. He watched them moving into their respective rooms, each with a girl on his arm, then Pang checked himself into a room next to theirs. After waiting there for two hours, he heard Jiao and his associates emerging, talking with those girls.

'Then Pang too stepped out, waving his hand at Xiahou like a satisfied customer, but after fifteen minutes or so, he hurried back, claiming he had dropped something of sentimental value in the room or somewhere along the corridor as he left in a hurry. The doorman recognized him, but once a customer had checked out, only the hotel attendant alone could go back into the room. Pang then asked for permission to take a look at the surveillance cameras at the entrance cubicle. Handing a one-hundred yuan bill as well as a cigarette to Xiahou, he said with a smile, "You have a cigarette outside, and I need just a minute or two to take a quick look at the camera."

'Xiahou pocketed the money, smoking outside, and thinking that it would do no harm for Pang to take a quick look into the camera monitors.

'About three or four minutes later, Pang stepped out, carrying in his pocket a memory stick that copied the camera contents, and he said to Xiahou that he must have lost the object of sentimental value somewhere else.

'One day later, a large number of pictures appeared online, those of Judge Jiao walking along the hotel corridor with a half-clad girl leaning on his shoulder, entering into the room hand in hand, and then emerging with the girl treading barefoot beside him in a bathrobe. With the pictures bearing the time and date, their meaning in sequence was unmistakable. So was the message. A corrupt Party-member judge, a disgrace to China's judicial system.

'"Human flesh search" ensued. Netizens had a wild time, like in a carnival, searching, watching, blogging, posting, commenting, and exposing Judge Jiao's sordid secret life with more pictures and material. They seized the opportunity to vent their frustrations at the system. Initially, the city government questioned the authenticity of the pictures and warned about the consequences of the irresponsible "smearing campaign".

'But Pang came out with his real name and posted a long statement claiming that he had repeatedly tried to approach the higher authorities without success, and that he had more pictures and evidence in his possession. As a result, the authorities abruptly changed their tune and promised to probe into Judge Jiao's scandal.'

She took a pause, heaving a small sigh. Apparently, she too had got a little carried away with the drama.

'So our office is supposed to make a statement about it?' he said. 'Yes, it concerns an important part of the judicial system reform. The scandal aside, the issue of the conflict of interest for people like Judge Jiao has to be taken seriously.'

'That's a good point. Some of our judges are not qualified,' Jin said, nodding. 'According to one netizen, Jiao was assigned to the judicial system after having served as a Party commissar in the army, which worked like an infallible political endorsement. He had a sort of law diploma through night classes for only one month. In fact, there're a number of senior judges like Jiao, who are in their positions simply because they are considered politically reliable for the Party authorities.'

'Things may have been improving. For young judges, they are required to have law degrees.'

'It may be true for the younger generation, but they are also required to pledge allegiance to the Party before law. The law tests are full of political questions—'

'These shall not come into our statement, needless to say,' he cut in. 'Yes, there're judges like Jiao, but as the *People's Daily* always says, they are few, far from being representative in today's China. Now we're all for the rule of law.'

'Law, like everything else, is under the leadership of the Party.'

He looked up at her sharply. These were not the comments

characteristic of a young secretary to her Party boss. Was she sent here to sound him out? She was perhaps too young for such a job, but he could not afford to let his guard down.

Then came another knock on the door.

He rose to open it again.

This time, it proved to be the delivery of the fried soup buns. And it was none other than Big Zhou himself standing in the doorway, smiling an apologetic smile.

'Sorry about the wait, Chief Inspector Chen,' Big Zhou said, taking a large plastic box out of a cotton-padded wrapper, along with the small packages of ginger slices and Zhenghai vinegar. 'Too many customers at the eatery today. But our special delivery is only for a valuable customer like you. The buns still steaming hot inside the cotton-padded wrapper.'

That special delivery was only for someone with a chief inspector title, Chen reflected, so Big Zhou was unaware of his having been deprived of the position. Big Zhou was stealing glances at the large apartment, and at Jin, who smiled back without bothering to introduce herself.

Chen thanked him and added a generous tip for the special delivery.

'Sorry, I ordered the fried mini soup buns before your arrival,' Chen said to Jin when the two were left alone.

'Fried mini soup buns! You have to eat them hot. Once cold, the soup inside gets greasy – quite unpalatable. The special delivery does make the difference.'

'Then you have to eat with me. It's from a neighborhood eatery, but the buns are delicious.'

'Well, I'm sort of on a diet, but I think I'll have a small one,' she said, picking one up with her fingers.

It was still hot, and she stuffed the whole bun into her mouth lest the soup would burst out. She appeared to relish its heat on the tongue. Licking at her fingers, she then had another bun, and still another. She finished four of them, before pausing to wipe her lips with a pink paper napkin.

'Sorry, I have finished half of your—'

'Don't worry,' he said, amused with the way she enjoyed them with such a youthful appetite. 'I think Big Zhou has given me three portions instead of two.'

'For a celebrated chief inspector, of course,' she said, crumbling the napkin into a tiny ball. 'Possibly four portions when he learns you're now a director at a higher level.'

'Only one portion when he learns I'm put on leave . . . or no special delivery at all.'

'Come on. He could not help being more impressed if he knew your new title, and if you had a little secretary working for you personally at your apartment.'

The unexpected lunch helped to animate the atmosphere between the two. The mention of a 'little secretary' carried a humorous echo of those spicy stories online. He did not have to be formal as he did in the office.

He got up to grind two spoonfuls of coffee beans, put them into a French press, and poured out a cup for her and another for himself. It might not be too helpful to his stomach, but he needed it for the discussion of the statement.

'The fancy coffee machine becomes the luxurious three-bedroom apartment of yours!' she said, sipping at the coffee, looking around in curiosity. 'And at the top section of the city, too.'

'Sorry, it's in a mess. I did not know—'

Her glance swept around, taking stock of the living room before coming to rest on the book on the desk. 'What are you reading, Director Chen?'

'A Judge Dee novel. A very intriguing book. An incorruptible judge in ancient China, in a sharp contrast to our Judge Jiao in today's society.'

He picked the book up and showed it to her.

'Yes, I have read a couple of them. In the Chinese translation, of course.'

'Oh, what do you think?'

'Judge Dee? He's something of a high-ranking mayor or a prime minister, but not a judge like in today's China, I think.'

'You're quite well read, Jin.'

'No, not quite. It's just because I did a history major in college.'

He remembered having read about that in her file. How had someone with a history major come to work at a government office? It was usually considered lucky, however, for young people to have such a civil servant position with all the benefits of the one-Party system.

'I think you're right, Jin, about the confusion regarding Dee's official position. Not a judge in the strict sense of the word, though he ruled some cases during his long official career. He's called a judge due to the lack of any real division between the executive and the judicial in the Tang dynasty. At that time, only an official with executive power could have made a difference at the court.'

'Well, is there any real division today?'

'That's a point.' He opted for a guarded response, once again taken aback by her satirical tone. 'That's why we have to reform. But back to Gulik, he was an encyclopedia of sinology. He surely knew better, and I think he just made use of the historical figure in the *gongan* genre of classical Chinese literature.'

'Yes, he was a man of great learning, he even did a book about the history of sex in ancient China,' she said with a smile. 'It's fun to read a Westerner's interpretation of the oriental sexology.'

'Oh, that.'

For a moment, he did not know how to go on. Perhaps he was too old – too old-fashioned, to say the least, sitting beside a young girl like Jin. It might be nothing for one of her generation to discuss with her boss about 'oriental sexology'.

'Now we've had our fried mini buns,' he said, 'it's time to go on with things in the office.'

For all he knew, the office could have been set up to make him gradually sink into oblivion, and for her watching constantly over him, whatever he chose to say or do there. But it appeared unlikely that his enemies would have needed something like a politically incorrect office statement to bring him down.

'For our judicial system, people have been raising a question online: Is the Communist Party or law bigger?' Jin said with a smile. 'The answer is implied in the question. So here comes an editorial in the *People's Daily*. "It is a false question raised with an ulterior motive to separate the two." Indeed, whatever question the Party authorities cannot answer must be false. Period. End of discussion.'

'And for our statement,' Chen said, choosing not to dwell on the Party-or-law topic, 'we'll say that our Party will fight corruption wherever it occurs, whoever gets involved, in whatever field, whether the offender is Party-member judge or not. In the meantime, we may also add that it is not proper and right for people to take things into their own hands. We have to trust our Party, to trust our law, and our voice will be eventually heard through the proper channel under the great leadership of our Party.'

'So we may as well copy paragraphs from the *People's Daily*.'

'But aren't we always busy cutting and pasting?'

Catching a subtle irony in his remark, she smiled with an amused light twinkling in her almond-shaped eyes. She looked young, smart and pretty.

'Yes, I've just read an official article this morning about the Judge Jiao scandal, concluding with such an invariable summary, "With the storm breaking out on the Internet, we shall take into consideration the political stability for the country – in the larger picture."'

'Did the article mention any specific measure the Party government would take for people like Pang?'

'No. The tone of the editorial is not that harsh, I think.' She added reflectively, 'They may have to make sure first what other evidence Pang could have obtained. Judge Jiao went there with a group of officials, like crabs bound together on the one and same straw rope. The surveillance cameras would not have focused on Judge Jiao alone. That's why Pang dared to come out with his real name. When cornered, he could have done anything.'

'You're talking like a detective, Jin. In the light of your theory, his choosing not to put all the cards on the table is wise, like an insurance policy bought for oneself. Consequently, the investigation may have to move on very cautiously, with the Party's interest before anything else.'

'Exactly, Director Chen.'

'Basically, our statement has to be just like the official article you mentioned. The corrupt judges have to be punished, but one tiny drop of rat poop should not be allowed to ruin a large pot of soup.'

'But it's not just one tiny drop, I'm afraid.'

'At the same time, we may well point out that Pang's end-justifying-means approach should not be encouraged.'

'A necessary balance in our office statement, I got you, Director Chen.'

'Another point. Any evidence obtained illegally like that will not be accepted at court in other countries. It's an issue of technicality.'

'That's brilliant, Director Chen. I don't think the *People's Daily* has touched on the issue. And the conflict of interest, too. You surely have done a lot of research for our office, Director Chen.'

'No, I've read some crime novels in English, in which such a point is often raised at court. Besides, I happened to have heard something about another judge.'

'Another judge scandal?'

'No. But have you heard of the Min case, or the so-called Republican Lady case? The judge assigned to the case happens to be one with a possible conflict of interest, like in Judge Jiao's scandal.'

'That's intriguing. I've read about the Min case, but without following it closely.' She added with a sharp focus in her eyes, 'The suspect is well known for her gourmet dinner parties. Something like that, right? I'll take a look into it.'

'Yes, something like that, but you don't have to go out of the way for it. I'm interested in it because I, too, am an impossible foodie. I have never visited her place. Nothing but an idiosyncratic curiosity on my part.'

He was known as a notorious foodie in the gastronomic circle, which might work as a pretext for his interest in the case. Then he moved on with a brief account of the Min case as assigned to Judge Liu.

'I'm not saying anything about Judge Liu being corrupt too, not the way some netizens are speculating,' he said. 'But Judge Liu could have been pissed off after staying so long on the waiting list.'

'Talking with you benefits me more, Director Chen, a lot more than reading books for ten years—'

'Spare me, please, Jin. Believe it or not, I was flabbergasted when you first told me about the Judge Jiao scandal. It's because I was reading a Judge Dee novel, and earlier in the day I happened to have just heard about the Min case with another judge in the background. What a coincidence! But back to the Min case, it does not exactly concern our office. I'm on leave, and you have a lot on your hands. Don't worry about it. Just an intriguing case, especially seen from the perspective of the judicial system reform.'

She appeared to be skeptical, at a loss for words, bewildered by his jumping from one judge to another, before she pulled herself together, nodding. 'As long as it is interesting,' she said vaguely, 'from the perspective of the judicial system reform.'

Sometimes words could be said to lead to something else, Chen pondered, like moving a white or black piece, seemingly purposeless, in a *go* chess game.

'This morning, I was reading the Judge Dee novel *Poets and Murder*,' he went on, changing the subject again, 'when it occurred to me that I might try my hand writing an article about it. The murderer in question was, I've just found out, none other than the celebrated poetess Xuanji in the Tang dynasty. I happen to have translated one of her poems into English.'

'That's a coincidence! The legendary chief inspector, and poet, critic and translator to boot,' she said with increasing familiarity. 'I think I've read an essay of yours – "Archetype of Femme Fatale in China's Collective Unconscious". A very original one with a sort of new historicist approach.'

'Now it's my turn to be surprised. You have read that article, detecting "a sort of new historicist approach"?'

'Don't forget my major in history, my Director Chen. But by the way, I've watched several Judge Dee TV movies, in addition to these books. So for your paper about Judge Dee, what can I do to help?'

He might have said too much, though he did not think she would make a report of it to the people above.

'No, it's just my way to prepare for the new job. To know something about the past, I think, before trying to do something in the present. As for the Judge Dee TV movies, I haven't watched any of them. Any of them well made?'

'I don't think I've watched enough to have a real opinion, but there're a lot of details not historically accurate in them.'

'That's no surprise. The directors may not have a history major, and they have to attract audiences in whatever way they can,' he said with a smile. 'Now regarding the statement of our office, our discussion may have covered the gist of it, I think. You go ahead with it. No need for it to be too long. One page should be enough. If there's any new development, we can issue another statement.'

'Yes, I'll keep you posted, Director Chen. And I'll include your point about the issue of technicality.'

'That's fine with me. But why?'

'That's a point not mentioned by others. The statement of our office under you should be different. You may receive the first draft from me this evening – Oh, do you have WeChat?'

'I've heard of it,' he said, surprised by the sudden change of subject on her part. 'I'm just too old to follow the latest technology trend, I'm afraid.'

'But it's so convenient. Especially for things like the lecherous judge with a naked girl in the club – you can find so much, and so quickly, on WeChat. Some posts may be blocked ten minutes later, but in another ten minutes new posts will pop up. Besides, it may also be easier to get hold of you for things in the office.'

'Really?'

'Yes, it's so easy to use. Give me your cellphone. Let me download the app for you.'

'But people spend hours and hours on it, I've heard,' he said, giving out his phone.

'Not if you don't have many friends. Just for your own circle. If you prefer, you may use it just to contact me. It's so user-friendly.'

He was not so sure about it, but it might be convenient to get messages from her if she proved to be his one and only contact on WeChat.

After installing it on his phone, she rose to leave, saying she had to work on the statement.

'Thanks for the fried soup buns, Director Chen. They were delicious.'

He walked her out of the door, and watched her stepping – almost scampering – into the elevator in her white tennis shoes.

The evening was spreading out like a man lying in bed on his convalescent leave.

For an unannounced visit, Jin's turned out to be quite a long one, particularly from a young secretary to her boss at his apartment. It was about office business, but was nonetheless a pleasant, scintillating talk between the two.

It was ironic, Jin contemplated, that Chen appeared to be more of an intellectual than a police inspector, the way he talked – not like a Party-member boss mouthing politically correct words all the time.

Nor did he look like a middle-aged man with any health issues, but it was little wonder, considering the theories she had heard about the real reason why he had been put on convalescent leave.

That he had not really been relaxing on leave did not surprise her, either. Perhaps nothing could be too surprising as far as the ex-inspector was concerned; someone had told her about him, adding that 'the impossible chief inspector is an enigma'.

Unexpectedly, she then caught herself thinking about things quite irrelevant.

What was he having for dinner tonight?

Possibly another portion of fried mini buns. While the taste was not bad from a street corner eatery, such an oily snack might not be helpful to his recovery. And his choice contradicted the gossips who said he was an impossible gourmet.

Whatever stories she had heard about him, he was not like any of those Party officials she had met before. His comments about the Judge Jiao scandal made sense. The office statement could not but be something in line with the expectation of the

higher authorities, and anything other would be counter-
productive. He'd sounded cynical, and it was not easy for
someone in his position to be cynical.

She thought she was not displeased at the prospect of
working with him if he was coming back to the office after
the convalescent leave.

And she began wondering what more she was supposed to
do as a secretary for him. She went over in her mind what he
had just said to her, trying to find some clues like a competent
assistant to an inspector in an investigation.

With his talk jumping from one case to another, from one
judge to another, she had been left more or less confused, but
among other things, it could be interesting to put the cases side
by side, 'especially seen from the perspective of the judicial
system reform'. That's what he had said about the Min case
toward the end of the talk, she remembered.

The streets followed in the dusk like an argument, but she
chose to ignore it.

Chen found it hard to concentrate on the Judge Jiao scandal
Jin had told him about. Not because it was not a case for him
or because he was no longer a chief inspector.

Party-member judges like Jiao were anything but independent of the one-Party system. It was just because of a
stroke of bad luck that Jiao had been caught on the surveillance
camera, and crushed in a 'human flesh search'. Many more
like Jiao were still out there, ruling as the judges politically
reliable to the Party authorities.

Still, he sat down in front of the computer, searching for
news about the ongoing scandal. An incredibly large number
of netizens appeared so indignant, showing solidarity with
Pang, and slamming the 'judicial system under the leadership
of the great and glorious Party'. The mayor promised to fire
Jiao from the position. So the request for the office statement
under Chen's name was part of the show needed for the
moment.

As for the statement, what else could he have said to Jin?
For that matter, he might have already said more than he should.
Jin was a vivacious young girl full of spirit, but he believed

she knew what to say in an official statement, the draft of which he was going to read and approve this evening.

But what he had said to her – on the spur of the moment – about the similarities among the judges kept coming back to his own mind.

Then thoughts about something else took over. The similarities between the two cases – the Min case and the Xuanji case – seized him again.

This time, he moved to put *Poets and Murder* side by side with the folder about the Min case. For whatever did not make sense in either of them, he marked with question marks in a notebook. In a strange way, police investigation seemed to work like deconstruction in post-modern literary criticism, focusing on the inexplicable. For both, it was imperative to find the clues and give interpretations, and with the evidence gathered to support the interpretations came the conclusion.

But the effort soon turned out to be too exhausting for him. So he used the French press for another cup of extra strong coffee. Immediately, he was beginning to feel uncomfortable in the stomach, but his cellphone dinged unexpectedly, with a different tone.

It was Jin contacting him on WeChat – with a profile picture of hers possibly taken in her college years, wearing a long queue, thread-bare jeans and flip flops. The message contained a Word document, a first draft of the office statement.

Jin had done her job fast. The statement covered all the talking points with a historical perspective. She did not forget to include the point about the ambiguous circumstances in which the evidence was obtained. So it showed at least one difference from the editorial of the *People's Daily*.

There was a short note at the end of it: 'Draft of the drafts. I'll send you the first real draft later, but let me know if you want to add anything.'

He did not think he wanted to add anything. Few would pay any serious attention to such an official statement of political correctness.

With the phone still in his hand, it rang again. Still from Jin, this time the screen showed several links to TV movies of Judge Dee investigations.

'Enjoy them. A master may really appreciate another master.'

He tapped on one of the links, *Early Adventures of Judge Dee*, and started downloading it. The picture quality was excellent, and he could not resist the temptation in spite of the small phone screen. It took only five or six minutes, however, for him to realize that the episode, while entertaining, had nothing to do with Gulik's work.

To his shock, in the cover image of another video, he saw Judge Dee standing in a wooden pillory cart with his hands and feet in chains, and a naked young woman in another cart following Dee's, with a phoenix-shaped headdress fallen at her bleeding bare feet, and a high bamboo sticker stuck behind her neck indicating her as one soon to be beheaded on the execution ground. It was devastatingly humiliating to be paraded like that in public, not just for the woman, but for Dee too. It was perhaps just another commercially-oriented TV movie made for the market, and he was in no mood to watch it. None of the TV movies would have had anything to do with Gulik's novels, let alone *Poets and Murder*.

In the socialism with China's characteristics, more and more people were becoming interested in the dramas focusing on the conspiracies at the court, such as the power struggle between the Empress of the Wu family and the Li family. The phoenix headdress at the feet of the naked woman seemed suggestive of her previous status as an imperial concubine, though Chen failed to recall anything like that in the period of the Tang dynasty. Nevertheless, it appealed to the audience.

He felt really coffee-sick.

The phone rang again. It was Lu this time.

'I've made several phone calls for you. And I got in touch with someone named Huang Zhongluo, a wealthy antique collector. Number one in Shanghai.'

'You know Huang?'

That came as a real surprise to Chen. Huang, the number-one antique collector, whose info he had just read in the list sent over by Old Hunter.

'Yes, he's been to my Moscow Suburb a couple of times,

but I cannot say he likes Russian cuisine that much. Too oriental-fashioned.' Lu added in afterthought, 'By the way, he's a regular at Min's private kitchen dinners. He invited you to breakfast at Old Half Place tomorrow morning.'

Lu had not only contacted one of the regular guests at Min's dining table, but also arranged a meeting for them. Huang, though not at Min's dining table that night, had been on the original invitation list.

'But I don't know him.'

'Don't worry about that. I told him you want to consult him about something in the antique business. He has heard a lot about you, and about your gastronomic passion, too. He agreed at once, saying it's an honor to meet with you. In a private room on the second floor of the restaurant. Around six thirty.'

'So early!'

'The water poured into the pot early in the morning is clear, with no residues from repeated noodle-boiling, and that will make a huge difference for the noodles. At least that's Huang's philosophy. So don't be late.'

'No, I won't. Thank you, Overseas Chinese Lu.'

It was a nickname he had been calling Lu since their middle school years during the Cultural Revolution.

Chen began wondering what he could possibly talk to Huang about the antique business. Of late, there were multiple Chinese TV programs about antique hunting and appraising. Apparently, it was a huge market.

But the train of his thought was derailed by another unexpected call through the special cellphone.

It was Ling, his ex-girlfriend, nowadays somebody else's ex-wife.

They had kept in touch through these years, albeit not that regularly. Like in an ancient Chinese fable about two fish in the sea, an immense distance between them, each too busy swimming and struggling against the tides, but aware of the other still being out there under the same sun, and occasionally reminiscent of the moments of their once being together.

He had made a point of giving her his latest special cell-phone number with a short text message without any elaboration. She understood, and she was calling him now – probably for a special reason.

'Long time and no speak, Ling. I was afraid you too had forgotten about me,' he said, trying to put a light touch of self-satire into the talk.

'How could people have ever forgotten about you? You are unforgettable after the investigation into Lai, one of the most prominent Red Princes.'

It was just like Ling, who came directly to the point. That Chen had ruffled high feathers was no news to her, but her making the phone call to him about it meant serious trouble for him. Her mentioning the Red Prince came as another unmistakably ominous signal.

The powerful Lai had fallen, but the group of Red Princes advanced to the top in the Forbidden City. While the downfall of Lai could have removed a competitor to the one sitting on the throne, the murderous details of the case had proved to be disastrous to the Party image.

'What's up, Ling?' he asked, noting for the first time the long, unfamiliar number on the phone screen. 'Are you calling from London?'

She had an office as well as an apartment in London, where she ran some sort of export and import business through her family connections, about which he knew nothing except that it was hugely profitable. She stayed for most of the time in Beijing, though.

'Yes, in London. Can you talk now?'

'Sure, I'm home alone.'

'I've heard about your new office position, and about your convalescent leave, too. I'm so worried for you.'

'I'm fine. No need to worry about me,' he said. 'It's just like a vacation. It may actually do me a lot of good.'

'You don't have to say that to me, Chen. Some people at the top have gathered enough files about you to fill a whole cabinet. About your investigation of the Red Prince, in particular. A too humiliating blow to the great, glorious façade of the Beijing government.' She then added in a hurry,

'Have you recently talked to someone surnamed Yao, a law professor in Shanghai?'

'A law professor in Shanghai?' he repeated mechanically before he recollected anything. 'Yes, Professor Yao, a law professor of the Shanghai Academy of Social Sciences. But it was nothing but a congratulatory phone call from him about my new position.'

'It was tapped.'

He took in a deep breath. Professor Yao had long been on a blacklist for his criticism of China's judicial system, known for his blog posts on several influential web forums. As for that phone call, what the two had talked about that day, he failed to recall any details. Yao could have said something about the problems under the one-Party authoritarian system, and about his expectations for Chen in the Judicial System Reform Office.

Whether it was because of Yao, or because of him, that the call had been tapped, he could not tell.

'They're talking about the conspiracies against the socialism with China's characteristics, the conspiracies through the joint effort of intellectuals and officials within the Party system—'

'What!' The accusation of conspiracies against the Chinese socialism sounded alarmingly familiar, just like another echo from the Cultural Revolution. 'Thanks, Ling. I'm no longer a chief inspector, but I still know how to protect myself.'

'If there's anything I can do, let me know, though perhaps not like before . . .'

He knew what she meant by 'not like before', catching a slight tremor in her voice. His father had stepped down from the powerful Politburo Standing Committee of the CPC. What she was capable of doing for the ex-inspector could be limited, though she would still go out of her way for him, like this phone call, or like the first time he had got into trouble because of the first major case he had investigated concerning a national model worker and an 'HCC' – a term used many years ago for high cadre's children, but nowadays known simply as a Red Prince.

He was struck with a sad sense of déjà vu.

But it was not déjà vu, not exactly. The fact that she had now learned so fast about his trouble, and from so far away in London, was more than alarming.

'Thanks for your call from London, Ling. I will be really careful.'

'I think I'm moving to London permanently, what with the changes inside the Forbidden City, and with the air pollution in Beijing.' She went on after a short pause, 'I have a two-bedroom apartment in London. Maybe I'll see you here. And you can stay in the apartment as long as you like. It's such a long time since we last saw each other.'

She had an apartment there, and had built plenty more business connections than she had started with. Thanks to her family background, she had also made quite a lot of money. She could live quite comfortably without having to work anymore, traveling between Beijing and London in leisure. But why was she telling him about her moving to London, and about her meeting him there at this moment?

Could that be another hint about the dire danger facing him; that he should flee from China?

If so, his appointment to the new office could have been a devious trap. On convalescent leave or not, he would have to talk to others about the problems of the judicial system, and whatever he said would then be gathered as evidence of the anti-Party conspiracies.

Things like that had happened in China, and they were happening again.

That's why she was making the call from London.

He could not help but feel grateful to her, and for the subtle suggestion, too. After all these years, it was now possible for them to be reunited – outside of China. Ironic as it was, it made some sense with her business established there.

What about him? He still had to make a living, but he knew he could not work as a cop in London. He might try his hand at writing in English, as a couple of American writers had suggested to him. He wondered, however, how far he could really go.

Putting down the phone, he was suddenly furious. He had been laying low on medical leave, and contemplating a different career, but those in power still would not let him off the hook.

And the video cover image of Judge Dee standing in the prison cart came shooting back to his mind. It was a real possibility.

Like Judge Dee, Chen had to fight back for his survival.

DAY TWO

C hen arrived at Old Half Place on the intersection of Fuzhou and Zhejiang Roads at six thirty in the morning.

It was still quite gray outside the restaurant, but its first floor was packed with early customers, most of them elderly, who had to shout loudly the numbers on the order slips, carry their breakfast trays by themselves from the sordid kitchen windows, and squeeze through the waiting crowd to their respective oil-smeared tables.

Not so with the clean, spacious second floor, especially with the pretentious private room overlooking the street below. An elderly waiter was leading him there respectfully.

Huang was already in the room, sitting at a mahogany table by the window, sipping at a cup of green tea with several small dishes of nuts and dried fruits aside the teapot. A white-haired and white-browed man in a scarlet silk Tang jacket, Huang struck Chen as singularly familiar. Then he recalled having seen the old man in a popular TV program about antique appraisal. He moved over and bowed low, his right hand grasping a set of books in a blue cloth box.

It was a collection of annotated *Three Hundred Tang Dynasty Poems*. Of excellent bamboo paper and traditional thread bounding, supposedly of the late Qing dynasty edition, it was probably of not too high value in today's antique market, but it would work as an excuse for them to start chatting.

'Thank you so much, Master Huang, for agreeing to see me this morning. It's such an honor for me.'

'You are most welcome, Chief Inspector Chen . . . oh, *Director* Chen.'

'Just call me Chen, Master Huang.'

The moment he seated himself opposite Huang, the waiter hurried over to open the menu for them with a proud grin. 'The knife anchovy noodles here. Ours is the one and only restaurant in Shanghai that serves this celebrated special. And now is the very best season to have them with the fish swimming back into the Yangtze River.'

'Long-jaw anchovy, but people simply call it knife anchovy because of its knife-like shape,' Huang said, an authentic authority on gourmet food, too. 'My treat today. Two portions of knife anchovy noodles. Anything else?'

'No. For me, it's always the noodles with Xiao pork in this restaurant. Too many tiny bones with the fish, I'm afraid,' Chen said, appalled at the price listed on the menu. *Thirty thousand yuan per kilo for the fish, minimum a hundred kilograms per bowl of noodles.*

Huang eyed him in surprise.

'And anything else?'

'A small portion of fried cabbage rice.'

'But you cannot have the knife anchovy noodles anywhere else in the city,' the waiter said, apparently disappointed.

'Don't worry about it,' Huang said simply. 'We will pay for the minimum expense for the private room. Eight hundred yuan per person, right?'

As the waiter reluctantly left with their order, Huang turned to Chen with a smile. 'You really don't care for the special fish noodles?'

'No, I don't. I had one bowl about twenty years ago. Nothing that special for the price. A lot of tiny bones. About thirty yuan per bowl at the time, I think. It's become so ridiculously expensive nowadays. What's the point having something you don't really like, however expensive?'

'That's the spirit, Chen. To tell the truth, I too don't like the fish that much. It's quite delicious, but with numerous bones. In my younger days, it was less than ten yuan a kilo in the food market, but as our fishermen kept catching relentlessly, the knife anchovy appeared on the list as a sort of endangered species. So the price shot up like crazy. For a bowl of knife anchovy noodles, it is said that the chef here has to put the fish scales, crumbles, bones, heads and tails into a cloth bag and boil it in a pot of soup for hours. And he then adds the tiniest bit of fish meat on top of the noodles. You can hardly find any trace of it.'

'It's definitely not worth the money.'

'No, it's not. But in our brave new world of conspicuous consumption, if I treat a distinguished man like you with only a bowl of Xiao pork noodles here, both you and I may lose a lot of face.'

'No, your agreeing to meet with me here today already gives me too much face. What's wrong with the Xiao pork? My dad used to bring me here for a bowl of Xiao pork noodles. It was such a treat, and it still is, not to mention the fond memories of those days. Of course, we dined downstairs at that time. I myself have come to this restaurant quite a few times, but never to the second floor before.'

'To tell the truth, it's just the second time for me, I mean in the private room on the second floor. What is served on the first floor is way cheaper, but with no difference in taste. It's just too noisy downstairs, we can hardly talk,' Huang said after taking a slow, leisured sip at the tea. 'Now we really have one thing in common between us. My favorite food is not expensive, either. In fact, it's not even in a restaurant. Nothing but the cheap street food.'

'That's unbelievable!'

'A rice ball at a street corner stall in Yangpu District, and that too with a lot of memories,' Huang said, turning out to be an energetically talkative old man – like another Old Hunter. 'It's almost thirty years ago since I first ate there. At that time, I worked at a neighborhood production group, earning seventy cents per day, and working like a deadbeat dog on three shifts. One chilly early morning, I passed by the stall on the way to the neighborhood production group, and bought a rice ball from a cotton-padded, coat-wrapped wooden container, with a fresh-fried dough stick put into it there and then. What a blissful first bite, it kept me energetic and happy for the whole day. And I've since been going back to the stall quite regularly, though I moved away, far away from Yangpu District years ago.'

'What an experience, Master Huang!'

'As luck would have it, the stall is still standing there, sticking to the traditional way of making a rice ball. The same taste just like the first time. Now that's a secret I've shared with nobody else. Once it's brought up in the media, the old business model would soon be gone.'

'Thank you for letting me into this secret. I'll definitely go there next week, and you can rest assured that I won't tell anybody about it, Master Huang.'

'The highest level of gastronomic enjoyment is to have what you crave in your heart. Whether it's well known or expensive hardly matters. Like in an old saying, "You're a man who really understands the music," Chen. But you're a man much more than that. For a man of my age, I think I can tell a thing or two about a piece of antique, about a special dish, and about a man, too.'

'Yes, you're the number-one antique authority in the city. Lu may not have told you about the favor I'm going to ask of you,' Chen said, taking the books out of the blue cloth box. 'Here is an old collection left behind by my late father. I should not part with it, I know, but with my mother moving into a nursing home for twenty-four-hour care service, it's getting too expensive for me to cover. That's why I think of selling some of the old books at home.'

With the generous payment from that mysterious client Sima, he would be able to send his mother back to the nursing home, but that sum would not last too long, considering the inflation, and he was truly worried about it.

'It's an honor for you to think of me, Chen. For a man of your position, you actually have to sell books to take care of your mother, which in itself speaks volumes about your filial piety, and about your integrity as one of the few honest Party officials in today's China, standing out like a white crane against those chickens of corrupt Party officials. They really fatten themselves like the red rats described by Tang poet Liu Zhongyuan.'

'No, I'm just old-fashioned. As Confucius says, there are things a man should do, and things he should not do. That's all there is to it. As for my mother, it's just like in another Tang poem, "Who says that the splendor of a grass blade can prove enough / to return the generous warmth of ever-returning spring sunlight?" That's the least I should do for her.'

'I'll take a good look at your books. Old and rare books

are not my forte, but I have some friends in the circle. Things can be quite complicated in our line of business.'

'That's so true,' Chen said, thinking he'd better not come to the point too quickly. And he might have to sell some more books. He knew very little about the business except its being so hot of late. 'And you surely can teach me a lot more about the antique business.'

'Well, people complain about the soaring house prices. But it's nothing compared with the soaring antique prices. I was so lucky as to stumble on a pair of Ming dynasty vases for nothing during the Cultural Revolution. The collectors, then scared shitless by the Red Guards, had to throw their once-treasured pieces away as "four olds". They were dirt cheap. And you did not have to worry about them being fakes either.

'But guess why they suddenly became hot cakes?' Huang went on, putting a boiled peanut into his mouth. 'It's simple. The government has printed way too much money, and the price for a bowl of knife anchovy noodles here really illustrates the fast devaluation of yuan. The interest in the bank can never catch up with the inflation, the economy is in an increasingly terrible shape, and no one believes in the system any more. So antiques become a sort of hedge for some people, who believe they will hold on to something valuable when the huge bubble eventually breaks.

'At the same time, it's also more than that. For some Party officials, they choose to take bribes not in cash, but with antiques. When busted, they can claim it's nothing but inexpensive knockoffs. And they can resell them too. It's just another way of people currying favor by purchasing the "antiques" – more likely than not fakes – from them and paying the full price.'

'I've never heard of those deals.'

'That's no surprise. These things are arranged and done under the table through connections.'

'For your line of business, you have to have a large network of connections.' Chen then added casually, 'Oh, I remember having just read something online about your being a regular guest to a private kitchen party. Little wonder, of course, for a man of your epicurean sophistication.'

'Well,' Huang said, looking up from his cup. 'You're talking about the murder case in Min's private kitchen dinner party, right?'

'Right. I have read speculation about it on the Internet. But let me assure you: I'm no longer a cop, and I'm not doing any investigation. Just a bit curious about the case, and about her dinner too.'

'The dinner at Min's is expensive, but she is a consummate chef and host. And some people went there not merely because of her culinary skills. It's more like an elite club, where she had her way of choosing her guests. You may be super rich, but you can still be put on the waiting list forever. Your appearance in her *shikumen* house speaks volumes about your social status. Some people attended the dinner party more for the sake of developing connections through her. That could be of immense importance in business, and particularly in the antique business. She's said to have relationships with people really high up there, though she's a cautious one, never bragging and boasting of the men she sees in secret—'

The talk was interrupted by the waiter coming back to the table with their order.

The Xiao pork noodles proved to be as tasty as Chen remembered, with a tiny dish of extra-thin sliced ginger that brought out the special pork flavor. Huang picked up a piece of half-transparent pork and buried it under the noodles in the steaming soup ritualistically.

'That's my father's way of enjoying the noodles too,' Chen said, watching.

'Yes, that's the way for the old customers in this restaurant,' Huang said, nodding. 'What was I saying? Oh, for some people, they went to Min's for connections more than anything else. For me, it's a lucky combination of gastronomical bliss and business opportunities. Some of her clients are super rich, and it's fashionable for them to dabble in antiques for fun as well as for investment. In our line, there're too many fakes, but it would not be that practical to buy or sell through auctions. So some connections of hers choose to do business through her instead. With her connections at the top, people do not have to worry about those shady transactions. She's introduced a number of customers to me at her private dinner table.'

'But you were not there that night, were you?'

'I'm coming to that, Chief Inspector Chen. About two months ago, a mysterious connection of hers wanted to sell a scroll of Tang dynasty paintings. I spent days researching it before I made sure that it was an authentic piece by Wu Daozi.'

'Wow, by Wu Daozi in the Tang dynasty!'

'It's worth a huge fortune. And based on my research and recommendation, a buyer offered a reasonable price for it, considering the fact that the seller did not have to worry about the fee and tax in auction, the tiresome paperwork, and the undesirable publicity. But at the last minute she told me her connection had chosen not to sell. I got very upset. It could have been arranged for a free appraisal from me. And she would never tell me about what really happened.

'So she arranged for a special dinner party as an apologetic gesture. I did not want to go, but it was not something so uncommon in the antique business. No point cutting off the nose to spite the face.

'I sent my nephew Zheng there instead. Zheng was of course more than willing to go. He had heard and read about her, and asked me questions about her dinner party with great interest. His appearance at her dinner table could also add to his status. He was overjoyed.'

'I see, it's your nephew Zheng—'

Huang talked on without waiting for the ex-inspector to say more.

'Not my real nephew, but from the same countryside, where people have a way of claiming one another as relatives. He came to Shanghai about ten years ago and ran a small printing shop, and then became a special assistant of mine in the antique business and made far more out of it. Younger and energetic, he's quite helpful for me.'

'You must have taught him a lot in the antique business.'

'No, not really. He simply runs errands for me. And he travels for me too. Domestically, as well as internationally. You have heard of stories about a large number of Chinese traveling abroad for fun and shopping, but there's also a small group of them going abroad for antiques.'

'For antiques abroad?'

'Not necessarily in those big cities through which Chinese tourists have already swept time and again. But in antique shops of small cities, Zheng searches around for hidden gems, and brings them back to sell for a much higher price to the crazy rich Chinese clients.'

'But how could he tell whether a piece is valuable or not?'

'Good question. I'm too old to travel long distances like that, but he goes wherever I want him to. When he sees something of potential value, he sends back pictures for me to make the call. He speaks some English, and that helps too.'

It was turning into a lecture about the antique business, possibly much longer than anticipated. Huang was certainly an interesting character, and it was also a very interesting talk, but Chen was not sure how much of it was really related to the investigation.

'Zheng must be a valuable helper.'

'That's why I let him go to her dinner party that night. It was an invaluable opportunity for him, I know. But I have no clue as to what really happened there that night. As a regular customer, I knew Min had grown quite dependent on Qing, her kitchen assistant. It may be not that easy to have someone equally capable as your help. So it was a setback to Min that she was leaving.'

'She was upset, but so upset as to kill, I don't know. But according to those pieces online, Qing was going to work for a man who had been a regular at her dinner table.'

'You're well informed, Director Chen. Yes, that's Rong. But Rong knows better than to fall for a "little provincial sister" like Qing. It's not unheard of, however, for an upstart like him to have a "sex maid", serving him both at the table and in bed.

'But what she might have dreamed of could be another story,' Huang said, finishing the last spoonful of the noodle soup, and looking at his watch. 'Sorry, I have to meet a client at nine thirty, Chen. That's why I wanted you out for the early breakfast. I'll ask around my associates about the value of old books. And I'll let you know soon.'

'Thank you so much, Master Huang. Next time should be my treat.'

The moment she got into the office in the morning, Jin started re-reading the 'final version' of the statement regarding the Judge Jiao scandal.

It was her first real job in this office and she wanted to do her best.

A draft of the office statement had been completed and emailed to Chen the previous night, and he had given his prompt approval without changing a single word of it.

Shortly after she sent the statement to the City Propaganda Ministry, the minister himself sent an email in response:

> An excellent job, Comrade Jin. Put it online immediately. It will also appear in the city government e-newsletter. Don't forget to include Director Chen's signature at the end of it. And that along with a footnote: 'Director Chen, while still on convalescent leave, looked it over and pointed out the inadmissibility of the evidence under normal circumstances – not just in China, but in other countries too. It's an insightful observation from an experienced chief inspector.'

It was beyond her to say no to such a footnote. She thought about calling Chen, but she decided not to. There was nothing he could do about it, either. Chen's signature as well as his observation about the issue of technicality had to be included, in the Party's interests.

In all probability, the statement would come out in other newspapers too, highlighting his comments about the inadmissibility of the illegally obtained evidence in the Judge Jiao scandal, perhaps with some more added sentences.

Finally, she pressed the send button after enclosing Chen's signature.

It was out of her hands. No use speculating about it anymore.

She looked up, her glance sweeping around the unchanging

view of the large yet solitary office. In the eyes of her relatives and friends, it was an unbelievable stroke of luck for her to land a city government job with excellent pay, and with unbelievable benefits and perks as well. Her parents had spared no effort pushing through on their connections for her.

But she was wondering whether it was truly such a good job for her. As whispered in the circle, the office itself had been set up as a temporary arrangement of convenience for the ex-inspector. Nothing but a show of social and political stability: the good, honest cop Chen still in a high-ranking position, albeit a different one. Those interpretations she had read online, even though some of them were blocked just minutes after their appearance, appeared to be even more disturbing. In fact, he had come to the office only once for a short visit – less than ten minutes. From day one, she had been taking care of the boring routine work all by herself.

And there was something else inexplicable about the office. For its 'official status', there should be a number of people working there, at least seven or eight, but she was the only one. A chauffeur, who had been officially assigned for Chen, never appeared.

Things were not too difficult for her, though. Her job consisted of receiving the reports delivered to the office, classifying them, putting them chronologically in a bracket, and for those possibly important ones, forwarding them to Chen's residence. Otherwise, she had the large but deserted office to herself.

With the office statement done, she was supposed to sit there, drinking tea or coffee, relaxing and WeChatting with her friends.

But what about the future of the office? If things she had heard about Chen's troubles were true, the office would be soon gone, along with Chen.

Could the existence of the office have meant something more than a political show enacted just for the moment? It might be too early for a novice like her to have anything taken for granted. But she believed she could be fairly sure about one thing. While a temporary job for him, it was a really important one for her. It would be a disaster for her – and more for her parents – if the office was gone along with her job.

Things seemed to have changed, however, with her visit to Chen in his apartment. It was the first time that she'd gone to talk to him, person to person, and not at all in a business-like way. Behind the shell of political correctness, she sensed a subtle touch of cynical parody in his talk, as if playing the one and same record, mechanically, from the Shanghai People Radio Station in her company.

The phone suddenly started ringing. The number showed it as one from the same government office building. About the office statement regarding the Judge Jiao scandal, she supposed.

However, it was from Ma Yuan, Chief of Staff for the city government, whose office was located on the top floor of the building.

'Can you come up to my office, Jin?'

'Anything wrong with the statement, Chief Ma?'

'No, I would just like to talk to you.'

'But I'm waiting for the possible feedback for the office statement. I'm all alone in the office, you know, for the moment.'

'Don't worry about it. I'll come down then.'

Ma was a man of real power and connections. It was an absolute surprise that he would choose to come down to her.

In less than five minutes, Ma strode into her office without knocking at the door, and he moved directly to the point.

'You've done an excellent job with that office statement. We've looked into your file, Jin. You're young, and with a college degree, and with some publications in magazines, too. You'll have a promising future in the system. You have discussed with Director Chen about the statement, haven't you?'

'Yes. After I tried to reach him several times without success, I went to his apartment yesterday afternoon because of the deadline. And after listening to my account of the Judge Jiao scandal, he made a point about the inadmissibility of the evidence,' she said guardedly, trying to respond in a proper way in spite of her confusion. 'He's truly experienced. The statement was done with his suggestions and approval.'

'What else did he say to you?' Ma added in a hurry, 'Make no mistake about it. We all know he's a capable police officer. But we have to know more. The office is new to him, and to the city government too, and we want to make sure that it plays its important role in today's society.'

'We did not talk that much – apart from the wording of the statement. Oh, he's been reading a Judge Dee novel in English—'

'A Judge Dee novel – why?'

'He said that he was reading by way of preparation for the new position. He believed that the knowledge about the judicial system in traditional Chinese society may be helpful to today's reform.'

'He is so serious! Director Chen has overworked himself, you know. And he can be a little eccentric,' he said, pointing a finger at his head, 'right there. That's why he'd better stay on convalescent leave for the moment. A bit of eccentricity is no big deal for an ordinary man, but he is one of extraordinary caliber. We have to look out, and that's also the opinion of a leading comrade in Beijing.'

She was more than alarmed, wondering whether she had said too much about Chen, but she had to go on.

'Thank you so much for telling me all this, Director Ma. Director Chen looked rather tired, I think. He appeared to have not been taking good care of himself, skipping meals, drinking too much coffee, and with a slight twitching under his right eye, but other than that, I could not see anything seriously wrong with him. Of course I will pay more attention, and I'll report to you about anything noticed.'

After Ma left the office, she tried to sort out her entangled thoughts. Despite the recognition of 'an excellent job', she felt bad. She could have said that she was incapable of reaching him, and that the office statement had been done through an exchange of emails. Now, she had to watch over her 'eccentric boss' for the Party government.

But it was so unfair to the ex-inspector. She had heard a lot about him even before she got the office job. Chen appeared to be a legendary officer of integrity with several successful investigations to his credit. In a one-Party system riddled with corruption, he was seen as one of the few conscientious cops still left working there – like the endangered species, as in a joke enjoyed by netizens.

As luck would have it, she had been assigned to a job working under him in the new office. That was a career she had never dreamed of, but she had told others with a touch of pride about her working for 'Inspector Chen'.

But it was turning into a situation that was becoming overwhelming for her. Instead of working for Chen, she was now supposed to work for the people above Chen – and possibly against him too. She had not been given this position for nothing. It was for the sake of keeping the ex-inspector under surveillance for the city government – like one of the numerous cameras installed everywhere in the city. To keep her job, she had no choice but to do whatever the Party authorities wanted her to. She was not in a position to say no.

Yet if she succeeded in gathering the information Director Ma wanted about Chen, and consequently having Chen eliminated, the office itself would disappear – along with her job in it.

It did not mean, however, that she had to do exactly as requested by Ma, she tried to reassure herself. She would still report dutifully to Ma, yet choosing carefully as to what was included in the report or not.

Should she try to alert Chen? It was a tough situation for him, and a tough decision for her. But he was probably well aware of it, much more than she could tell.

Instead of jumping to a decision, she started thinking about what else she could do for him. With the office statement delivered, there seemed to be little else for her to do.

It was then she thought of his comments about the Min case again, which involved another judge with a possible conflict of interest. Chen seemed to have brought it up offhandedly, but she wondered what he was really up to. His comments made her think that he could have been following cases in secret, like in those stories she had heard about the tireless chief inspector.

If so, was what he had said about the Min case meant as a clue for her?

Whatever her enigmatic boss might have up his sleeve, the Min case was a complicated one. At least she could try to gather more information about it.

And she was just learning the ropes, she told herself, doing some preparatory research for her job. It would be justifiable for her to take a look into a much-talked-about case – in line with her responsibility at the Judicial System Reform Office. She might start by doing a background check on the Min case. It mattered not whether Chen had specifically asked her to do so or not.

And it might not be too difficult for her to develop a profile about Min in her own way. Preferably in a way that was not easy for the ex-inspector to follow at the moment. He was supposed to stay on convalescent leave, not move around actively like an inspector.

She took out an iPad, clicked on a VPN, a 'wall-climbing' app she often resorted to like other young people, and focused on the politically sensitive aspects of the Min case. She was not sure whether Chen had access to those websites.

Immediately, she found the speculations about the case had escalated into a hurricane on the Internet. In a fairly long article about Min's *shikumen* house, there was a quite detailed description of the place, along with its location and surroundings.

The neighborhood turned out to be walking distance from the office. No more than fifteen to twenty minutes away. She took a look at her watch.

She could take an earlier lunch break. A longer one if necessary.

Shortly after nine, Chen was stepping out of a taxi at the Shanghai Academy of Social Sciences on Central Huaihai Road, contemplating an open 'mountain road' for himself by paying a visit to Professor Yao there.

The plan had been made after his getting the phone call from Ling last night, and after re-reading an old book about the art of war titled *The Thirty-Six Stratagems*.

In the early days of the Han dynasty, as recorded in *The Thirty-Six Stratagems*, General Xin had to lead his troops out

of Hanzhong, but aware of his enemy staying there on high
alert, ready to strike with superior force the moment General
Xin's soldiers came in sight, he made a show of building a
mountain road out of Hanzhong in the open, but at the same
time he constructed a path through Chenchang in secret, thus
taking the enemy by surprise. It worked out as one of the most
successful tactics, later called 'building a mountain road in
the open to surprise a stronghold through a secret mountain
pass'.

Since those people who kept Chen under surveillance knew
about his contact with Professor Yao, his visit would be
watched and reported.

He had been to the academy many times before. The
Literature Institute there had recently held a forum about
modern Chinese poetry and had invited Chen as the keynote
speaker. Earlier, he had also had a collection of classical
Chinese poetry translations published by the SASS Press.

In the morning light, he found himself more inclined toward
the scenario that the phone conversation with Yao had been
tapped because of him, as an ex-inspector. A bookish intellectual, Yao had said things unpleasant to some officials, but
nothing seriously threatening to the Party authorities.

Not so with the ex-inspector.

So his talk to Professor Yao about a Judge Dee project could
cause a distraction to those watching over him closely in the
dark. His concentration on a historical figure in the Tang
dynasty instead of any investigation at the present might serve
as a fictional mountain road.

But Professor Yao was not in his office that morning. Chen
approached the head of the Law Institute instead, a middle-
aged associate professor surnamed Hou. Director Hou received
him with the due respect.

'You must have heard of my new position, Director Hou,'
Chen said with a smile. 'I'm still on convalescent leave, but
I cannot afford to sit at home doing nothing all day long. It's
a new responsibility for me. A cop all these years without
having done any systematic study of our judicial system, I
have to get myself prepared for the job. And a visit to your
institute is like making a short cut for me.'

'You are being so modest, Director Chen.'

From the puzzled expression on his face, Chen guessed that Hou had heard stories about his trouble. In terms of the Party cadre rank, however, Chen's was higher. Not to mention the possibility of his finding his way back into the Party's favor.

'What can we do for you at our institute?'

'Well, I would like to spend some time in your library. It's easier to browse than the Shanghai Library, I've heard, with so many law books on open shelves. It's a credit to your institute.'

'Thank you, Director Chen. It's true that our library is known for its well-arranged categories for research. You can take out any books you want.'

'In preparation for the new job, I think I'm going to write a paper about Judge Dee.'

'An academic paper about Judge Dee in the Tang dynasty?' Director Hou did not try to hide his astonishment.

'Yes, the very Judge Dee. Professor Yao is known for his expertise on the history of China's judicial system. So I would like very much to consult him about it, but he's not in his office this morning.'

'Professor Yao's away at a conference in Guangxi, but he has published quite a number of academic works. I'm not sure if any of them are related to Judge Dee, but they are quite possibly related to the Tang period. They are all kept here in the archive of his academic achievement.'

'That's fantastic! Can you do me a favor and make a list of those papers related to the Tang period? When Professor Yao comes back, I will discuss more with him. Judge Dee was a representative of the judicial system in ancient China. So a paper about the legendary figure may also touch on the urgency with which we need to push forward the reform today.'

'You always have your original perspective, Chief Inspector Chen – sorry, Director Chen.'

'No, you don't have to say sorry about that. I'm having a hard time getting myself adjusted to the new position. So I have to do as much research as possible, and to consult with experts like Professor Yao.'

'We will all be greatly honored if we can be of help in any way,' Hou said, rising with Chen reverentially.

Chen then moved into the library. It appeared to be fairly small, but cozy, convenient, with the clear classifications and open shelves. Looking around, he turned to move down from the top shelf a set of thread-bound volumes of *Annotated Tang Dynasty Law*, a rare reprint during the Republican period, with a label saying 'Read in library only'. He put the set on a table near the entrance, where he was pleasantly surprised at the sight of an English book, *True Crimes in Eighteenth-Century China: Twenty Case Histories*, written by a contemporary sinologist named Robert Hegel. Ironically, he sometimes found reading the English translations of law studies easier than the original in classical Chinese. Was it because there were no exact words or phrases for these judicial concepts in the Chinese language? For this English book, he thought he could order it from Amazon. The new office had a large budget, which came with its status.

He talked to someone like a librarian sitting in a corner, who gave him permission to copy pages from the *Annotated Tang Dynasty Law*. He started doing the job there gingerly, page by page, as the time-yellowed paper appeared to be so fragile. It was then that Director Hou came bursting into the library.

'You don't have to do it yourself, Director Chen. I'll have someone copy whatever you want.' Hou must have dug out the newspaper with Chen's office statement in it. 'You really have made an excellent point about the inadmissibility of the evidence in Judge Jiao's case. In this global age, we'll have to learn those good points from the West too. It's a pity that some of our net mobs totally ignored that.'

'Yes, that's a technicality issue. A lot we can surely learn, not only from the West, but also from China's history.'

It was a politically correct comment, also demonstrative of his correct attitude toward his new position. With Hou's connections to the city government, Chen's visit to the institute would probably soon come into a report on the desk of the higher authorities, though it was far from enough to get him out of trouble.

'Also, I've just thought of one who can help you with your Judge Dee project. Professor Zhong of the Literature Institute.'

'Professor Zhong Longhua?'

'Yes, that's him. Tell you what, he has actually served as a consultant to a Judge Dee movie.'

'Really! I did not know anything about it. Thank you so much, Director Hou. I'll write down the number of the pages to be copied here. And I'll go to talk to Professor Zhong right now. The Literature Institute is on the second floor, correct?'

'Correct.'

Chen made his way down to the Literature Institute.

He had met Zhong Longhua before, in the institute as well as at the Shanghai Writers' Association. A senior research professor specializing in Tang poetry, Zhong was also a member of the association, in which he belonged to the classical literature group, and Chen to the modern poetry group.

Moving down the stairs, Chen came to a stop on the landing and took out his phone to check the links to the Judge Dee TV movies Jin had sent him the previous day. Sure enough, Zhong's name appeared as a special consultant for one of the TV adaptations. And in a quick web search, he found in an interview that Zhong had been writing a literary biography of Xuanji, with parts of it published in magazines. It would make a more than plausible pretext for him to consult Zhong about the Tang dynasty case.

The people in the institute came in just two days a week for meetings and political studies, and at the end of the year submitted a list of their publications for the work evaluation. But that morning, with the recent re-emphasis on political studies, all of them were there.

Chen was lucky enough to immediately catch sight of Professor Zhong working at his desk. He looked pleasantly surprised at the sight of Chen stepping into his office.

'What favorable wind has brought you over here today, Director Chen?'

'The wind from the Tang dynasty, the rain from the Chang'an Palace.'

'What a poetic director!'

'No, I'm just paraphrasing Wang Changling's line.'

'Yes, "the moon of the Qing dynasty, the pass of the Hang dynasty". It's such an honor to have you come to visit our small office.'

It was not a too-small office, but Zhong had to share the space with four or five colleagues, who wondered whether they should leave the two of them alone there.

Greeting them, Chen seated himself in a chair opposite Zhong, not minding the presence of Zhong's colleagues in the office.

'Today I'm here as a student of yours for Tang dynasty poetry. I have always admired your excellent work in the field, Professor Zhong.'

'You're flattering me, Director Chen. You have translated a collection of Tang poems, so there's a lot we two can discuss on the subject. Are you translating another collection of Tang poetry?'

'I'm planning to. Possibly for an enlarged edition. But for the moment, I'm reading a Judge Dee novel about Xuanji by the Dutch sinologist Van Gulik. A very intriguing book, with the tragic poetess as one of the central characters, so I have a number of questions about Xuanji and Judge Dee. You are the authority on the subject, I know. I've just read the interview about the biography of Xuanji you have been working on. And you've also served as a special consultant for a Judge Dee TV movie—'

But their talk was interrupted by the entrance of a middle-aged researcher Chen did not know, who turned at the sight of Chen, said something vague in exasperation, and withdrew from the office.

'Let's go downstairs to a quieter place,' Zhong suggested. 'There's a café on the first floor of our main building. Not fancy, but quiet. We often meet with our guests there. Only the coffee is not freshly ground.'

'Don't worry about the coffee. I'll pass. I've had too much coffee of late.'

It turned out to be quite a large café in the office building, with its customers mainly from the academy. For the moment, only two or three people were sitting near the counter, drinking and reading.

Chen and Zhong seated themselves near the further end of the room behind rows of white-painted magazine shelves, which provided a sort of privacy enclosure.

Zhong ordered a cup of black tea with lemon for Chen, and a cup of black coffee for himself.

'You were talking about Judge Dee,' Zhong said, smiling an apologetic smile.

'Yes, believe it or not, I became interested in the Judge Dee novels because of a poem by Xuanji, which Gulik quoted partially in *Poets and Murder*. It's one she wrote for Wen, her first lover, I believe.'

'That's little wonder for our poet-detective. I too recognized the poem in the Chinese translation of the novel. But you know what? The translator did not know the poem in the original, so the translation is not that readable back into Chinese.'

'What a pity for such a superb mystery. The combination of the poems and the love affairs and the murder truly held me spellbound. And I have to consult an authority like you.'

'You've come to the right person, though not an authority as you put it. Yes, I've done a biography of Xuanji, which will come out next year. As for Van Gulik's work, I read the Chinese translation years ago. I don't remember all of its details, but I did recognize the heroine in *Poets and Murder* as Xuanji. It was the most sensational real murder case in the Tang dynasty.'

'What do you think of the case?'

'The case in Gulik's Judge Dee story or the case in the Tang dynasty?'

'Both.'

'Well, in the Judge Dee story, the main character is Judge Dee, and Xuanji is just one of the intriguing characters thrown in for Judge Dee's sake. To be frank, a rather unconvincing character in the story.'

'Please enlighten me further, Professor Zhong.'

'I'll start with a short bio of Xuanji, though you may have read about her too. Cut me off any time you want.

'Xuanji was born of a poor, hardly educated family, but

unlike the children from such a family background, she showed extraordinary talent in poetry as a teenager. In the Tang dynasty, however, there was no way for a young girl to come to the fore through poetry writing. No permission for a female candidate to participate in the civil service examination. It was not even considered as a good idea for a woman to be educated, since her role in life was seen, in the light of orthodox Confucianism, to be that of obeying her father before marriage, of obeying her husband after marriage, and of obeying her son after her husband's death. But poetry writing was so popular at the time, and soon Xuanji attracted the attention of men of letters, among whom she met with Wen Tingyun, a renowned poet. Wen appreciated her beauty as well as her poems. Though she was more than thirty years younger, Xuanji fell for him. It was said the two wrote a number of passionate poems for each other. Things did not work out for them, though. According to some later critics, it was because Wen was a plain man, very self-conscious in the company of women, but according to others, he was too ambitious for an official career. It was romantic to have an affair with a poetry-writing girl like Xuanji, but quite another matter to marry her. Whatever the interpretations, Wen did go out of his way for her by introducing her to Zi'an, a younger man of letters with a far more promising future. Zi'an fell for her, but he was married, with a wife from a prominent family, which meant a lot to his future career. It was out of the question for him to divorce his wife for Xuanji's sake. So they lived together in the capital for a short period without the knowledge of his wife. When his wife too came to the capital, however, Xuanji had to stay away, missing him day and night.'

'Yes, she wrote a poem for him titled *Look out from the Riverside*. It's included in the collection I have translated, so I remember.'

'That's an exquisite poem, for Zi'an had to be frequently away for his official responsibilities, or in the company of his wife, who became furious with Xuanji being a secret concubine. Zi'an had no choice but to send her into a Daoist temple, promising to get her out in a year, but he remained as henpecked as before, doing nothing for her. Despairing, with no end to her waiting, she abandoned herself to affairs with men who came to the temple for her beauty or poetry.

'The next part of her story got somewhat blurred. She continued writing poems, and being a Daoist made it possible for her to lead a more bohemian life by taking customers like a high-class courtesan in the temple. Then something inexplicable happened. In a moment of jealousy, she beat her maidservant to death, who was said to be carrying on with one of her lovers. She buried the body in a flowerbed outside the temple. But people came to notice flies buzzing and circling the flowerbed the next day, so the bloody body was discovered. Xuanji was found guilty and executed.'

'What a tragic story! Thank you so much, Professor Zhong. For her affairs with Wen and Zi'an, I think I can find traces in her poems. But can you tell me something more about the murder she committed in the temple.'

'To begin with, the historical material about the murder case is scanty, and unreliable. It was not recorded in the official Tang history. Nothing but a brief mention of the case in a collection of anecdotes and stories titled *Little Tablets from the Three Rivers* from the ninth century. Some pieces in the collection are supposedly based on real-life stories in the mid-Tang period. The piece about Xuanji is one of the most well known. According to it, when Xuanji scolded the maid, the maid talked back, and Xuanji beat her to death in a blind fury. With the body discovered, she pleaded guilty and was executed because of it.

'But the part about Xuanji beating her maid to death in an uncontrollable rage is open to question. Xuanji's suspicion about the maid was not backed by evidence or witness. How could a talented poetess have suddenly turned into an insane murderer? Some critics thought it might have been a cover-up for something or someone else.'

'A cover-up, that's novel.'

'Also, according to the anecdote in the collection, the judge or the magistrate who sentenced Xuanji to death happened to be one who'd had his advance to her rejected earlier, but that could have been a matter of hearsay. She was such a notorious courtesan, and a high-ranking magistrate would not have made any serious advance or proposal to her. So things might have been more complicated.

'But more than a thousand years later, with no historical records available, the best you can hope for is one scenario which sounds a bit more likely than another. There's only one thing I'm sure about in the background of the case. Those romantic affairs might have been popular in folk literature, but she was not seen as one acceptable in the official discourse at the time.'

'In other words, Xuanji was also found guilty as someone unacceptable to the dominant discourse in the Tang dynasty.'

Zhong nodded broodingly over his cup of coffee.

'Perhaps because of the scanty material, instead of having Judge Dee investigate the Xuanji case, Gulik was so clever as to put her in the background of another case, in which she appeared to be even more a victim of passion.'

'Indeed, you know such a lot about the historic details, Professor Zhong. To tell the truth, I'm coming to you today not just because of my curiosity with the Xuanji case as depicted in the Judge Dee novel. I'm thinking of writing a paper about Judge Dee and the Tang judicial system. Possibly with the Xuanji case as an example. As a police officer for many years, I could not help reading Gulik's novel like a real case, and analyzing it from my experience.'

'A brilliant idea, Director Chen. It's a real case. You're in a unique position to do so, having majored in English literature, read the book in the original language, translated the Tang poems, and written some yourself. Not to mention your experience as a chief inspector.' Zhong paused, taking a sip of the coffee before he said, 'And it's very good timing. It's a series well known in the Western world about a Chinese hero. Politically correct. In fact, a considerable number of Judge Dee books were translated and published, including *Poets and Murder*.

'And the movie producer had a long talk with me about it. It's much easier for the censorship official to approve a Judge Dee movie – given it was long, long ago in the Tang dynasty, and nothing to do with the socialism with China's characteristics today. No problem to represent such a Chinese myth as Judge Dee.'

Their talk was interrupted again by a young man barging into the café with a book in his hand.

'I don't want to interrupt, Chief Inspector Chen, but I was told that you're here talking with Professor Zhong. I've got to come to say hi to you. My name is Guan, a young colleague of Professor Zhong's, and I'm a huge fan of yours, not only of your investigations, but of your poems too. And here is a copy of your poems I cherish so much. Would you please sign your name on it for me?'

'Indeed, *who does not know you under the sun?*' Zhong said, beaming with pride. 'It's just like the line in Gao Shi's poem. You have your fans everywhere.'

'You don't have to say that, Professor Zhong. I'm just learning such a lot from you about the Judge Dee case.'

'Of course, Chief Inspector Chen is the Judge Dee of the twenty-first century. You are just being too modest. Since you have a lot to talk about with Professor Zhong, I don't want to take more of your time. But is there anything I can do for you?' asked Guan.

'Perhaps you can make a copy of the manuscript of my book that's coming out early next year. Director Chen may find it interesting.' Zhong took out a flash memory stick. 'Do it in the Director's office, with the laser printer, quicker and better.'

'Of course, Professor Zhong. It will be done in no time. Again, thank you so much, Chief Inspector Chen. Your signature has made my day.'

After Guan left with the book, Zhong said with a serious expression, 'I have a suggestion for you, Director Chen.'

'Yes?'

'Don't worry about your research paper. Write a Judge Dee story instead.'

'Why, Professor Zhong?'

'I've been doing my research on the Tang dynasty poetry for over thirty years, and published books and articles. But what I got paid for them through all these years is less – you may never believe – than the fee for a special consultant in a Judge Dee TV movie. What a shame!

'And it's not a matter of money. It's a third- or fourth-class script about Judge Dee, but the TV producer came to me and made an offer too good for me to say no. Needless to say, I then had to do my part providing the background knowledge for the movie.'

'Surely they could not have done it without your generous help. And your name adds to their credit too. But why that suggestion of yours to me?'

'Money aside, you can write a far better story. A story worthy of Judge Dee, Xuanji, and worthy of the Tang poetry, too. And you'll have a far larger group of readers for your story. Fans like Guan have so much expectation of you. A legendary inspector in contemporary China writing a legendary judge in ancient China. Imagine the response from your readers.'

'I'll think about your suggestion, Professor Zhong.'

'For such a project, I'll help the best I can. Any historical details you may need for your book – and then for a movie based on your book – just ask.'

'You're moving too fast, Professor Zhong. I've not written a single word for the story yet, and you're already talking about a movie based on it. One small problem, though. Judge Dee and Xuanji did not live in the exact same time period. Not the way it is depicted in Gulik's novel.'

'There is a simple explanation. It was the most sensational case in the Tang dynasty, with love, poetry, sex, jealousy, murder, fox spirit, and what-not, all the exciting elements in the one case. And Judge Dee, the most celebrated judge or detective at the time. Gulik could not have resisted the temptation to put them together.'

'That's true. It's a temptation for me too.'

'A couple of movie companies have contacted me about a truly worthy Judge Dee movie. I'll talk to them tonight. Wait for my phone calls.'

As if on cue, Professor Zhong's cellphone started dinging.

'Oh, it's a message from the head of our institute. He wants me in his office.'

'Of course, you go there now, and it's time for me to go somewhere else too.'

'Fine. I'll call after the talk with the producer. China's movie market is huge. Western producers are trying to squeeze in like crazy. This is a safe topic. Chinese Sherlock Holmes.'

It took Jin less than twenty minutes to arrive at Min's neighborhood, but quite a while to locate the neighborhood committee tucked in the intersection between Jinling and Madang Roads.

It was not an uncommon scene for the dramatically changing city of Shanghai. One section so crowded with the new high rises, but half a block away another section still scattered with shabby *shikumen* houses in which the neighborhood committee office looked like a time-yellowed postcard kept by her parents.

The front of the neighborhood committee office was partially obscured by a mobile food stall sporting rows of uncooked dishes beside a coal stove and several woks. The chef was busy stir-frying for the customers sitting on benches around the rough, unpainted wooden tables.

She stepped into the office, where she introduced herself to a silver-haired woman half-dozing on a chair near the door. Taking out her business card as the secretary for the Shanghai Judicial System Reform Office, she thought she had a perfect pretext to learn some background information regarding Min.

'My office is in the city government building at the People's Square, it's so close—'

'The head of the neighborhood committee is not in the office. It's lunch time. I'm just a retiree sitting here for the moment,' the old woman said without showing any interest, her face shrunk like an aged walnut.

'An office in the city government building at the People's Square?' an old man exclaimed excitedly, emerging from a back room carrying a plastic food container and leaning over for a closer look at the business card in Jin's hand.

'Yes. We've heard about the Min case in your neighborhood. I'm not a cop, but I just want to do some background research for my office.'

'About Min, you have come to the very man for information, Secretary Jin. I've lived in the same lane with her for years, watching her growing up as a little girl still wearing a short pigtail. She was with her parents in that small *tingzhijian* room at the time, not in the multi-million yuan *shikumen* house of nowadays. Everything you want to know—'

'You're opening your big, reckless mouth again,' the old woman said in apparent disapproval, her silver hair glaring in the sunlight.

'Don't worry. I am not a journalist, and whatever you're telling me here, it won't be put into a report,' Jin said to the old man. 'And you're doing a great service for the government. So your name, old comrade?'

'Bao Guoqing. I'm here just to warm my lunch in the microwave. I used to be a neighborhood patroller.'

She was surprised that Bao had to go to the neighborhood committee office for the use of the microwave. Evidently, he was not a well-to-do one. Then she thought of the food stall outside, recalling the stories she had heard about Chen's interviews as an inspector – done over the dishes and cups with interviewees. Why not? Bao too could talk more freely out there, not worrying about any interruption from the old woman. 'How about having a simple lunch with me outside?'

'But I have my lunch box with me.'

'You can save it for the evening. My treat.'

Bao readily moved outside with Jin, grinning from ear to ear. The old woman looked at the two of them, shaking her head without getting up from the chair.

Outside, there was not much for them to choose at the food stall. She had a portion of Crispy Bells – fried tiny tofu-skin-dumplings – which were supposed to be crunchy and delicious, though she was concerned about the repeatedly used oil at the place. He fell to a full platter of double steaks braised in reddish soy sauce with green cabbage heaped on top of white rice.

'Not bad at all,' Bao said with a satisfied sigh, finishing the first steak and wiping his mouth with the back of his hand. 'I used to be an activist here, patrolling the neighborhood. Those days, those peddlers stood in awe of a neighborhood patroller. It's really a changed world now. And it's not for nothing, I know, for a young office lady from the city government to treat a poor old retiree like me. So you just go ahead with your questions.'

'Thank you.' She took out her cellphone and pressed *record*, as if checking a message.

It was not going to be used as evidence. She did not have to worry about its legality.

Emerging from the Shanghai Academy of Social Sciences, Chen did not have any idea about where to go, but he turned left on Huaihai Road.

Half a block away, he saw a long line of people waiting, leading to a delicatessen window of an old-brand restaurant, *Happy Village*. The delicacies were cooked in the traditional Shanghai style, such as chicken immersed in yellow rice wine, smoked fish head, pork belly braised in red sauce, all of them quite palatable, sold at the delicatessen window at half the price of what was charged inside the restaurant.

He did not feel hungry, even with his breakfast so early in the morning. He decided to walk on for a while. He thought he needed a little more time to digest what he had just learned from Professor Zhong.

The visit to the academy had turned out to be a random harvest in several respects. For starters, he had spread the word about his being busy collecting material for a Judge Dee project. It could have taken him months to learn by himself what he had learned from Professor Zhong in one morning, if he was really going to write something about Judge Dee. It was also a good idea, incidentally, for him to work on a Judge Dee story instead of an academic paper, which he had not done for years. Nor could he afford the time for the research needed for it. A story would be different. With the material obtained through the shortcut, he should be able to put together a piece with fairly reliable historical details.

And the prospect of a bestselling book, and then of the movie adaption, as Professor Zhong had presented, was not without temptation. The ex-inspector had to think about his mother, if not himself. She should want for nothing in her last years at the nursing home.

At the same time, he was ambitious about creating a truly worthy book, like Gulik's, which people would read for years and years, as in a line by the famous Tang poet Du Fu, '*Writing is for thousands of autumns.*'

Then his thoughts began to wander, jumping from Gulik's treatment of Xuanji's efforts to protect her secret lover, to Min's statement about her not being with anyone during the night despite her sleeping naked.

He moved past the restaurant-circling line, in which one of the customers was absorbed with an e-book instead of talking to others, tapping on the tablet, as the line edged forward to the delicatessen window at a snail's pace.

And he turned round, walked several steps back, and went into a bookstore. It was perhaps coincidental that he found on the front shelf three Judge Dee stories in Chinese: *The Lacquer Screen, The Phantom of the Temple, The Chinese Lake Murder*. Judge Dee had become so popular in China. Chen was not sure about the translation quality, but it could be faster for him to read skipping one page after another in the Chinese translation.

Carrying the books, he then found himself moving in the direction of the New World, and thinking about a Starbucks there, when his special cellphone started ringing.

'Something new . . .' Old Hunter said in a hurry.

'Something new . . .' Chen responded, repeating. 'Yes, we should try something new. How about the Starbucks in the New World? They serve green tea too.'

'Green tea in Starbucks?'

'Yes, green tea latte, among other varieties. The café is located near the northern entrance of the New World. It may not be up to your tea standard, but worth trying for a change.'

'OK, see you there in fifteen to twenty minutes.'

So Old Hunter must be somewhere nearby. It would take Chen less than ten minutes to walk from the bookstore to the café.

The Starbucks appeared to be packed as always, extremely popular among the young white-collar workers in the area, but compared to other bars and restaurants in the New World, the price for a cup of coffee there seemed to be reasonable.

He was lucky enough to find a table outside, ordered a

tall cup of black coffee, and opened *The Lacquer Screen*. It was not a cold day. Sitting there with the book in his hand, he thought he looked just like one of those regular customers at the café.

He had just finished the first ten pages of the novel, sipping at the coffee, when Old Hunter strode over to him and slumped in the chair opposite.

Not too surprisingly, the green tea latte ordered for the old man did not appeal to him; he appeared to be frowning at the first sip, though without saying anything about it.

As it turned out, Old Hunter had intended to invite him to another café, much more fashionable and expensive than Starbucks.

'How about the garden café of the Moller Villa Hotel. People say its coffee is excellent, very black, and very strong. Expensive, but it's worth the money. The atmosphere of the garden is absolutely mesmerizing. And we can have privacy in a small tent, if you prefer. With the new expense allowance from our client Sima, it won't be a problem.'

'So it's the café in the garden of Moller Villa Hotel on the corner of Yan'an and Shanxi Roads,' Chen said, his heart sinking with the knowledge.

The hotel, meticulously preserved because of its singular history, was a rediscovered legend among the rich and successful of the city. It was said that Eric Moller, a businessman who had made his fortune through horse and dog racing in Shanghai, had this fairy-tale-like mansion built in the 1930s. Originally designed in accordance with a dream of his little daughter's, it proved to be an architectural fantasy. After 1949, it was used as a government office for years before being turned into an elite hotel, redecorated and refurbished, with its interior design and original details meticulously restored, and with a new building in the same style added next to it.

But what worried Chen was something else about the hotel.

'When did you become so picky about cafés, Old Hunter?'

'You've been to the hotel before?'

'Yes, for an investigation a few years ago.'

'So you know . . .'

Old Hunter did not have to go on. He knew Chen knew what it really meant.

Min was *shuangguied* in that hotel under the government surveillance, which came as no surprise to him. In an earlier investigation, a high-ranking Party official had been kept in the hotel, and then murdered. A complicated case that had led to the downfall of the then Party Secretary of Shanghai.

It was ironic that the building, originally built out of the fantastic dream of a little Norwegian girl, symbolic of unbelievable wonders of the brave new world, had turned into the secret detention place of the *shuangguied*, under the twenty-four-hour surveillance of the Shanghai government, with its staff members trained and experienced with the workings of the *shuanggui* system.

Perhaps there was just one thing new in Old Hunter's description of the garden café. During that investigation, Chen had noticed only the in-house hotel guests drinking coffee in the garden. Nowadays visitors could also enjoy the service, as well as the view of the mystery-wrapped garden.

'For a veteran tea drinker like you, how did you manage to find out about the hotel garden café?'

'It's through Mr Sima. He's really well connected, you know. We have no clues about where Min is kept.'

The case must have had a higher political stake than they knew of, something more than making an example of a Republican Lady.

What was Old Hunter able to achieve by going there in the company of Chen? Some reconnaissance around the hotel, probably. But no possibility of their sneaking in for contact with Min. The hotel was so closely guarded by its well-trained staff, who would recognize Chen whether in a garden tent or not. Not to mention the many surveillance cameras installed there. According to the latest report online, the number of surveillance cameras was catching up with that of China's entire population. It was getting worse than in *1984*.

No point taking the risk, he concluded. He had been lucky so far, but the luck could be running out at this very moment.

'Sorry, Old Hunter. The city government has just requested

an office statement about a Party-member judge scandal. I have to be really busy for a while.'

'But you're on leave, Chief.'

'After our visit to the matching corner in the park, my secretary came to my apartment with the urgent instruction from the city government. She is working hard on it, and I'm waiting for her phone call right now. But I'll give you a call in a day or two. Don't worry. The strong black coffee in the hotel garden may be too much for my stomach, but we'll go to the hot water place you recommended. Black tea agrees with me more.'

As Old Hunter disappeared out of sight, dragging his feet, Chen kept stirring the lukewarm coffee with the spoon.

What difference could he possibly make? It was a question to be asked not just of this investigation in the company of Old Hunter. For years, he had been holding on to the belief that he was capable of making a difference by doing a conscientious job as a cop within the system.

With all those years wasted, he finally came to the realization that such a difference existed largely in his imagination. What's more, he was not a cop any more.

But what else could he have become?

And what could Judge Dee have really become?

It then occurred to him that he should check with Jin, who might tell him something more about the real Judge Dee in the Tang history, in addition to any developments at the office. Talking with her about the Judge Dee project might serve as the mountain path too. It was not unimaginable that some people could try to ferret out things about him through her.

Chen took out his cellphone. But just before he pressed the number, the screen showed a WeChat message with the emoji of a young girl in a mandarin dress saying 'Hi,' waving coquettishly, her bare, slender arm as white as the lotus root in a Tang dynasty poem. He knew nothing about the use of emojis, and he texted back: 'Oh, what's up, Jin?'

'We got some feedback from the city offices and media about the statement made by our office. Very positive.'

'That's good. It's to your credit.'

'No, it's all under your guidance, Director Chen.' She added another emoji of a girl covering her face in embarrassment before she typed, 'Let me call through the WeChat phone. You just need to press "accept".'

'That's fine.'

Perhaps she had a hard time trying to reach him through his ordinary phone. But he was not in a hurry to give her his special phone number.

It turned out to be a video call. He was pleased to see her young, animated face flashing across the phone screen. It appeared she was not in the office.

'For the office statement, the footnote-like comment was added by the Minister of the City Propaganda Ministry. He insisted on it, as if the inadmissibility of the evidence had been its one and only merit.'

'For the Party newspapers, they have to worry about a lot of things. Pang's success may inspire copycats, and that's something the government authorities want to prevent. Any news about the development of the case?'

'Judge Jiao was officially *shuangguied*. It's a matter of time for him to be charged. In the meantime, Pang said in an interview to the *Liberation Daily* that he saw justice finally being done, and that he would not do anything like that in the future.'

'That's good. Thank you so much, by the way, for the links to the Judge Dee movies too.'

'After our talk yesterday, I've watched another Judge Dee DVD, and gathered some information about the judges we discussed.'

'The TV movies are really interesting,' he responded, noting the plural 'judges' in her comment, wondering whether she had gathered some info about the other judge as well.

'And there're some more, not about Judge Dee, but about the case similar to the one in the Judge Dee novel. It's so heated on the Internet. I collected some of them through a VPN, as people put it, by "climbing the firewall".'

'Ah,' he said, surprised by her going out of her way for him.

'I've printed out a bunch of them for you – but where are you? The background is noisy.'

'At a café in the New World. This morning, I too did some research at the Shanghai Academy of Social Sciences. About Judge Dee, you know. Now I am reading another Judge Dee novel in the Starbucks here.'

'Really! I'm near the intersection of Madang and Huaihai Roads. Really close to the New World. I would like very much to make a detailed report to you about the office statement – and about something else.'

'But—' he cut himself short. 'You're welcome to join me at the Starbucks.'

'Then I'll be over in about twenty minutes. You just wait for me there. Twenty minutes at the most.'

'That will be fine with me. No hurry. I'm enjoying the novel.'

Jin's insistence on coming to the café came as another surprise for the day, but it more or less supported a well-meant fib he had just told Old Hunter.

Walking through the tables outside the café, Jin appeared more like a young fashionable office lady in a well-tailored light gray dress and black high heels.

'What would you like to drink, Jin?' he asked as she took the chair opposite. 'My treat today.'

'A green tea latte with ice for me, Director Chen.'

'That's original.'

'Why?'

It was more coincidental than anything else. At this same table, Old Hunter had just frowned at the green tea latte. For the old man, the way to enjoy tea was, invariably, by pouring hot water over it, breathing at it vigorously, watching the green leaves rising to the surface and sinking back to the bottom, before taking a slow, small sip.

But she was so different, taking a large gulp from the latte, crunching the ice with her white teeth, and wiping the sweat from her face with a paper napkin.

'So you are working at the café instead, Director Chen?'

'No, not exactly. At home, it's just so easy to find all sorts of excuses to be lazy. A new TV episode, or a portion of fried soup buns delivered like yesterday. And you end up doing nothing for the whole day. But at a café, you feel obliged to do something for a cup of coffee's worth.'

'You're kidding. That's the last thing you have to worry about.'

'As I've told you, I had a talk with Professor Zhong at the Shanghai Academy of Social Sciences. He suggested that I write a story based on *Poets and Murder*, so I need the time and the coffee to digest what I've just learned from him.'

'A story! That's original. But why not? You are a poet as well as an inspector, and you can do a better job than Gulik. To say the least, much better than the stuff for these Judge Dee TV movies.'

That was a comment similar to Professor Zhong's, but it would be too long a discussion for the moment.

'You said you have something to talk to me about, Jin.'

'First, the office statement,' she said, taking out her cellphone for him to see the statement published in the city government e-newsletter. It gave top position to the office statement, high-lighting his comment about the inadmissibility of the evidence under normal circumstances.

And then she brought up some microblogging posts, in which he was represented as lending his name to the govern-mental handling of the scandal. Some netizens seemed not to be too pleased about it, even though his comment was true.

'A fantastic job, Jin. I really appreciate it. For the routine work in the office, as I've said to you, you can make decisions without having to discuss them with me first. Of course, I would like to work with you at the office. It's just my energy levels may not yet be up to it.'

'And another thing, Director Chen. This morning I did some research for the office and talked to someone in Min's neighborhood.'

'Hold on, you mean Min, the Republican Lady I told you about yesterday?'

'Yes, that's her. As a secretary of the office, I believe it's my responsibility to do some research into the background of the Min case, which is turning into a most sensational one on the Internet. And I happened to find in a blog post that neighborhood was not far away,' she paused to take anoth. gulp of the drink, the ice tinkling in the cup. 'So I went to Min's neighborhood committee, but no one was there during lunch time. I ended up talking to a once-neighborhood patroller named Bao, and I recorded the conversation with him.'

This time Chen was more than surprised. But for his bound hands, he himself would have done the same as a cop, but she moved fast. He failed to recall what he had said to her about the Min case, but some of his words could have been taken as subtle hints to her.

'I'm amazed, Jin. You did not have to go out of your way for this. We're not doing any investigation, but I'll listen to your recording back home – just the die-hard curiosity of an ex-cop,' he said guardedly. 'And before my coming to work in the office, I may need more of your help with the Judge Dee story. Your expertise will make a huge difference regarding the accuracy of historical details.'

'That's great!' she exclaimed, draining the tea. 'But I'd better hurry back to the office. I sneaked out during the lunch break, you know. Already been out for quite a long while. Oh, you know how to listen to the recording, Director Chen?'

It was his turn to get confused. The cellphone might have the function, but he had never used the phone for recording. On a moment of impulse, he took out his special phone.

'It's a phone with its number known only to the people I trust.'

'Thanks. I won't give it out.' She took it from his hand and demonstrated how to listen to the recording.

'Now I'm sending the recording to your special phone through WeChat, and you can start listening to it over your cup of coffee here.'

'It's so smart of you, Jin.'

'Let me know if there's any other research I can do for the office,' she said, ready to rise before turning to add casually, 'By the way, Director Ma, the Chief of Staff for the city government, came down to our office this morning. He's so concerned about your health. He wants me to keep him posted about you – with all the possible details.'

.hanks, Jin. The only problem with me is that I cannot
~ properly on leave. At night, I keep tossing and turning in
~d with irrelevant thoughts racing through my mind, like a
~ulb burning hot before bursting. So I wake up still so tired
in the morning. That's why I tried to work a little instead on
something light like a Judge Dee story, which may actually
help me sleep better. It's a practice suggested by Dr Xia, an
old friend of mine.'

She nodded with a knowing smile instead of saying
anything, as if seeing through why he was complaining about
his health problem.

Chen remained sitting there alone, taking the lid off another
cup of coffee as he started listening to the recording.

What he heard first was something like the mumbled noises
and voices in the background – '*Small croaker with pickled
cabbage soup, milky white soup*' . . . '*Fried stinking tofu with
a lot of pepper sauce*' . . . '*Sliced pork in fish sauce with
garlic . . .*'

So the interview could have been recorded in a neighborhood eatery. She had not worked with him before, but she
seemed to have conducted the interview after his own fashion
– over lunch. Shaking his head, he listened on.

> *Jin: Let me say again, Old Bao, I'm not doing any inves-
> tigation here. But it's turning into the most-talked-about
> case on the Internet. I mean the Min case, so we have
> to learn as much as possible about its background, and
> the first-hand information from an experienced neighbor-
> hood activist like you would help greatly. You said you
> have lived in the same lane with Min?*

> *Bao: Yes, all these years. Tell you what, Secretary Jin!
> Whatever happens to the shameless bitch Min, she
> deserves it. She can dream of her spring-and-autumn
> dream about getting away so easily this time!*

> *Jin: So she has done something like this before? Please
> tell me from the very beginning.*

Bao: Indeed, it's a world turned upside down. I moved into the lane in the mid-sixties. At the beginning of the Cultural Revolution, her family was driven out of the shikumen *house – to a small tofu-like* tingzhijian *room in the lane. Believe it or not, that* tingzhijian *room is just under my wing room.*

Nowadays people keep on saying all kinds of things about the Cultural Revolution. And about Chairman Mao, too. But think about it. Those years, how many working-class families had to live squeezed together like in a can of sardines? More than twenty, to say the least, in a house the size of Min's, with each family huddling in a partitioned room. You call that fair? No, definitely not. Not to mention all the dividends her family received after the Party government turned private companies into state companies in the mid-fifties.

Min was born toward the end of the Cultural Revolution, I think, possibly one or two years after it. In that tingzhijian *room, she grew up to be a young slut. When she graduated from high school, she already had men circling her like flies around a piece of rotten meat. Her family then had a change of fortune. Her grandfather was said to be a patriotic banker before 1949, with rich, influential relatives coming back from abroad. So a district official came to her family, offering compensation for their so-called loss during the Cultural Revolution. Anyway, hers was then called a 'good family', and she had rich and powerful men swarming into the lane for her, with flowers in the open, and with money in secret. Shortly afterward, the whole* shikumen *house was handed back to her family like on a platter. It was supposed to be in accordance with the government policy, but it was achieved through all her connections – in bed.*

Jin: The city government had a new policy regarding private properties at the time, but it's also true that few were lucky enough to get their house back.

Bao: Exactly, she also got so much money from those men, without having to work a real job for a single day. She kept the tingzhijian *room in the lane, in which her maid Qing stayed instead, and bought several new apartments near the New World for her parents and younger brother. And she moved into the completely refurbished* shikumen *house – all for herself – a full-time high-end slut in a fancy brothel.*

Jin: A fancy brothel? You mean she had customers coming and paying for sex with her?

Bao: Um, probably not a hooker or prostitute in the common sense of the word – she's called a mingyuan. *It's a term used before 1949 in the Republican era, meaning a precious flower of the high society. Nothing but a high-class courtesan in reality. Anyway, she then started to have the weekly dinner party at home. Obscenely expensive, about ten thousand yuan per person for a private dinner with her, usually with seven to eight men at a round table. In the old days, such a dinner party was called a flower party in a brothel, and if people paid a price high enough, then overnight—*

Jin: You think it could be something like sex orgies with those people in the shikumen *house at night?*

Bao: I have never been inside the shikumen *house at night, so I could not be sure about that. But it's more than possible that the man who paid the highest price would have her for the night. Anyway, can you believe anyone would pay ten thousand yuan simply for one meal?*

Needless to say, such wild parties could not but hurt the image of our lane. People complained about it to the neighborhood committee, but they were told that she was untouchable.

Jin: Because of the government standing behind her?

Bao: Not the government itself, but the head of the neigh-borhood committee heard something about one of her visitors being a top government official. And he knew better than to tell us about it.

Jin: She must have had powerful connections to get back the shikumen house and the permission to have those parties there. It's little wonder.

Bao: And she calls her party a salon. An outrageous salon just like in the old days. It is now the new society under the Communist Party, but she's still after those things under the KMG during the Republican period. Hence her nickname Republican Lady.

Jin: Nickname aside, have you seen or heard suspicious things about her and her men before or after those wild parties at night?

Bao: To give a devil her due, I myself have not seen men sneaking in and out of the shikumen house in the middle of the night, but some of her neighbors saw something there in the early hours.

Jin: Can you tell me the names of those neighbors?

Bao: Well, you can ask the neighborhood committee about it.

Jin: That's fine. But can you tell me anything you noticed about that particular night, Old Bao?

Bao: That evening, I went to my son's in Hongkou District, and I got back to the lane quite late. Around eleven – five or ten minutes earlier or later. Now you have mentioned it, I remember I noticed someone waiting near the entrance of the lane, waiting for his car after the party.

Jin: How did you know he was a guest at her party waiting for his car?

Bao: It's a common scene – people waiting outside for their cars after her party. And he looked like one from her party – dressed in an expensive-looking suit. Her guests usually come in their own cars, and with their own chauffeurs. Ours is a narrow side street. Too narrow for a taxi to come in, and difficult for a car to park. For her wealthy visitors, they simply have their chauffeurs pick them up after the dinner party. Some of them have their bodyguards, too. So you can see those guests of hers waiting outside for cars late at night.

Jin: You have a good point. Now about the maid named Qing, you've just mentioned that Qing stayed in the tingzhijian *room underneath you.*

Bao: That's true. Qing helped at the shikumen *house during the day, and came back to the* tingzhijian *room for the night. Occasionally, she might have stayed overnight in the* shikumen *when there were too many things for her to do, but I cannot say for sure.*

Jin: Do you think Qing knew about what might have happened after dinner between Min and her guests?

Bao: I don't think she knew that much about things after dinner in Min's bedroom.

Jin: A different question. For a young girl like Qing, do you know if she had any secret visitors?

Bao: You mean . . . Oh, I see what you're driving at. If she wanted to spend the night with someone, it would probably not be in that tingzhijian *room, what with her neighbors constantly moving about, and with little privacy because of the makeshift partition walls being old and thin, and the door incapable of being shut closely. You imagine for yourself. People could easily find out what the other is doing in the next room.*

Jin: What do you think of her then?

Bao: Like the master, like the maid. For one thing, she dressed more and more shamelessly. Bare shoulders, bare back and bare thighs. For her men, you bet. I did not see her carrying on with other men in the open, but other neighbors in our building said they had seen a man leaving the tingzhijian *early in the morning.*

Jin: I see. Just one more question, Old Bao. With the shikumen *houses in the lane practically joined with each other, a break-in at night could have been heard or noticed by her neighbors. Have Min's neighbors mentioned anything unusual about that night.*

Bao: No, not that I have heard of.

Jin: Thank you, Old Bao. If you think of anything else, you have my number, and you can contact me any time. Perhaps we can do another lunch talk just like today.

Apparently, that was the end of the conversation between the two. The ex-inspector himself might not have pushed any further either. Those activists could be so energetically suspicious about things in the neighborhood, but they had little or nothing substantial for support.

Bao's account of Min came from an unmistakably hostile perspective, which had to be taken with a pinch of salt. If anything, the mention of a man seen sneaking out of Qing's *tingzhijian* room in the early morning confirmed Feng's statement regarding a possible relationship between Qing and Rong, but it could have been another man.

All in all, Jin had done an excellent job, doing what was expected of an assistant to a chief inspector, rather than a secretary at the office. And she had done all that, he supposed, because she was aware of the difficulty for him to do so under the circumstances.

There was a tacit understanding between the two. He had

not said a single word about his attempting to probe into the Min case, nor given any instruction about what she should do.

And her comment made just before she left the café came like a Parthian shot – a subtle warning that people like Director Ma were anxious to finish him off.

In China, things could be like a scroll of traditional landscape painting, in which the blank space presents more than what is represented.

He decided not to speculate too much. In the worst case scenario, he would declare he had not told her to do anything about the case, and she could claim she had done it merely as research for the office. It would be justifiable for her, a secretary of the Judicial System Reform Office, to be concerned with a case talked about so much online.

Having just put the cell into his pocket, Chen pulled it out again. He took another gulp of the coffee and dialed Kong Jie, the Party secretary and editor-in-chief of the *Wenhui Daily*.

They had known each other for years, long before Kong became the Party boss of the influential newspaper. Kong had published Chen's poems in *Wenhui Daily*. And two or three years earlier, they had been together in a 'pen meeting' for a week in the city of Chengdu.

Kong was one of the few who had not tried to avoid the ex-inspector after his being put on convalescent leave.

'I guessed you would call,' Kong said, picking up the phone on the first ring, seemingly anticipating the phone call. 'You must have heard something about me of late.'

'Well, I'm calling you for a reason you may never have guessed. I was at the Shanghai Academy of Social Sciences this morning, talking with Professor Zhong about Judge Dee in the Tang dynasty. I've been thinking about writing a paper on Judge Dee – partially in preparation for my new office position. The judicial system in ancient China vs the judicial system in the present-day China, so to speak, but he suggested that I write a story about Judge Dee instead. What do you think?'

'That surprises me, Director Chen. If it's not a long paper, it can be published in *Wenhui*. A lot of readers will be interested in it. How a present-day detective approaches a Tang dynasty detective. Dee is popularly rediscovered, you know. But . . .'

'But what?'

'But I, too, would suggest a story – instead of a research paper. For a simple reason, Director Chen. A comparative study of China's past and present judicial system may be too sensitive a topic at the moment. For such a paper, there are things you may have to touch on. Like the concepts of separation of powers or judicial independence. Now, here's something between you and me. We've just gotten specific instructions from above that articles embracing or even mentioning these concepts cannot get published in *Wenhui*. The ideological control is getting tighter. Just about a month ago, China's Chief Justice Qiang declared that the Party government has to "draw out its sword" against the concept of "separation of powers".'

'Yes, I've read that speech of Qiang's,' Chen said after a pause. 'Don't get me wrong, Kong. For my new office, I just have to learn a lot of things, but I see your point. Yes, writing the story about Judge Dee may be a more practical alternative.'

'A short story is a totally different story. It can also be done as a comparative study for your purpose, but you don't have to bring in any present-day case, or any theoretical discussion. *Wenhui* can easily publish it. No problem at all. So go ahead and tell me about the story in your mind.'

Chen moved on to tell him briefly about the storyline before adding something at the end of it.

'I have not done any historical fiction before, but my new office assistant has a history major. She may help with historical accuracies, at least at a level comparable with Gulik's.'

'More than comparable, I bet. And if it's a novella instead of a short story, *Wenhui* can serialize it. Surely a boost to our newspaper circulation.'

'With the material gathered so far, it can be done for a novella, I think.'

'Then it's settled. Don't give it to anyone else. *Wenhui*'s exclusively. For a novella, we'll pay the advance. It's a shame for a Westerner – Dutch, I think – to write bestselling books about a Chinese legend. Our timing is perfect. A couple of TV movies have been made of Judge Dee. Such a subject matter won't have to worry about censorship.'

'Indeed, you're such a persuasive chief editor. I'll think about it, and I'll keep you informed.' He changed the subject abruptly. 'Now you just mentioned that I must have heard something about you of late. Is this about what happened at that private kitchen dinner party? Let me say this to you first, Kong. I'm no longer a cop. Not doing any investigations. From what I've learned, the case is in the hands of Internal Security, and I know better than to land myself further into the mire. But as an ex-cop, I'm just being curious.'

'Curious about what, Director Chen?'

'An influential Republican Lady she may have been, but why should Internal Security have rushed in and kept her *shuangguied*? If anything, it has served only to bring about a lot of wild speculations. Far from helpful to the political stability.'

'You're no outsider, whether engaged in an investigation or not. People had been paying attention to Min's private kitchen parties for a long while, but she seemed to be untouchable. Why? Because of the men behind her.'

'Men behind her?'

'Because of their special relationships.'

'Among the guests at the private dinner parties?'

'Among the special guests. Those she entertained not just in the dining room, but in her bedroom, too. No one really knows anything for sure, and she knew better than to talk to others about it. All that I have heard is also very hazy, fragmented. Possibly nothing but hearsay. People may be just clutching at the wind and shadow, as in an ancient Chinese proverb.'

It would be useless, Chen knew, to push an experienced Party-member newspaper boss like Kong to get into the details.

'There's something else I happened to overhear about the case. People above seem to have been pushing in different directions. Opposite directions, I would say. Like in a poem by Xu Zhimo, *"In which direction the wind is blowing, I don't know."*'

'Thank you for sharing the info with me, Director Chen.'

'And there's another puzzle for an ex-cop: Min does not have a motive for the murder. Of course, I don't know too much about the case.'

'We're all shocked.'

Apparently, Kong was not too eager to talk to him about it. With his background, it was hard for Kong to guess how much Chen knew, and more importantly, how much harm could be done if he shared whatever info he had with Chen.

'It's developing into a huge storm on the Internet. If the investigation of such a high-profile case keeps dragging on, it can bring about a lot of negative publicity for the people concerned – even for someone like you, who just happened to be at her dinner party that night.'

'I'm well aware of that.'

'If you think of anything else about the case, let me know. I may be able to have a word or two through my own connections. With the real murderer caught, the storm will soon blow over. Between you and me, I don't think Internal Security will do a real investigation on the murder case. But let me repeat, I'm not doing any investigation, so please don't say a single word to others about it.'

This would have served as a hint to the well-seasoned editor. He was talking to him not as a cop, but he still could help in his way. Kong had better come up with some useful information.

Since they were just chatting about the possible serialization of the Judge Dee novella in the newspaper, it could also have sounded like an exchange of favors.

'I really appreciate your offer of help, Director Chen. Of course I'll call you if I think of anything.'

Back home around eight, Jin's parents were watching TV in the living room. They had left a bowl of Yangzhou fried rice for her on the table in the dining room. She gestured to them to go on watching their favorite comedy.

She changed into an old T-shirt and pajama pants, put the rice into the microwave, made an instant egg drop soup, and then carried the rice and soup into her own rooms. The warmed rice smelled nice, golden-looking against the green pea, chopped pork and peeled shrimp.

She finished the fried rice without really tasting it. It was probably not too bad. She then moved into her bedroom. Closing the door after her, she seated herself at the small desk by the window.

After her talk with Chen at the café, she had thought that the afternoon would be an uneventful one, but to her surprise, phone calls from quite a number of newspapers came in, mainly about the office statement, particularly about the issues of the technicality regarding the evidence. She had to repeat again and again the point Chen had made in the statement. It had been a busy and stressful day.

The music from the TV in the living room made it difficult for her to do some quiet thinking. Outside the window came an occasional pigeon whistle trailing through the evening sky. Nowadays, it was a sound rarely heard in the city.

At the Starbucks, Chen had talked more with her about Judge Dee than anything else. He seemed to be so into the project, having visited the Shanghai Academy of Social Sciences for the purpose. It might work out, as Professor Zhong had suggested, for him to write a novella instead of a critical essay. And she might be able to help with details of historical accuracy.

But how could the ex-inspector have been preoccupied with such a literature project without being aware of the critical situation for himself?

She did not think Chen could have been so bookish at a moment like that. Or was he making the writing of the Judge Dee story a cover for something else?

He did not talk much about the Min case, but he did not try to dissuade her from doing the so-called research for the office. Like her, he'd used the word 'research' instead of 'investigation' throughout the talk.

'*I'm so glad that you are doing research into the background of the case. The way it's developing, we may soon have to issue another office statement.*'

That's what he had said at the café before she left, she remembered.

Was he trying to make it sound like routine office work? If so, she was in a position to go on as long as she pleased.

Once again, she thought it premature for her to jump to any conclusions. The little info she had gathered about the case might not mean anything; Chen could have obtained it through his own channels, one way or another.

No more TV noise came from the living room. Her parents must have gone to bed. It was late. She remained clueless.

With a ding on her cellphone, a WeChat voice call unexpectedly came through from Chen. She was relieved that it was not a video call. Her room was in a mess.

'A question, Jin. How did people tell the time in the Tang dynasty – especially at night?'

'At night, the night watchman would knock a wooden knocker while patrolling around, announcing the second watch, third watch, fourth watch, fifth watch . . . but no sixth watch.'

'Is that about the same length as one hour?'

'No, actually the first watch is about seven to nine p.m., and the fifth watch is about three to five a.m.'

'So is it OK to say, for instance, "after a couple of hours of a sleepless night, Judge Dee got up".'

'I think it's OK. It's a story for today's reader.'

'Thanks. Really good to know. So many things were different in the ancient China.'

'What else is a secretary with a history major for?'

'By the way, I had a talk with Huang Zhongluo this morning about an old book – not of the Tang dynasty, but of the Qing dynasty – which he may help to sell in an auction.'

'An auction?'

'Oh, it's left behind by my father. I should keep it, but the expense for my mother's nursing home is getting too high.'

'Sorry to hear that, but Huang Zhongluo, hold on. The name sounds so familiar, I must have come across it in the last few days.'

'Possibly in your research about Min's private kitchen dinner party. Huang did not go there that night, but he's a regular at her parties. During our talk at the noodle restaurant, Huang happened to mention another guest named Rong, who would have hired Qing. Rong was said to be a lover rejected by Min. And coincidentally, in the Xuanji case, the Tang dynasty judge too could have been a would-be lover rejected by her.'

'Wow!'

'The world is weird, and more than we think. But it's late. Time for you to go to bed. Good night.'

'Good night, Director Chen.'

By now sleep was the furthest thing from her mind.

So he was actually writing a Judge Dee story, as he had told her. She might do some more checking into things related to the Xuanji case, as represented in the Judge Dee novel. If Director Ma chose to ask her again about the ex-inspector, she would have something more concrete to say.

That the Tang dynasty murder appealed to Chen was understandable. Things did not add up in the case. For one thing, Xuanji did not have a motive . . .

Could the same be said about Min?

Was that the reason that he brought up Huang out of the blue? The ex-inspector might be an eccentric man, but she did not think it could be a coincidence for him to meet with Huang regarding an auction at this juncture.

If not, it could only mean that he was probing into the Min case with a pretext. Jin picked up a pen to draw two lines in parallel on a piece of paper—

The train of her thought was interrupted, however, by a light knock on the door. Her mother was standing in the doorway, carrying a bowl of white tree ears stewed with rock sugar.

'You've been so busy with your new job. Your boss has just called you?'

'Yes, just another call about the work in the office.'

'What kind of a man is he?'

'An enigmatic one. I don't think I really know that much about him. But he's a decent man, though a workaholic too, I believe, even on convalescent leave.'

'So he makes you work hard too.'

'No. Not really. Just some routine paperwork.'

'Don't overwork yourself. The white tree ears may be a boost to your energy.'

'Thanks, Mom. It's late, you should go to bed. Don't worry about me.'

The white tree ears tasted sweet. She finished the bowl in three or four large spoonfuls.

But she found it difficult to pick up her earlier train of thought again. She decided to stop cudgeling her brains out in the dark. Perhaps she would be able to think more clearly the next morning. Frustrated, she kicked off her slippers and flung herself across the bed.

With a couple of pillows propped against her head, she sent out several messages to her WeChat friends, who might have some info related to the Min case. It was such a hot topic online at the moment, and her interest in the case would not appear suspicious.

Sure enough, one of her friends named Xiaoxiao chatted back with a link to an article about Shang, the 'number-one real estate developer' in Shanghai, who had also attended Min's private kitchen dinner party. Xiaoxiao added a line, saying 'He's a distant uncle of mine.'

Then Jin recalled one thing Chen had said to her in the WeChat call. 'Coincidentally' – in reference to Rong and the judge. She was a bit confused, but it was anything but 'coincidentally', the way he brought it up. She reflected, staring up at the time-yellowed ceiling. Could his mentioning Rong and the judge have been a cue, pointing at the direction for her to follow?

She jumped off the bed, moved barefoot to the table, and added a few words to the piece of paper.

Kong called Chen late in the evening.

'I've tried hard recollecting details about the dinner party that night, Director Chen, but some of them may be totally irrelevant.'

'Any details may turn out to be helpful, Kong.'

'I had met the other two guests at her dining table before – Peng Jianjun and Shang Guanhua – but Zheng Keqiang was there for the first time. Peng, Shang and I were all on quite friendly terms with Min. Otherwise we would not have been invited to the *shikumen* house on a number of occasions. For

Zheng, it was simply because Huang Zhongluo could not make it and sent his nephew there on his behalf. In fact, it was a dinner specially arranged for Huang as an apologetic gesture.'

'An apologetic gesture for what?'

'She has a huge network of connections. As an antique dealer, Huang makes a fortune not only by buying or selling through auctions, but by dealing in secret with those Big Bucks clients. That's an open secret in the circle. And he secured a number of deals through her connections.

'But of late, he was said to have suffered a sizable loss because one of her connections did not deliver. I don't know any more details. So he had reason to be mad with her, but he still sent his nephew over there that night. To keep up appearances, I think, since they still might have business to do in the future. As for Zheng, it was a wonderful dinner for free. And then an unexpected opportunity to help the tipsy beauty to her bedroom as well. We're too old for the job.'

Chen listened without making any interruption. He had not told Kong about his meeting with Huang that morning. The unpleasantness between Min and Huang was not exactly news to him.

'After helping Min back to the room, did Zheng say anything to you?'

'No, not really. We were all about to leave. He said he was going to wash his hands in the restroom because she vomited on him. And then he stepped out a couple of minutes later. I was still waiting outside for my car.'

So they confirmed each other's alibi again. And Kong must have been the man waiting for his car, as seen by Bao around eleven that night.

'But I recalled something else,' Kong went on. 'Not that night, but about half a year ago. That day, a friend of mine brought me a large box of live Yangcheng crabs from the lake. I carried the crabs to the *shikumen* house as a surprise for Min. When I got there, it was noon. I knocked on the door, and to my surprise, a middle-aged man in black opened the *shikumen* door to me. He did not look like a guest there. More like a bodyguard stationed outside in the courtyard. A stranger never seen before, he demanded I show my ID with an authoritative air, and he then said that she was still sleeping, and that I should leave. I wanted to leave the crabs in the courtyard, but he told me not to bother. So I left carrying the crabs, unable to shake off a feeling that someone was inside with her. What's more, as I walked out of the lane, I noted another stranger in black standing at the lane exit, looking like another bodyguard.'

'That's really something. Possibly a number of bodyguards for someone really important staying with her inside. Hence all the security measures.'

But that too merely confirmed something he had suspected from the beginning. The mysterious client Sima could also have been working for that 'someone really important'.

DAY THREE

Jin was stepping into the office at eight thirty in the morning, humming, when she got a text message from a WeChat friend named Yaping.

'Just read your message from last night. Guess who else was at Min's party that night? Kong Jie, the editor-in-chief of *Wenhui Daily*. I've learned from my cousin working in the newspaper. It's confidential. The Party authorities made a point of withholding the names of the people attending the dinner party that night.'

With *Wenhui*'s number easily available on the Internet, Jin picked up the phone. Her call was transferred to Kong.

But Kong said no to her request for an interview on the grounds of his being too busy with a major conference just getting under way in Beijing. Upon learning that she worked for Chen in the new office, he changed his tune.

'Oh, you should have told me earlier, Jin. Director Chen and I talked just yesterday about a Tang dynasty story he was going to write – possibly for our newspaper.'

'A Judge Dee story?'

'That's right. He is really a wonderful boss to work with, isn't he?' Kong then added, 'I'll let you know about my schedule when the conference is over.'

It was still a no, Jin knew, putting down the phone. Chen, too, had contacted Kong, which she supposed was not just for the discussion of a Judge Dee story.

She thought about modifying her approach by going to visit the other possible interviewees directly instead of making a phone call first. She was nobody, but those people at Min's private kitchen dinner party were somebodies. They saw no point meeting with a little secretary in the midst of a sensitive case.

And to the interview list she added Rong, though he had not been at the dinner party that night. Chen had mentioned him, 'coincidentally', in parallel to the man rejected by Xuanji in the Tang dynasty case.

Chen was startled out of another dream by a weird screaming sound.

He remained so disoriented that it took him more than a minute to glance at the alarm clock, which showed it was already nine thirty. He had had a hard time falling asleep the previous night, and around four thirty, with the first gray light peeping through the window, he had taken two more sleeping pills.

In the glaring sunlight, he realized that the sound was coming from his cellphone buried under a pile of newspapers, still shrilling. He picked it up in a hurry.

'Huang was killed,' Old Hunter was practically shouting into the phone. 'The antique collector who had been originally invited to the dinner that night, but unable to attend for some unknown reason, you remember?'

Of course he remembered. Just the previous morning, the two of them had been together at the Old Half Place, enjoying the Xiao pork noodles, and talking about the antique business – among other things.

'How?'

'I don't know any details yet, but his body was found early this morning in a side street.'

'In a side street where?'

'Quite a distance from his home.'

'You don't think that it's a coincidence, do you?'

'No, there's so much more behind the scenes. Yesterday, Sima called us a couple of times, sounding desperately anxious, and threatening too, though he chose not to tell us any specific reason. Zhangzhang is worried, but it's too late for him to back out. Hold on, Chief,' he said, 'I've got a text message from Yu. Possibly more details about Huang's death.'

'Forward it to me.' He then added, 'I think I really need a cup of coffee. I slept so badly last night, I'm still groggy because of the sleeping pills. There is a café not far from my apartment. Just on the street corner. Join me there in twenty minutes.'

*   *   *

Less than twenty minutes later, Chen had just read a couple of lines of Detective Yu's text message when Old Hunter came striding into the café and joined Chen at a table in the corner. He started off without so much as taking a sip of the coffee.

'I was talking with Yu on the phone all the way here, Chief. For once, Detective Xiong shared some info with him this morning.'

'Xiong's under too much pressure, considering the possible connection to the Min case.'

'Yesterday afternoon, Detective Xiong had contacted Huang as one of the guests on the original dinner invitation list. Huang failed to make it to the dinner party that night, and he did not offer a credible explanation about his absence to Xiong. Still, Huang had his solid alibi – at home with some client – and Xiong did not push.

'And early this morning, Xiong got a report that Huang's body was found on a side street in a slum section of Yangpu District. The death time was estimated between five thirty and six a.m. In appearance, it points to a chance robbery that went wrong, but the wallet remained in his jacket pocket, with a small amount of money untouched.

'And here's the question. For a man walking there at such an early hour, he would most likely turn out to be one of the not-well-to-do locals in the neighborhood, not carrying much money with him. The amount in his wallet confirmed that. If so, how could the criminal have chosen such an unlikely target?'

'Yes, that's the question.'

'Various interpretations came up among Detective Xiong's team. For instance, a local good-for-nothing loser, having lost all his money in an overnight Mahjong game, got too distraught and preyed on Huang on the spur of the moment. But the circumstances of the crime scene hardly contribute to the scenario. Apart from the fatal blow to the back of his head, Huang's body showed no other wound or bruise. It can be assumed that an old man like Huang would not have put up much resistance when confronted with a ferocious thug, so why did the latter have to kill him? More importantly, the little money Huang carried was untouched.

'And then the discovery of Huang's identity raises another question. For such a wealthy man, why should he have appeared there at that time? It was a forgotten slum in the midst of all the new skyscrapers. The pebbled street was too narrow even for a car to get through. And at quite a distance from Huang's home, too. At least half an hour by car. People cannot but wonder why a rich old man like Huang should have been there at all. To take a morning jog or to make an antique business deal?'

'No, not at that time, not at that place.'

'According to the residents in the neighborhood, they had not noticed anything unusual that morning. It must have happened very fast. One blow to his head, and the murderer fled out of sight. Coincidentally, like Qing, Huang's head was also hit by a heavy object.'

'What do you mean by "coincidentally", Old Hunter?'

'Could it have been a sign that Huang was the murderer at the *shikumen* house? At least one man under Detective Xiong saw it that way. What happened to the maid in the *shikumen* house, now to Huang too. Karma.'

'That's way too far-fetched.'

'And some netizens have even whispered about a possible relationship between Huang and Min.'

'What about the possible relationship between the two?'

'For more than a year, he came to her *shikumen* house almost weekly. An impossible gourmet he might have been, but his wealth alone could not have secured such a regular seat at her table. You know about the popularity of the private kitchen dinner; people could have waited forever for an opening at her table. And he had been with her, going out of his way to help her get back the whole set of old mahogany furniture taken away by Red Guards during the Cultural Revolution, at a time even before she became known as a Republican Lady. Also, Huang usually arrived earlier than other guests – on the grounds that he enjoyed not only the delicacies on the table, but also the smells from the kitchen beforehand. They were really close. So he might have the key to the *shikumen* house—'

'But what's the motive for him?' Chen said, cutting him short.

'They might have broken up for some reason not known to others. After all, he was in his mid-seventies, and for a young courtesan it was more than possible for her to have some young lovers on the side. So he flew into a murderous rage.'

'In that scenario, Huang should have targeted Min instead of Qing.'

'But he could have tried to frame Min, according to some Holmes-like netizens,' Old Hunter said, shaking his head. 'And then the young lover retaliated.'

Old Hunter as well as those netizens seemed to know nothing about the recent squabble in the secret business relationship between Min and Huang, which, confirmed by Kong, could have served as a slightly more plausible motive. But even in that scenario, Qing would have been the unlikely target.

'For an alternative scenario, with Min's connections to people high up, and with all the political complications in the background, Min could have told Huang something she should not have, and Huang had to be silenced like Min – though with the appearance of a botched mugging.'

'That's an original theory, Chief, but if that's the case, it means the killings could possibly go on beyond Qing and Huang. Min might have told it to some others.'

'Whether or not there's an intimate relationship between Min and Huang, it's inconceivable for a man in his seventies to break into the *shikumen* and kill a young maid at night. I don't think he even had the strength for the job. But back to the time and place of Huang's murder case – whatever the possible scenario, the murderer could have been a man familiar with Huang's morning routine.'

'But it's difficult to investigate along that direction. For that forgotten corner in Yangpu District, there's no surveillance camera installed—'

Old Hunter's cellphone started ringing, interrupting their talk, and he cut himself short to take the call.

'I see,' Old Hunter said succinctly. 'I'll be back immediately.'

'What happened?'

'Sima is at the office again. Possibly with some new info.

Zhangzhang is at his wits' end.' Old Hunter rose. 'I'll talk to you soon.'

'Take your time. I think I'll give Yu a call.'

Around one in the afternoon, Chen made his way back to the Old Half Place.

He had skipped breakfast, but he was not hungry. A bowl of Xiao pork noodles would not appear tantalizing to him at that moment, he knew. Nevertheless, he wanted to come.

Old Hunter had called back, but with nothing new, except that Sima too had learned about the death of Huang, and that he had demanded a meeting with Chen, which Old Hunter and Zhangzhang could not promise – not on Chen's behalf.

Detective Yu had not called back yet. Detective Xiong must have been too busy with the investigation of the new murder case in Yangpu District, and it would take some time for him to give the information to Yu – if he was willing to do so.

Chen felt Huang's death as a personal blow. Though the two had met only the day before, the ex-inspector felt as if he had known the old antique collector for a long time.

And he did not want to rule out the possibility that Huang's death was related to the Min case, though he failed to figure how the two could have been related. None of the scenarios Old Hunter had discussed with him appeared to be credible.

What's worse, he failed to shake off the feeling that he was in some way responsible for the old man's death. It could have been because of his meeting with the antique collector in the noodle restaurant. The onset of a splitting headache gripped him.

The Old Half Place was still open for business, but at that time of the day, there were only three or four customers eating downstairs.

Absentmindedly, he moved upstairs. The waiter of the previous day recognized him.

'Afternoon, sir. You're the one with Master Huang in the private room yesterday morning.'

'Yes, that's me. I would like to have the same room this afternoon.'

'Is Master Huang also coming today?'

'No, not today.'

The waiter apparently knew nothing about the old man's death. There was no point breaking it to him.

'As you're Master Huang's friend, and nobody will come to the private room at this hour, you can order whatever you like there, without having to worry about the minimum expense for the private room.'

'Thanks. I will order something, but first a pot of Pu'er tea, Master Huang's favorite, just like yesterday.'

'That's really nice.'

After the waiter put the tea set on the table and closed the door after him, Chen poured out two cups, just like the day before.

He was not a superstitious man, but he wanted to pay his last respects to the old man. He also wished that the spirit of Huang could come here, drink the tea like before, and reveal something to him.

Detective Xiong too had probed in the direction of Min's connections, which included Huang, in relation to the case.

But Chen remained more inclined toward Huang's account of their recent unpleasantness over the unsuccessful deal. He failed to see how that could have led to the murder.

In a chief inspector's position, he could have tried to use some of his connections to delve deeper into the murky background. As it was, however, most of his connections appeared to be avoiding him.

So he was making an effort to go over what Huang had said to him here, the day before, in this very room. The background scene might be able to stir up memories, he contemplated, raising the tiny tea cup as if to someone sitting opposite.

It was then his cellphone buzzed. Again, a WeChat message from Jin.

'Like yesterday, there's something I would like to report to you. Perhaps we could meet somewhere and talk over a cup of coffee. My treat today.'

The tea spilled out of the cup. The phrase 'like yesterday' sounded surrealistically ironic. He was here because he wanted to be alone, recollecting over the cup of tea as if still in the company of Huang like yesterday.

Without something special to report, she would not have asked him out just for a cup of coffee. Besides, talking could help his thinking. He had talked to her about his meeting with Huang. Why not something more today?

So he typed his response: 'At Old Half Place on the corner of Zhejiang and Fuzhou Roads. Private room on the second floor.'

'Old Half Place. I know where it is. Not far. See you in about half an hour.'

Her message came together with an emoji of a hungry girl burying her face in noodles. He wondered how she could have so many emojis at her disposal in the phone.

Opening the menu, he thought that he could have a bowl of noodles for himself, and some specials dishes for her. The minimum expense for the private room, if need be, should cover all of them.

The arrival of Jin had immediately made a difference to the ambiance of the traditional noodle restaurant. For Old Half Place, most of its customers were elderly, dressed plainly in black or blue.

This afternoon, Jin was wearing a striped satin twill shirt, beige skinny-fit pants and ankle-strap sandals. She would have appeared more in her element in the garden café of Moller Villa Hotel than an old-fashioned Chinese restaurant.

Stepping in light-footedly, she closed the private room door after her, casually, as if at home.

'I've done some more research for our office. I talked to Rong today.'

'The man who hired Qing—'

'Yes, he would have hired her, but she died before she was able to report herself to work in his household.'

'So you have the recording of the talk – like yesterday?'

'Like yesterday' came like the haunting refrain of a somber poem that early afternoon.

'Yes, I've brought it over for you. Perhaps nothing really new or surprising in it. You may listen to it in your leisure time. Also, I've made a phone call to Kong Jie, of *Wenhui Daily*, but he said you had already contacted him.

No point my meeting with him, but I just want to keep you posted.'

'You've done so much for the office, Jin. It's simply amazing. I'll listen to the recording of your interview with Rong. As for Kong, I contacted him for the Judge Dee story. He liked the idea so much he suggested a serialization of the story – possibly a novella – in the newspaper.'

'That's great news. Congratulations, Director Chen! So this is a cup of tea for me?' she said, pointing at the other tea cup on the table.

'No, it's for—'

He stopped mid-sentence at the sight of the waiter entering the room with a long-billed bronze tea kettle.

'Whatever specials you recommend for her, within the range of the minimum expense for the private room, and for me, still a bowl of Xiao pork noodles.'

'We have a large sample platter with all the specials in small portions, so your girlfriend may choose whatever she likes, and for you, the same Xiao pork noodles like yesterday,' the waiter said with a grin and withdrew.

'So you were here yesterday, Director Chen?'

'Yes, I was here yesterday morning, in this very room, with Huang.'

'And you discussed with him here the possible auction of the books left behind by your father?'

'Huang was an impossible gourmet, also a regular guest at Min's dinner party, as you may have learned in the background research of the case. He invited me here yesterday, but he was killed earlier this morning.'

'What!'

He then started telling her about what had happened since their meeting. It was not just that he wanted to talk to her about his sadness at Huang's death. After the interviews done in the name of the office research, she must have guessed what he was really up to, but she was clever enough to help without saying it in so many words.

But the waiter was coming back with their order on a cart. Like the day before yesterday, she started working on the impressive array of specials with the appetite of a young, energetic girl: a tiny bowl of the knife anchovy noodles, half a steamer full of soup buns, crab-shell cake . . .

He put his chopsticks into his Xiao pork noodles with no appetite, but he knew it was going to be another busy day for him. He'd better eat something.

'You have a piece too,' she said, putting a tiny soup bun into a saucer of vinegar in front of him.

If he wanted to investigate further – and he really wanted to – he had to enlist her help. And he could not keep some things from her.

He resumed his narration about Huang's death this morning, and she listened without making any interruption.

'So I'm here to pay my last respects to him,' he said, after recapping the murder case as well as some of the theories surrounding it, 'in memory of our meeting yesterday.'

'The meeting of two impossible epicureans.'

'A real gourmet, he liked what he liked, regardless of the price. It's true he might have paid a lot for the private kitchen dinner at Min's *shikumen* house, but he also had a real passion for the inexpensive yet typical Shanghai street food. Years ago, when he worked for seventy cents a day at a neighborhood production group in Yangpu District, he turned into a loyal customer of a cheap rice ball stall, and he still went there nowadays with galleries and billions of yuan under his name – to the same rice ball stall in the early morning. Oh, I'll be damned!'

'What, Director Chen?'

'From what he told me, he had not shared the secret of the rice ball stall with anybody. He lived alone, with an hourly maid for some cleaning work. So who could have known about his morning routine on Wednesday?'

'What do you mean?'

'The murderer could have been someone familiar with his Wednesday morning route.'

'That sounds logical to me. Judging from what you told me about the crime scene, he could have followed Huang all the way there, or waited for him and jumped out to attack as Huang came into sight.'

'I should have thought of it earlier. Much earlier, Jin. Now,

I need to ask you a favor. Can you find out for me where
Huang used to live – about thirty years ago – when he worked
for the neighborhood production group? And where the rice
ball stall there is – possibly not far from his old home or
the neighborhood production group? My hands are tied for the
moment, you know.'

'I know. And I'll find it out for you as soon as I get back
to my office. No problem at all.'

'On second thoughts, there's another favor I need to ask of
you. You went to Min's neighborhood committee yesterday,
right?'

'Right. But it was lunch time, so I did not meet with any
member of the committee.'

'Each and every neighborhood in the city is installed with a
surveillance system. Particularly for a lane like Min's, there're
a considerable number of cameras, I believe. Talk to the neighborhood committee about it, mention my name to the
neighborhood cop if needs be, and check the contents of
the video in the surveillance system for Friday the week before
last. No need to go through the whole day, just two short
periods, one from ten forty-five to eleven fifteen, the other,
eleven forty-five to twelve thirty that particular night.'

'So one's the time period of those guests leaving Min's
dinner party, and the other, of the murderer sneaking into the
shikumen house and killing the maid?' She was looking up
with candid questions in her large, clear eyes.

'Yes. I'm not doing any investigation, as I've said, but I
have a feeling that Huang's death may be related to the Min
case in a way still beyond my knowledge. Possibly even related
to my talk with Huang yesterday morning, too. So I want to
do something for the old man.'

'For the delicious meal he treated you to, my conscientious
director. And in return, I will also have to do my best for your
generous meal in the private room this morning,' she said,
smiling a teasing smile, and helping herself to a spoonful of
the knife anchovy soup. 'Just joking, Director Chen. As the
office secretary, it's my responsibility to run small errands for
you when you're on convalescent leave.'

*   *   *

Like the day before, he started listening to Jin's recording of her interview with Rong, drinking the lukewarm tea, the moment she walked out of the private room.

And she was right about it. There was hardly anything new or unexpected in Rong's words. It was no surprise. Rong had no motive for the killing. And he had his solid alibi. That night, he was on a flight from Nanjing to Beijing for some business. He even showed Jin the plane ticket stubs. And he had a young secretary traveling with him, and checking in at the same hotel.

If anything, Rong admitted that he had been intent on inflicting harm on Min. He had hired Qing for similar private kitchen dinners so that he could have told others that Min was a total 'fake', with all the specials actually prepared by Qing in the *shikumen* house instead.

But with Min already having gotten into trouble like that, he thought he did not have to do anything more. He hardly felt anything about the death of Qing.

'It's karma. Min deserves it,' Rong concluded callously, 'whether she killed Qing or not.'

On her way to meet Shang Guanhua, the 'number-one real estate developer in Shanghai', Jin did a quick Internet map search in the taxi. Putting the info together, she sent it to Chen as the taxi pulled up at Shang's office.

The meeting with Shang had been scheduled the day before. On the invitation list to Min's dinner that Friday night, Shang was another Shanghai number one, in addition to the late Huang Zhongluo.

'Let me open the door to the mountains, Jin. I think I know what you want to talk to me about. The Min case, right? With one number one already gone,' Shang said, shaking his head vigorously in his spacious office on West Nanjing Road, 'I have no idea how long I can still hang around here.'

'What do you mean, Mr Shang?'

'Once you're labeled as the number one, you become a target for many. Like me. Like Huang. And all the people talking about the connection with Min at her private kitchen dinner could not but make the situation even worse.'

'How could it be made even worse?'

'With the housing prices soaring like crazy, people keep complaining about the profit made by real estate developers. But we have to build houses on the land, which the Party government alone can sell – with higher and higher prices. And it's not just a matter of money. To secure a lot, we have to go through connections upon connections for it. And Min's the one with the connection at the top. It was through her help, for instance, that I got the lot in Xujiahui, which brought me a sizable profit, but she took about half of it, claiming she had to give it to the Party official in charge of the land allocation.'

It was not news to Jin. She had read and heard a lot about those shady deals between business people and Party officials. It was just like in an old proverb: all the ravens under the sun are similarly black.

But why was Shang so worried about himself because of his connection with Min?

'Have you read the new editorial in the *Liberation Daily*?' Shang went on without waiting for a response from Jin. 'The Party government is not now boosting the state-run enterprises. With the Party being the state, and the state being the Party, you know.'

Before she could move on further with the interview, however, Shang got a phone call with some urgent business. He left with a profusion of apologies.

It might be as well, though. Politics aside, she did not think Shang could provide anything really relevant to the case.

It helps to talk.

After his meeting and talking with Jin in the Old Half Place, and listening to the recording between Jin and Rong, Chen was determined that he would leave no stone unturned.

He was holding the phone, about to send another message to Jin, when an email came in from Professor Zhong of the Shanghai Academy of Social Sciences.

'The producer would love to meet with you this weekend, Director Chen. He's so excited about your Judge Dee story.'

'Not this weekend, I'm afraid. Too busy with office work.

Something unexpected. Perhaps next weekend, and I may be able to tell both of you something more about the storyline.'

And then he composed a WeChat message for Jin: 'Gather the pictures of those guests at the dinner table for me. Except Kong.'

Almost immediately she responded. 'No problem. They're somebodies, most likely with their pictures available online.'

She was right. He could have done the search himself. Perhaps he was just too old-fashioned to be an inspector in today's China. Was it really time for him to start a new career? A Judge Dee story could serve as the first tentative step.

But then Old Hunter called. 'Anything new, Chief?'

'Nothing so far. But have you checked Huang's family background?'

'Yes, a preliminary check. Huang's a widower. His wife died about thirty years ago. He had not remarried, nor been involved with any other woman – except for his regular visits to Min's dinner parties. He had no children. For an old man living alone in his seventies, he had an hourly maid coming in for household work once or twice a week. And a part-time private chauffeur on call. Both his niece and nephew work and live in Beijing. They have just been informed of his death, so they are coming to Shanghai in a day or two – for inheritance as his closest relatives. Huang may have left behind a huge fortune.'

'I see. Can you find for me the name and phone number of his part-time chauffeur?'

'I'll text you immediately.'

And almost immediately, the text message came from Old Hunter.

Chen had to change a couple of times on the subway before reaching Zhabei District, where he met with Huang's chauffeur surnamed Xi at his home near Zhabei Park.

Xi was a tall, robust man in his mid-thirties, speaking with an unmistakable He'nan accent, while taking care of his two- or three-year-old daughter.

The ex-inspector introduced himself as Huang's friend, having had noodles with Huang the previous morning. He also produced his new business card.

'Yes, I know. After the breakfast, I picked him up at the Old Half Place for a meeting with a client. And he spoke so highly of you in the car.'

'You did not drive him to the noodle restaurant yesterday morning, did you?'

'Huang was a considerate old man, hardly ever requesting my service early in the morning. My wife has a small dumpling place with a lot of morning customers, so I have to take care of the baby at home. On the occasions of his going to the Min party in the evening, he usually told me the schedule days beforehand, so my wife and I could make the arrangement accordingly.'

'Did he ever mention to you something about a street corner rice ball stall in Yangpu District?'

'Not as far as I can recall. He mentioned many restaurants and eateries, you know, but he did not necessarily have to request my car service. Not all the time. There's a subway train going direct to that section of Yangpu District. The subway station is only a five-minute walk from his old home. And from time to time, he would also call for a taxi. For a wealthy old man like him, the taxi money is nothing.'

'That's true, Xi.'

'And he had another driver on some occasions. A young relative of his. Huang actually bought a luxurious car for him. When I could not do the driving, that young relative would help. At least Huang told me so.'

'Did he mention to you the name of that relative of his?'

'He could have told me about it, but I do not remember. Sorry, Director Chen.'

'Let me give you a personal phone number of mine,' he said, adding the number on the back of his business card. 'If you remember anything—'

But before he was able to finish the sentence, he felt his special phone vibrating in his pocket. He took it out in a hurry.

There were already several WeChat messages left by Jin.

The first one must have come when he was on the train to Xi's home.

'Where are you, Director Chen?'

Ten minutes later, just an emoji of a young girl scratching her head.

And then another short message: 'Not far from Madang Road. Be there soon.'

He guessed that she was making the visit to Min's neighborhood committee.

The latest message had come in more than an hour after the previous one. This time it proved to be a fairly long one.

'I tried to reach you several times but without success. I've got it from the neighborhood committee. The neighborhood policeman really helped, saying that he knows of you, and that it's an honor for him to do something for you. No questions whatsoever asked by him. You may need the info as soon as possible, I believe. It's a huge file. So I've just dropped the memory stick in the mail box of your apartment building.'

Jin had been moving really fast. He too was going to hurry back home.

It might be as well, he thought, since he had learned all he could from Xi. He would go back over the recorded interview with the chauffeur later, though he did not think he had got anything for a possible breakthrough.

The moment he got back to the apartment, Chen took out the memory stick from the mail box. He put it into the computer in his study and clicked 'play'.

The video consisted of two sections – each one for the time period as requested by Chen.

The first section covered the part of Min's guests moving out of the lane after the dinner party that Friday night, with the video focusing on the front entrance of the lane. As he had learned from Kong and other sources, the video confirmed Min's guests coming out to the lane entrance around eleven, first three of them – Peng, Shang, Kong – and then a minute or two later, a younger one – Zheng. Peng and Shang immediately left in the cars waiting there for them; Kong waited for a couple of minutes more, alone, before Zheng too came out, exchanging a few polite but meaningless words with Kong, waving his hand before heading in the direction of Huaihai Road. In the meantime, Kong's car also arrived for him. The section of the video lasted about thirty minutes.

The next section was originally supposed to cover the time period from eleven forty-five to twelve thirty, but Jin had downloaded the video contents for a longer period, with a note indicating that it started almost immediately – just one or two minutes after eleven fifteen, with two girls entering the lane. Also, the video included the recordings from cameras installed at both the front and back entrances of the lane.

'I have no idea about what you may really want to examine in the video,' she wrote in a note wrapped around the memory stick. 'So there's no gap between the last person leaving the lane at eleven fifteen and the next one entering it. And with some people still seen entering and leaving the lane after twelve thirty, I downloaded a bit more. After one fifteen, no one was visible there. I waited for another ten minutes and then called it a night.'

Again, it was thoughtful of her. Even more thoroughgoing than the ex-inspector, he admitted with a touch of self-satire.

He drew a blank, however, after watching carefully through the two sections. With the faint light of the lane, the video quality was not good, presenting only fuzzy images of people coming in and out, but he did not think he saw the same person in both the first and second section.

Still, he could not shake off the feeling that there was something he had missed.

Around eight thirty, Detective Yu emailed back with some of the information Chen had requested.

Detective Xiong had double-checked the surveillance cameras near the crime scene in Yangpu District. As a forgotten corner of the city, the number of cameras was less than elsewhere, but there was at least one installed on either end of the short side street. No footage of suspicious things or people was available there that morning.

It was possibly because of the blind spots that the cameras

couldn't reach, but more likely because of the murderer knowing how to stay out of the angle of the camera.

In the latter case, the murderer must have done some homework about the area beforehand, which further ruled out the possibility of a chance street mugging gone wrong.

DAY FOUR

After another night of broken, restless sleep of no more than three hours, Chen woke up around four thirty. Looking out of the window, he thought he could still see the round moon waning in a deep gray sky.

He saw no point forcing himself back to sleep. It would be useless, he knew.

Nor any use trying to make a phone call to others. It was too early in the morning.

The outside appeared enveloped in fog or smog. Hopefully it would turn out to be the former, which would then disperse with the sunrise.

He decided to wear himself out by working on an outline of the Judge Dee novella, as he had promised Kong. Once he became utterly worn out, he might be able to drop off for another couple of hours.

For one thing, he would try to include in the novella some of the love poems between Xuanji, Wen and Zi'an. Or at least a group of Xuanji's poems. Possibly for an appendix, as at the end of *Doctor Zhivago*.

And one titled 'Lament of the Inlaid Lute' came to mind.

> *Still, no dream comes to her,*
> *the split-bamboo-made mat cool*
> *on the silver-inlaid bed.*
> *The deep blue skies appear like water,*
> *the night clouds, insubstantial.*
> *The cries of the wild geese journey*
> *as far as the Xiaoxiang River.*
> *The moon continues shining, undisturbed,*
> *into her celestial abode.*

It was a poem written by Wen for Xuanji, Chen was pretty sure about that. 'Celestial abode' usually referred to the place for a goddess or a Daoistess. Therefore, an unmistakable reference to Xuanji in the Tang context. Wen missed Xuanji, but he expressed his feeling by portraying her sleeping alone on a night with the blue sky like water, and the clouds insubstantial. It was indeed a masterpiece.

For another, the storyline had to be somewhat different – based on the real Xuanji case, but more loyal to the historical figure of Dee Renjie.

His efforts lasted for no more than ten minutes. It was difficult for him to concentrate on a story based on the long-ago case, with a real murder case going on at the present moment. His thoughts kept jumping from things in the ancient Tang dynasty to those in the present-day China.

He ended up feeling dog-tired, but still not sleepy. Staring up at the ceiling, he had a different idea about what he could do in the early morning.

He would walk out, heading straight to the rice ball stall on that street corner in Yangpu District.

He retrieved the WeChat message from Jin last night after she'd delivered the memory stick into his mail box.

'The neighborhood production group in which Huang worked is long gone. From his home to the production group at the time, the route should be like this – see the map attached. The street corner rice ball stall he would have passed should be on the intersection of the Jungong and Pingliang Roads.'

Then he retrieved the email from Detective Yu again. After comparing the two messages, he thought he had something like a reliable map in his mind.

Looking up at the clock on the wall, he realized it was about the time for him to walk out – the time that Huang used to walk to the rice ball stall.

With the help of Jin's message, the map and the GPS on his phone, Chen managed to locate the side street, which was practically as narrow as a lane.

It had been a slum area in the pre-1949 era. Some of the 'Workers' New Village' houses had been built there in the mid-fifties as a sort of government project to showcase the dramatic changes in the socialist new China. They were mostly two-storied buildings with minimum facilities, which nonetheless represented an improvement at the time.

For some unknown reason, the old houses there had since been forgotten, despite the waves of relentless urban development in recent years. The area was consequently known as one of the 'lower corners' or 'forgotten corners', where the remaining inhabitants were simply too poor to move into new apartments elsewhere.

Along a narrow street, winding and forking into narrower sub-streets, he made several wrong turns before catching sight of the rice ball stall at the street corner in question. The chef was about ready to call it a day, rubbing his hands in contentment over the nearly empty wooden rice container.

Chen approached him in a hurry.

'Sorry, it's all gone.'

'I'll have whatever is left for a rice ball,' Chen said in earnest. 'A small one – just one or two bites will do. An old gourmet friend has recommended your rice ball to me.'

'Really! But I do have some old customers here. No salted egg yolk for the rice ball?'

Chen looked up at the items listed on a small blackboard menu hung on the door behind the rice ball maker. The menu showed the changes with time. The rice ball nowadays could be made with salted egg yolk or shredded pork in addition to the traditional fried dough stick.

'Don't worry about it. Nothing but the rice ball with a fried dough stick for me. That's the original, and that's the best, according to my old friend.'

'That's interesting. I have an old customer who comes practically every week. Rain or shine. He wants nothing but the rice ball with fried dough stick. An old gentleman with his glasses as thick as the bottom of a beer bottle, he never bothers to look up at the menu.'

'I think that's him. Did he come this week?'

'Yes, he came yesterday. Like always, he bit into the ball the moment he got it from my hand. "Have to have it warm," that's what he always says. And it is still warm today too, thanks to the cotton-padded army coat. It keeps the rice warm.'

So saying, the chef scooped up the remaining rice from the container, put in half a fried dough stick, rolled it into a ball, and handed it to Chen.

Like Huang, Chen bit into it at once; it tasted warm, soft, satisfying.

Taking another small, slow bite, he felt grateful for one thing that had happened to Huang just before he met his untimely end. At least the old gourmet had enjoyed his favorite rice ball on the last morning of his life.

Huang's last epicurean bliss aside, it made sense for such a street snack stall to survive in the area, Chen reflected, chewing at the inexpensive yet delicious rice ball, which was probably what most of the people in the neighborhood could afford.

But it was unbelievable for a wealthy old man like Huang to come all the way to the street corner stall – not without the knowledge of his formative years at the neighborhood production group in the poverty-stricken area.

Nor did it make sense for the violent mugging to happen there so early in the morning.

Chen went on taking extra small bites, like Huang, relishing the rice ball to the last bite. The ex-inspector did not think he would ever come back to the street corner stall.

He then took a walk around the crime scene, which was no more than five minutes' walk from the rice ball stall.

Equally poverty-ridden, desolate, with some of the old houses demolished, and some stubbornly still hanging on, and some broken walls sticking out of the debris, the lane-like road made possible a short cut for the local residents to Pingliang Road, but at that early hour, hardly a single soul was visible.

So, what could have been the possible connection between the Min case and the Huang case?

Nothing, except that Huang had been a regular guest at Min's dinner parties, and they shared some not-that-illegal business connections in secret.

If anything, the early morning venture served to confirm only one thing for Chen. For the killing at that unlikely hour, and in that unlikely place, it could not have been a reckless mugging that went wrong.

Heading back toward home, he felt so drained in spite of

the rice ball. He had got up too early. The subway train began to feel insufferably overcrowded, and he became increasingly bugged by the various scenarios of Huang's murder, none of which appeared to be that convincing to him.

But an unexpected phone call came in from Jin as he got off the train. He looked at the time on the phone. It was not eight o'clock yet.

'Sorry to call you so early. Last night, Director Ma called me. It was quite late, so I did not report to you then as you might have gone to bed.'

'What was Director Ma's phone call about?'

'Regarding the conclusion of the Judge Jiao scandal, the *Liberation Daily* made a point in its editorial about the nation-wide system called "Heavenly Eyes" – the surveillance cameras installed everywhere – making it impossible for the culprits to go undetected and unpunished in today's China. Some netizens have responded in a surprising way, condemning it as much worse than in *1984* in terms of the authoritarian governmental control. So Director Ma wanted me to ask you whether our office would issue another statement about it.'

'An endorsement of the practice of "Heavenly Eyes" in the name of our office? No, I know so little about the so-called surveillance system. Nor have I read George Orwell's *1984*. So I don't know what to say about the situation. Besides, I don't think I'm up to the research about it any time soon – you know my health problems.'

Things in China really were getting worse than in *1984*. He knew, but he did not have to say it. People also knew.

'I see your point. But where are you, Director Chen? A lot of traffic noise in the background.'

'I'm just taking a walk out in the morning. The fresh air may do me some good.'

'Yes, you're still on convalescent leave. By the way, have you checked the air quality forecast this morning? The polluted air won't be helpful to your recovery. Hopefully you're not jogging. In an article I've just read, jogging in the polluted air can have disastrous consequences. I'll talk to Director Ma about your health issues. Don't worry about it, Director Chen.'

* * *

When he got back to his apartment, he sat at his desk by the window, his mind a blank.

He took out a piece of paper, on which he had drawn a number of dots around the Min case in the last few days. They refused to be connected, however, with a straight line. He dropped some words in the margin of the paper, with two more lines drawn in parallel, but all his efforts led to nothing.

Looking out of the window, he saw a white-haired woman picking up a bundle of old newspapers dumped near the neighborhood trash can, wiping a hand across her mouth and grinning from ear to ear. A bright red convertible sped through the grayness of the morning, a young girl beside the driver throwing some scraps out into the wind, laughing like silver bells.

Then he tried to piece together the fragments of what he had thought of when still lying in bed in the morning, before making the trip to Yangpu District. But some of the ideas, so vividly poignant to him at the time, turned out to be neither clear nor logical as he re-examined now.

In frustration, he laid himself down on the sofa, stretching out and pulling over a throw, ready for a nap. He had never felt so tired before.

A convalescent leave might be what he needed after all, he concluded, staring up at the water-stained ceiling with a touch of self-satire as he began dozing off.

He did not know how long he had slept on the sofa before he became aware of being stranded in another horrible dream, which faded fast in confusion as he was startled awake by a phone call from Old Hunter.

'Horror!'

'What, Old Hunter?' It seemed as if the old man had intruded into his dream.

'Come to the Old Teahouse right now, Chief.'

'Which one?'

'The one not far from the Writers' Association on Shanxi Road, you know.'

He knew.

Old Hunter met him at the teahouse close to the overpass at the intersection of Yan'an and Shanxi Roads. It was an old-fashioned teahouse they had visited several times together. Old Hunter simply referred to it as the 'Old Teahouse'.

From their mahogany table, Chen thought he could catch a glimpse of the steeple of the Moller Villa Hotel at a distance across the street. He could not help but begin to wonder at Old Hunter's choice of teahouse.

'Another shocking development this morning,' Old Hunter said straightforwardly, not at all like a Suzhou opera singer, though with a purple-sand pot of tea, and a white folding fan placed in front of him on the table, he still looked like one.

'What happened?' Chen said, without so much as taking a sip of the tea.

'Someone broke into Min's hotel room last night.'

'Something happened to her?'

'No, she was not hurt.'

'But she has been kept in an undisclosed location guarded by Internal Security, hasn't she?'

'If Sima was able to find out she was being kept in the Moller Villa Hotel, so could others. That's where I wanted to take you out for coffee, you know.'

'Yes, I knew. I've been there before, for the investigation of another *shuanggui* case. I was afraid people might have recognized me there.'

'According to Sima, Min was initially kept in an undisclosed detention place, but with the case becoming so high-profile on the Internet, journalists were anxious to get hold of her for spicy and salacious material. Consequently, she was secretly moved into the hotel for better security. She stayed in a luxurious suite, where she lacked nothing, almost like an all-paid vacation. The Shanghai Police Bureau was then told to send someone to the suite, so no one would be able to approach her there. Wanxia was chosen for the twenty-four-hour job.'

'Wanxia of the homicide squad?'

'Yes. It's no longer a case for the homicide squad, but Party Secretary Li insisted that a policewoman be sent to the hotel, as Internal Security had a hard time finding someone appropriate at short notice. To be fair to Li, it was not considered a dangerous job. She would simply stay in the guest room, and sleep there too. Naturally Min was not pleased with such a "human surveillance camera", but she had no choice. Last night, Min went to bed earlier than usual, complaining of a headache. Wanxia remained alone in the living room, working on her laptop. Around nine thirty, a hotel attendant in uniform knocked on the door, and pushed in a cart with a special night meal.

'As recorded in the surveillance camera in the room, the attendant said to Wanxia with a bow, "Compliments from the hotel, the fresh egg noodles made by a special noodle machine in the hotel."

'Wanxia must have taken it as something common in a fancy hotel. Without waking up Min, she finished the noodles with the four small dishes—'

'Across-bridge noodles, I think. Tiny dishes served separately as the toppings.'

'Less than ten minutes later,' Old Hunter went on without responding to Chen's comment on the noodles, 'she was doubled over, holding on to her stomach in unbearable pain. She dialed the front desk for help. The hotel people lost no time putting her in a car and rushing her out to a hospital nearby.

'She was hurting really bad, but she still had the presence of mind to tell the people in the car about what had happened earlier in the hotel room.'

'You mean she was poisoned by the egg noodles?'

'The hotel management later confirmed her suspicion. There was no order for room service from Min's suite. Neither any night meal sent as the compliment of the hotel, nor any in-house special noodle machine. As a rule, the hotel orders noodles from a workshop on Changle Street every morning.'

'What then—'

'She lost consciousness in the car. No life sign of hers was visible when they reached the hospital. Wanxia did not make it—'

But Old Hunter was unable to go on as a phone call came in to Chen from Detective Yu, interrupting their talk.

'I've just told Detective Xiong, Chief, that you're talking

with someone at the teahouse, which is close to the hotel. He
has no objection to your coming over there for a look.'

So Director Chen would be said not to be doing any investigating, but just taking a look at the scene in the hotel since
he happened to be in the neighborhood that morning. A
convenient pretext with a tacit understanding between them.
Detective Xiong must have been so stressed out.

'You have so many things on at the agency, Old Hunter,'
Chen said, rising. 'You don't have to go to the hotel with me,
but we'll have our tea again soon.'

Old Hunter nodded, draining the tea.

Detective Xiong met Chen at the hotel entrance guarded by a
pair of crouching oriental stone lions.

Xiong was a tall, wiry man in his early forties with a severe
receding hairline, which became more pronounced with his
hard-knitted frown that morning.

'Detective Yu must have told you about what happened at
the hotel last night, Chief Inspector Chen. So let's go to her
room suite.'

Detective Xiong seemed to think that it was Detective
Yu who had briefed Chen, but at that moment it hardly mattered
who had done the briefing for the ex-inspector.

'Detective Yu feels so bad about it,' Chen said vaguely. 'It
was through his introduction that Wanxia came to work in our
police bureau, I still remember.'

The suite Min had stayed in turned out to be a spacious
one in a northern European style with Asian elements blended
in, especially with the crouching-tiger-shaped attic windows
and exposed ceiling beams.

Min must have been moved somewhere else in an extreme
hurry by Internal Security, with her bed still unmade and
several pieces of her clothing left behind in disarray in her
bedroom. Even Detective Xiong did not know her whereabouts
for the moment.

The living room was in a worse shape, with the food cart
still left there, but plates and bowl gone, and a glass cup shat-
tered on the floor, possibly knocked over when Wanxia fell to
the floor.

A lone white leather sandal – probably Wanxia's – lay in a corner, as if anchoring the silence of the room.

'We've just got the hospital report. Poisoned,' Xiong said grimly. 'The doctor was positive about it. It's murder.'

Chen had met Wanxia a couple of times in the bureau. A young police academy graduate, intelligent, hard-working and informed, with a real passion for the job. Detective Yu had thought about getting her into the special case squad, and Chen had approved. She'd told him that she had intended to work with him, having heard so much about the 'legendary chief inspector', he remembered, but she ended up being assigned to the homicide squad under Detective Xiong.

For the first time, Chen knew he had to step up to the investigation of the Min case as a cop, even though nominally he was no longer one.

'It's changed. Utterly changed,' Chen said abruptly, without elaborating the point. 'So the man who sent in the egg noodles was not an attendant working at the hotel?'

'No. The hotel people checked further. It was discovered that another room ordered the special across-bridge noodles that evening – along with the four special dishes – slices of chicken, *jinhua* ham, bamboo shoots and shrimp, plus a bowl of green bean sprouts – exactly what was sent to Min's room.'

'Anything unusual about the man who ordered the noodles in that room?'

'For starters, he wore a pair of amber-colored glasses – even in the evening. Oh, he also wanted to have the soup delivered separately in an insulated cup. When he was ready to eat, he said, he would be able to put the noodles into the steaming hot soup along with the toppings himself.'

'A real pro who knows how to appreciate the across-bridge noodles. The steaming hot soup and the noodles have to come in separate bowls. That way, no worry about the noodles getting sodden for having stayed too long in the soup. It's a request not unexpected from a gourmet customer.'

Detective Xiong glared at Chen for the untimely gastronomic lecture.

'Anyway, he asked the hotel attendant – the real one – to

leave the cart in the room. He would have the noodles when he liked.'

'So his ID info left at the front desk was—'

'Fake,' Xiong said. 'He was careful enough to remove all his fingerprints from his own room, and to wear gloves when he pushed the cart into Min's. On a surveillance camera installed outside the room, an attendant appeared in the corridor leading to Min's room around nine thirty, knocked on the door, and pushed the cart into the room. Two or three minutes later, the attendant re-emerged, without the cart.'

'That's so obvious. But one question, Detective Xiong. Did he still wear the amber-colored glasses while pushing the cart into Min's suite?'

'No. He wore a face mask like a chef or one working in the hotel kitchen.'

'Coming out of Min's room, where did he go?'

'Surveillance cameras covered only part of the corridor. There's no knowing where exactly he turned, going out of sight. The night manager at the front desk remembers seeing a man in a gray T-shirt walking out of the hotel shortly after ten. No luggage. The manager believed that he would either take a short walk in the garden, or out on Shanxi Road at the center of the city. Some of the customers from overseas may walk out later because of the jet lag. Nothing suspicious about it. The surveillance camera at the hotel gate confirmed that the man in the T-shirt left the hotel shortly after Wanxia was rushed out to the hospital, and the camera there did not record his coming back for the night. And the next morning he was gone without a trace – without having checked out of the hotel.'

'Thanks for all the info, Detective Xiong. But who could have committed such a well-planned crime?'

'No clue whatsoever yet. It's really a well-planned one, no question about it.'

'Have the people at the front desk recalled anything about the circumstances of his checking in?'

'When he checked in, he was wearing a gray suit, as the front desk manager recalled. Then they also found out that he had given the suit to the hotel for dry-cleaning, without taking it back.'

'So people did not recognize him when he walked out . . .' He did not finish the sentence, as something elusive flashed across his mind, but it was lost in a confusion of thoughts.

'I don't think so. Internal Security immediately raised the alarm at the hotel after Wanxia's phone call, and the murderer wanted to wait until he saw the commotion break out in Min's suite. Then he left. It's planned down to every detail. The fake ID, the amber-colored glasses, the face mask, and the room service ordered to his room. Of course, the hotel uniform too, but that's not too difficult a job for a pro like that.'

'And his choice of the across-bridge noodles too – with the soup in a separate insulated cup – was a calculated move indeed. No one would have suspected anything about a gourmet practice like that.'

'You surely know a lot about gourmet food, Chief Inspector Chen.'

'But do you think the attempt was not meant against Wanxia?'

'That's a good question.' Xiong then added hesitantly, 'Against Min?'

'The murderer had no idea that Min had gone to bed earlier because of her headache, and that there was someone else sitting in the suite that night.'

'It's a possible theory, I think. But Min was kept in the hotel because Internal Security wanted her to talk   in an arrangement unknown to others. So who would have tried to murder her there?'

'Some other people who didn't want her to talk.'

'What do you mean, Chief Inspector Chen?'

'It's just a thought, Detective Xiong.'

Chen chose not to elaborate. Some people could have tried desperately to silence Min once and for all, he contemplated, because she might break under the pressure. But what secrets could she spill?

He did not think it would be about the murder at the *shikumen* house.

About those deals between Min and Huang? Those shady but not necessarily illegal deals involved a huge amount of money, but they were not uncommon in the socialism with China's characteristics. Whatever Min could say, it would not be such a big deal. And now Huang was already dead.

About her clandestine relationships with those really powerful people high up? Chen did not want to rule out that possibility. Particularly in the context of the intense power struggle at the top between the Red Princes, those from the families of the first-generation Party officials, and the Youth Leagues, those from ordinary families. So it was not Min personally, but the fact that her relationship with the people from one group could be used by another group in the cut-throat fight for the ultimate position in the Forbidden City. Her testimony against the man – or the men – involved with her could cause a political earthquake.

What about Huang then? In a way, it might throw some light on his death too. A regular visitor to the *shikumen* house, Huang could have learned something about Min's private life. But for a sophisticated *mingyuan* like Min, she would have known what to say, or what not to say, to an old businessman like Huang, despite their business deals.

Chen decided not to say anything about all this to Detective Xiong. It was just a possible scenario, but unsupported by any investigation he had done.

And for that matter, he had hardly done any investigation in the way of a real cop. For the moment, he was but a tea drinker who had happened to be in a teahouse located not far from the hotel.

'What did Internal Security say to you, Detective Xiong?'

'Nothing so far – except they had to rush Min to another unknown place, and—'

But it was almost like a cue. Detective Xiong's phone started ringing at that very moment. It was none other than Internal Security who wanted him over at their office for discussion. Xiong had to leave in a hurry.

Chen too rose to leave. Moving out toward the hotel gate, he saw people having tea and coffee in the hotel garden. They were talking, drinking, laughing, undisturbed by what had happened last night. Some of them were probably not in-house guests. There were a couple of colorful tents on the lawn, in which people could have privacy, like in a private room in a fancy restaurant.

Perhaps he should have come with Old Hunter a couple of days ago. Perhaps he could have discovered something here.

Usually, Jin would not read messages during a meal. According to her parents, it was not helpful to her digestion. But for her, it was not one of the ordinary days.

She'd had an email from Chen, with the letterhead of the Judicial System Reform Office. Strictly official business, so to speak. It started with a seemingly disarming pleasantry:

Dear Jin:

I hope the note finds everything well with you. I'm better, though still not well enough to come to the office. And I appreciate all the work you have been doing for the office.

But I cannot afford to stay at home doing nothing all day long, so I've started working on the Judge Dee story, more or less by way of preparation for my new job, as I have told you.

I truly admire Van Gulik's masterful treatment of the Xuanji case in Poets and Murder. *I think I also understand the reason for some of the changes made in his novel. Still, there are things so puzzling about the case. With your college major in history, you may help with your expertise about the things in the Tang dynasty. Naturally, you don't have to feel obliged to do so, as you are busy with the office work, I totally understand.*

In Van Gulik's novel, Xuanji doesn't want to talk because she is anxious to shield the high-ranking official she loves, but apparently some other people want her to talk. Was it because of the secret fight between the two factions at the top during the early Tang dynasty?

For another thing, the implausible motive for Xuanji. The maid might have carried on with the man behind Xuanji's back, but it was quite another story for the man to fall for the maid. The Tang dynasty was one that set great store by the family background. It was hard for

Wen or Zi'an to formally accept Xuanji with her low-level background – how much more so for a maid serving in Xuanji's household?

As for the capital punishment, I'm not familiar with the Tang dynasty law. I know a story titled 'Carved Jade Buddha Image', in which a general was not even condemned, let alone punished, for beating a maid furiously to death for her eloping with an artist.

And here I may well tell you something about a habit of mine. Sometimes I talk to myself about the inexplicable in an effort to clear the entangled thoughts. Writing this mail to you is like talking to myself, just a bit more serious, more in a logical way. Needless to say, you don't have to go out of your way to do anything because of it. And I thank you for patience with my monologue.

Chen Cao

P.S. I am at the Moller Villa Hotel for something totally unexpected this morning, but the hotel garden tea looks so wonderful on the well-kept lawn. I would like to treat you to an afternoon tea there some other day, for all your marvelous work and help. And thanks for TV links and the memory stick too. They're truly helpful.

Jin took a deep breath, read the email again, and made herself a cup of tea.

The email was meant as a sort of discussion with her, she understood, in a language intelligible to them alone in the given context. The messages in it were related not so much to the Tang dynasty Xuanji case in the Judge Dee story, as to the Min case of the present moment. The two cases shared striking similarities, especially so for those points he made when read between the lines.

The point about some people wanting Xuanji to talk and others wanting her not to talk, she took as a subtle reference to Min being in a similar situation, but the research she had done so far about the Min case failed to give her any clue in that direction. For the moment, all she could think of doing was approaching the other two guests at Min's dinner party.

Of the two, Peng Jianjun was a man in his sixties, who had recently gone through an advanced chemotherapy for his colon cancer. It was inconceivable for him to have the strength to commit the crime. As for Zheng Keqiang, he was just someone sent over by Huang on his behalf for that night, and she could not see any possible motive for the first-timer to the *shikumen* house to become involved in the murder on the same night.

She was touched, unexpectedly, with the point about his writing the email to her being like talking to himself. At least he no longer saw the two of them just as the Party-member boss and his secretary. The ex-inspector was said to be a romantic poet, but judging by the few poems of his she had read, she was not too sure about it. But she could have read too much into the message. For an 'old-fashioned man' like him, he might have just wanted to express his appreciation of the 'research' she had done for the office.

What about the implied message, then, in the cryptic post-script regarding the afternoon tea in the garden of the Moller Villa Hotel 'for something totally unexpected'? She immediately started web-surfing. It did not take long for her to find bits and pieces about the hotel being used for keeping *shuang-guied* Party officials. Min had also been put into an undisclosed location like a *shuangguied* official, as Jin had unearthed in a blog post. It was strange, but a lot of things were strange in the Min case. Then, in a couple of short WeChat posts, some netizens mentioned a disturbance – possibly a murder – committed at the Moller Villa Hotel the previous night.

What if something had happened to Min in that hotel? The posts provided no reliable details about the disturbance, or about the identity of the victim. But she had an instinctive feeling that the victim was not Min. Otherwise everything would be finished. So why this sudden, strange email from Chen?

Whatever the possible scenarios, Chen had not simply been to the hotel garden for tea, which would not have been described as 'something totally unexpected'. Was he actually requesting more help from her, albeit by way of discussing a Tang dynasty case?

It was a calculated move. Aware of others hacking into

his emails, he wrote in a coded language accessible to her alone. In the meantime, it continued the show about his interest in a Tang dynasty story as a cover for his investigation on the sly.

As for the flash memory stick mentioned in the postscript, he seemed to have found it helpful, though without going into any details. She found herself singularly gratified. With the aid of the neighborhood cop, she had not met with any problems getting the contents of the surveillance system in Min's neighborhood. Still, she had no idea about what he could have wanted to do with it.

In spite of his assurance that she did not have to go out of the way for the 'office research', the message could have been read as a suggestion for her to continue as before. And it would not hurt for her to move further along the line of enquiry.

After all, Chen had his hands tied. It was not convenient for him to openly investigate, and to approach the people possibly involved in it. But she could. As long as she took precautions, she should have no problem.

Chen found himself bogged down at a critical juncture where he could not afford to be bogged down.

So many things were happening in quick succession, so many things appearing inexplicable in the messy entanglement, that it was even more mind-boggling to examine the possible connections between them.

Things were related, he was nonetheless convinced, in a way he had not been able to grasp yet. It could take him a lot more effort to get to the bottom of it. The problem for him, however, was that he had to remain on convalescent leave. Any open move into the investigation could not only get him into more trouble, but alert the people behind the scenes as well.

Instead, he picked up the Judge Dee novel again, thinking it was ridiculous for him to be in the mood for the book. Nevertheless, it might help to clear his mind by doing something different for a change.

It turned out to be unexpectedly depressing for him to dip

into the novel at that moment. Judge Dee too was overwhelmed with similar troubles in the Tang dynasty.

So he started to read a Chinese collection of Xuanji's poems instead. It occurred to him that one of her problems – whether a murderer or not – was that she went after too many things. Poetry, celebrity status, idealistic passion, literary fame, romantic affair, wealth and security. In a simpler life, she might have found a man who truly cared for her like in her poems.

But there was no blaming Xuanji. No one is capable of stepping out of one's world of self-interest. The same could be said of Min.

Once again he came across the poem partially quoted in *Poets and Murder*, and he tried to do a tentative translation of the whole piece. Xuanji's poem was titled 'A Letter to Wen Tingyun on a Winter Night', an exquisite one written for her first lover, the famous Tang poet, about the unquenchable yearning she had for him on a cold, lonely night. On a moment of impulse, he translated into English, a version different from Gulik's rendition:

> *Thinking and thinking, I search hard*
> *for the lines I can recite*
> *under the lamplight, too nervous*
> *to spend the sleepless,*
> *long night under the chilly quilt,*
> *with the leaves trembling*
> *in the courtyard, fearful*
> *of the coming wind, and*
> *the window curtain flapping*
> *feebly under the sinking moon.*
> *Keeping myself busy or not,*
> *I cannot help being kept aware*
> *of the unquenchable yearning*
> *inside. My heart remains*
> *unchanged through all the vicissitudes*
> *in life. The parasol tree being*
> *no place for perching, a bird circles*
> *the woods at dusk, chirping,*
> *and chirping in vain.*

In Gulik's novel, it was said to be a poem written by Xuanji for the guests of a banquet. Translating it, he felt like doing a closer reading. In the English version, the Dutch sinologist seemed to have taken some liberties. In the fifth line, Gulik opted for 'lonely coverlets' instead of 'chilly quilt'. His version was more faithful to the original, and the adjective 'chilly' also more poignant in that it was not just getting colder in the depth of the night, but the poetess felt 'chilly' under the quilt because of her loneliness. The line 'long night under the chilly quilt' appeared to be particularly striking in terms of objective correlative.

But something else in the line made the ex-inspector come to a sudden stop. Something amiss, elusive yet critical he had felt earlier during the day.

Thinking and thinking, he succeeded in recollecting what he had momentarily sensed at the hotel, where Detective Xiong had described the suspect walking out in a T-shirt instead of the gray suit he had worn when he checked in. It did not make sense with the evening getting cold, but it did with people's wariness of the omnipresent surveillance cameras in today's China.

He stood up, took out the memory stick that Jin had left the day before, inserted it into the computer, and replayed the video, which he had already watched a couple of times.

Judging by the background research and the pictures of the guests at the *shikumen* house dinner party provided earlier by Jin, the four guests appeared to be moving out of the lane around eleven in the first section of the video. The first three were all in suits and ties, but Zheng, the last one moving into the scene, was in a long, light-colored jacket. It seemed not to be the proper dress code for the occasion, but Zheng could have hurried over to the *shikumen* house with the last-minute notice from Huang.

Then Chen moved on to the second section of the video. Because of the poor light, the video quality was not that good, presenting only blurred pictures of people passing through the lane, but this time he paid more attention to the clothes they wore. Halfway through it, he stopped the video, catching sight of a man in a white shirt with a light-colored jacket draped over his arm, and re-examined the image. It was not a cold day for May, but with the temperature lower at night, it did not make sense for one to go out earlier wearing the jacket and come back with the jacket over his arm – if the person in the jacket in the first section and the one with the jacket over his arm in the second section proved to be the same. Chen was not absolutely sure about it, though he thought he saw a resemblance.

It made sense, however, if the man in question was wary of the surveillance cameras at the entrances of the lane. With people talking about the cameras installed everywhere, especially after details of the Judge Jiao scandal coming out online, a would-be criminal could have taken some sort of precaution for himself.

But the ex-inspector had another unanswered question. Checking through the video again, he failed to see any trace of the man in question afterward. In other words, he could have been a resident in the lane returning home late at night, and the light-colored jacket nothing but a matter of coincidence. Chen gazed at the computer screen. The video ran to an end at one twenty-five – already much later than he had requested.

But what if the man in question had come out again later than that?

He did not like the idea of having Jin go to the neighborhood committee again. It could raise unnecessary alarm.

Chen took out his cellphone, hesitated for a minute, then dialed the special number of Mr Gu.

Mr Gu was one of the few he had never really figured out. A highly successful businessman, Mr Gu had been the first one to see the incredible potential in the development of the New World, which turned out to be one of the most fashionable landmarks in the city of Shanghai. As the chairman of the New World Corporation, in addition to the mega business/shopping center of the New World, the numerous real estate developments all around, he'd also made a number of successful investments and become one of the top Big Bucks in China. He claimed himself as a fan and friend of the chief inspector, though Chen remained wary of getting too close to him, in spite of his willingness to help, and sometimes going out of

his way for the inspector during difficult investigations. They
had not contacted each other, however, for quite a while.

In China's fast-changing political landscape, a number of
entrepreneurs had gotten into trouble of late, as the Party
government made an abrupt shift, trying to boost the state-run
enterprises at their expense. In an apparent attempt to turn the
clock back to Mao's time, 'official scholars' began clamoring
about the 'state capitalism', the 'Red emperor' or the 'historical
justification for the Cultural Revolution', like cicadas in the
summer. Chen did not want to add to Mr Gu's problems.

'What a pleasant surprise to get your call, Chief Inspector
Chen. You must have recovered well.'

'Well enough to call you, I think.'

'Anything I can do for you today?'

'Nothing really important, I know you too have a lot of
things on your hands, but do you know any people at the
Pacific Ocean, the luxurious shopping mall close to Madang
Road? To be more exact, people in a position to do something
in the garage of that shopping mall? It's not far from your
New World.'

'Well, I know the general manager of the Pacific Ocean,
but not too well. He is a man with a governmental background.
But why, Chief?'

'A garage like that must be equipped with surveillance
cameras. I'm wondering whether there are backup copies available there.'

'Backup copies?' Mr Gu went on in a hurry. 'Sure, there
are backup copies. As a rule, the video contents can be retrieved
one way or another for what happened up to a couple of
months ago.'

'It happened just a couple of weeks ago. Friday the week
before last. I need to check for that one particular night – for
no more than several hours.'

'Then no problem at all. The day before yesterday I
happened to interview a store manager from that shopping
mall, who has applied for a senior executive position in my
New World Group. As long as it's still in the surveillance
system, it will be yours.'

* * *

About one hour later, Chen arrived at Judge Liu's office for an unannounced visit, and with an unprecedented approach.

It was in the impressive building of Huangpu District government, towering over Fuzhou Road. Despite his knowledge about his being kept under watch, the ex-inspector knew he had to step out in the open. He could not afford to leave any stone unturned.

He had thought about turning to Old Hunter or Detective Xiong for help. For a private investigator, however, Old Hunter was in no position to do anything about an unrelated case. As for Detective Xiong, there was little he could do about the death at the Moller Villa Hotel with Internal Security in charge, no matter how intent he might have been on avenging Wanxia, a young officer working under him.

So Chen had no choice but to pay a visit to Judge Liu in person.

Judge Liu was a youngish-looking man in his mid-thirties, who appeared pleasantly surprised with Chen's visit to his office.

'It's such an honor for me to have you as a visitor in the office today, Chief Inspector Chen,' Liu said with sincerity in his voice. 'I still remember the day you came to give a lecture at our university. What a wonderful speech!'

'Thank you, Judge Liu. But I'm no longer a cop, as you know. At the Judicial System Reform Office, the job is so new to me. Working on one case after another through these years, I've not done any systematic study of our judicial system. So there's a lot of research work I have to do for the new position. A friend of mine at the Shanghai Academy of Social Sciences has recommended you to me, saying: "Judge Liu is not just a capable young judge, but also an emerging scholar with a considerable number of publications in the field." In my effort to learn the ropes, I hope you will offer me help and suggestions, Judge Liu.'

'Just call me Liu or Little Liu, Chief Inspector Chen. For me, you're always the one and only Chief Inspector for the city of Shanghai. A true legend. Indeed, it's such an honor, as I've said, if I can possibly do anything for you, I will.'

'Yes, there's been all kinds of talk about our judicial system reform. For instance, one of the heated topics online of late is whether the Chinese Communist Party is bigger than law or the other way around. In other words, shall judges prove to be loyal to the law, or to the Party? In *People's Daily*, it is simply brushed aside as a bogus question – "In the last analysis, our judges uphold the law under the leadership of the Party." But to a number of people, that does not answer the question at all. There will be such an amount of work for the new office, I'm afraid.'

'That's true, Chief Inspector Chen,' Liu said, nodding. 'I was particularly impressed with one point made in that lecture of yours. You said that for all the tremendous progresses made in recent years, there's still a lot of room for improvement in our system. So let each of us do his or her job conscientiously in China's unprecedented reform, and one's self-realization may eventually be achievable in something larger than one's self.'

He could have said that at the time, when he still believed in China's reform under the leadership of the Party, but could he say the same thing today?

'I had just graduated then, but I went back specially for your talk. I was the one sitting in the front row of the audience, applauding non-stop.'

'Really! Sorry I did not know that, Liu.'

'Of course you could not have known the people sitting down there that day. It truly means a lot for you to come to my office today. Whatever I can do for your research, you just name it.'

'Thank you. I surely appreciate your offer to help.'

'You are still on convalescent leave, aren't you?' Liu said, having obviously heard stories about the trouble for the ex-chief inspector.

'I'm still on leave, you're right about it, but I have to do something to prepare myself for the new job.'

'But I've just read your office statement regarding Judge Jiao's scandal. And your point about the inadmissibility of the illegally obtained evidence is a much-quoted one in the newspapers.'

'I cannot claim credit for the statement, which was mostly

done by my secretary, Jin. She's been doing most of the work for the office, and I've stayed at home for weeks.' Chen added in afterthought, 'You have heard the interpretations about my convalescent leave, I presume.'

'There are interpretations and *interpretations*. The latest one I have heard, for instance, is that the Beijing government wants to set up a judicial system reform committee, like the one under you in Shanghai, but at a much higher level, directly under the Central Party Discipline Committee. And you are shortlisted as one of the candidates for that Beijing position.'

Chen shook his head without saying anything. He too had heard of it, but he did not think it likely. The Red Princes nowadays proved to be too powerful even for someone like Comrade Zhao, the ex-secretary of the Central Party Discipline Committee, who had been something of a patron for the ex-chief inspector. Still, he did not have to explain it to Liu.

'Anyway, I'm trying to write a novella about Judge Dee in the Tang dynasty – by way of preparation for the work in the office. How the judicial system worked in the Tang dynasty, and how it works today. A comparative study with a historical perspective may help with the job.'

'That will be nice, really nice.' Liu was surprised, at a loss about what to say in response.

'And I've just finished reading Van Gulik's *Poets and Murder*. It's a Judge Dee novel based on a real Tang dynasty murder case, of the well-known poetess Xuanji killing her maid in a fit of jealousy. But there were a lot of things that did not add up. Gulik made a clever change, turning a poet/official into an accomplice, and moving the poetess to the background of another hardly related murder case. But things in his treatment remain inexplicable. For one, Xuanji did not have a credible motive for the murder.'

'That's inexplicable . . .' Liu said, sort of echoing, still unable to say anything proper in response.

'What's more, in the source material for Gulik's novel, the Tang dynasty magistrate, or I should say mayor in charge of the trial with no separation between the executive and the

judicial power, was no judge in today's sense of the word at
the Tang time – was said to have been rejected as an admirer
by Xuanji. So people came to see the trial as an unfair one.
Such a twist of revenge on the part of the magistrate was
probably concocted just to make the story spicier. Gulik did
not include the hearsay in his book, and I don't believe it
either. In the Tang dynasty, affairs were common between
courtesans and poets or poet/officials, but were not taken seriously. What the magistrate wanted with her was just something
like a one-night affair, or even less, and it was no big deal for
either of them.

'After all, the magistrate was a high-ranking official at the
time. Unpleasant as her rejection might have been, it would
be unlikely for him to risk his reputation by retaliating like
that. He had to take into consideration the public opinion about
his handling of the case. Also, the early Tang period was
marked by the relentless fight between the Li and the Wu
factions at the court, and the magistrate might have been under
untold pressure to take over the case, so he had to be extra
careful.'

'You're really insightful, Chief Inspector Chen!' Liu could
not help exclaiming.

By now Liu must have come to understand the real purpose
of Chen's unannounced visit. All his talk about the Xuanji
case in the Judge Dee novel served merely as a pretext, a Tang
dynasty case in parallel to a present-day case, which was
assigned to Judge Liu. Liu stood up, paced a few steps as if
looking for something, and sat down without finding it.

'You may have heard something about the Min case, Chief
Inspector Chen,' Liu said, with a sudden serious edge to his
voice. 'About those speculations online about me as the judge
assigned for the case.'

'Let me say this first, Liu,' Chen said, looking Liu in the
eyes. 'I'm not doing any investigation. I have to take care of
things at my new office. Not to mention my so-called convalescent leave. Frankly, I know better than to get myself into
more trouble at the moment.'

It was true, and he thought he sounded candidly convincing
– perhaps even to himself. The noise of busy traffic along the

street seemed to be surging up through the office windows on the twentieth floor.

Liu looked up and took a pack of cigarettes, lighting one for himself after and offering another to Chen, who declined, waving his hand.

'So what do you want with me, Chief Inspector Chen?'

'Make no mistake about it, Liu. I'm not here as a chief inspector. It's just that the Min case bears a number of similarities to the Xuanji case in the Judge Dee story. As people often have a joke about it: once a cop, always a cop. I simply cannot help being curious about it.'

'Curious about what particular aspects of the Min case in relation to the Xuanji case?'

'How about telling me what you know about the Min case, Liu?' Chen added after a short pause, 'Of course, there're also dissimilarities between the two cases. For one, in a week after the death of Qing in the *shikumen* house, two more murders happened – of Huang and Wanxia – both of them possibly related to it.'

'You may be disappointed, Chief Inspector Chen. As a matter of fact, I know very little about the Min case. As for those speculations online about my "having a grudge" against Min, they're totally groundless. For an internet celebrity like Min, she was much discussed, as you may imagine. I think it's about half a year ago. I had a cup of beer too much and joked with friends that I might be a judge known in the circle, but I would have been put on the waiting list of her private kitchen dinner forever, even if I had tried with all my might. It was nothing but a joke in a bar, but it turned into a story that I was snubbed by her. When the Min case broke out, I did not want to take it, but it's in the hand of Internal Security. What could I possibly do?'

'Yes, I've heard about the involvement of Internal Security from the very beginning.'

'But there're some things a bit unusual about the Min case. Usually the practice of *shuanggui* is adopted for damage control in the cases of corrupt Party officials, and those *shuanggui* cases come to judges at the end, just like a show – with the arrangement made by the government people beforehand about what the *shuangguied* is supposed to say or not say in the courtroom. The only thing for a judge to do is to read the pre-written script with the deal cut and dried in the closed room. Consequently, there is no damage to the image of the Party authorities. But this time, as soon as I was given the case, phone calls started coming in, seemingly with different, even contradictory, messages from people above telling me what to say as the judge.'

'That's unusual. Tell me more about what people above want you to do, Liu. Leave out nothing, whether you think it important or not.'

'Of course I'll leave nothing out for you, Chief Inspector Chen.'

Then Liu started telling him about what he knew about the Min case, with some details.

It did not surprise Chen that Internal Security were trying so hard to make Min talk, for which they also wanted Liu to put pressure on her, though the judge had no idea about what exactly they wanted to hear from her. It was a matter of course that they chose not to tell him everything. What they really wanted to learn from Min, Chen became more convinced, involved people high above, possibly at the very top.

And at the same time, some other people in Beijing had also called Liu, wanting him to report the progress of the case in detail, and to 'abide by a judge's principle'. Naturally, they did not tell him anything about the real reason either. It was probably for the same reason that the mysterious client Sima, while seeking the help from Old Hunter's agency, had chosen not to tell the truth either.

As Liu lit another cigarette, Chen took one too, to the judge's surprise.

Obviously, Sima and the people in Beijing cared not about what might have happened to Min, but about what she might say under pressure. The murder of Huang must have thrown them into a panic. It had dawned on them that Min would not be released any time soon, with the case getting more compli-cated. And with her remaining in *shuanggui* indefinitely, they had to worry about the worst-case scenario. As it seemed to them, it was only a matter of time for her to talk under the mounting pressure.

That suddenly shed light on a number of aspects of the case. And on those of the related cases too.

'From a cop's perspective, the heart of the matter is to have the real murderer caught as soon as possible,' Chen said at the end of Liu's account. 'As long as Min remains in her vulnerable position under *shuanggui*, some people above may continue to put pressure on her, and others may push in a different direction – for whatever reason, we don't know. Hence the possibility of more victims like Huang and Wanxia. In other words, only with the true criminal put away could the vicious cycle come to an end.'

'You're so right about it, Chief Inspector Chen.'

Still, he tried to get something more specific from Judge Liu.

'Between you and me, Internal Security is not that experienced in investigating a homicide case. I'm on leave, but I may still be able to see something they do not see, and say something to my former colleagues in the police bureau, and to some of my connections above too. After all, Wanxia was a colleague of mine.'

'She was a very young policewoman, I know.'

'And I'm truly worried about the possible development of the case. The longer it drags on, the more the collateral damage. Not just for people like Huang and Wanxia, but also for those not directly related. It's like in a proverb: the fire devouring the city gate could prove to be a disaster to the fish in the small pond.'

'Yes, I may be like the fish in the small pond. But what else can I possibly do, Chief Inspector Chen?'

'What else can you remember about things those people said to you? Things that struck you as strange, unusual.'

'Now you mention it, there's something puzzling me. I know nothing about Wanxia, the young policewoman killed at the hotel. Nothing from Internal Security. But some people in Beijing called me, asking for a report about it.'

'Who are those people?'

'Not Internal Security, but people really high up there, that's about all I can say, Chief Inspector Chen.'

That's what he had suspected, and it was about all he could get out of Judge Liu. It was useless pushing for more.

Like in another Chinese proverb, when the roof starts leaking, it must keep on raining all night long.

The moment Chen got back to his apartment, he received a phone call from Old Hunter with Zhangzhang in the background, chipping in with a word or two, and coughing uncontrollably. The cry for help proved to be too much for the ex-inspector, who, with no time even to digest what he had just learned from Judge Liu, was astounded with the latest from the PI agency.

Sima, the mysterious client, already knew Chen had been to the Moller Villa Hotel. So he'd demanded to meet with Chen in person; failing that, to know what Chen had discovered there.

But how could Sima have learned about his visit there so fast? In fact, Chen went to the hotel because of the unexpected request for help from Detective Xiong. He had not told anybody else about it.

And 'what Chen had discovered there' mattered a lot to Sima, apparently, but why? It reminded Chen of what Judge Liu had told him. The people in Beijing had also requested a report about what had happened at the hotel.

Sima seemed to be like 'ants crawling on the hot wok', raising the amount of the bonus by twenty percent if the agency could succeed in getting Min out, but at the same time warning them that the agency might as well be closed overnight if they failed to deliver.

It was a serious threat. For a client like Sima, with his official background and his connections, it would be a piece of cake to have a PI agency shut down.

Chen decided not to tell Old Hunter about what he had done so far. Possibilities here and there, but nothing definite for a breakthrough. It was out of the question for him to meet with Sima. Or to tell Sima about his discussion with Detective Xiong in the hotel.

For whatever undisclosed reason, it might be justifiable for

Sima to engage the agency to clear Min's name, but not for him to be so anxious about Chen's findings in the hotel.

Unless Sima and the people behind him were related to the murder in the hotel.

But what was the point in paying the agency such an incredibly high fee in the first place?

For the incredibly high stakes involved in the Min case, which explained the huge amount paid to the agency to get Min out, but failing that, possibly even higher stakes for Sima and the people behind him if Min broke down under the pressure.

Exhausted with those speculations, he made himself another cup of black tea.

After half an hour of tossing and turning in bed, and still failing to put the pieces together, Chen knew he would be unable to fall asleep, but he did not want to take sleeping pills. He got up instead, lighting a cigarette.

Was it possible that some of the pieces might not have belonged to the one and same puzzle, he contemplated in the spiraling smoke rings? If so, he might as well shift to focusing on just one piece – the latest one.

He checked his emails and printed out the case report about the murder in the hotel. It had been forwarded over by Detective Yu. Detective Xiong had made no progress. Still too reluctant to openly seek Chen's help, he'd shared the report with Detective Yu. After all, it involved one of their colleagues.

But Chen had a hard time relating it to the other two murders. The murderer of Wanxia must have known the hotel inside and out, most likely via inside information. It had been done in a way that was so different from the first two murders.

While all of the three victims could have been seen as related to Min, he could not lose sight of the fact that the hotel murder could have been done by a professional with a government background, which made the situation even more politically sinister than he had first imagined.

A street mugger, who could have run across Huang at an unlikely moment, at an unlikely location, would not have obtained any clues regarding the whereabouts of Min. The hotel might have been known in the circle as a special place for the *shuangguied* Party officials, but no one could have suspected that someone like Min would actually be put there.

Supposing the motive for the hotel murder was to silence Min, then what about the first two? The Party authorities might not have been pleased with Min's celebrity status as symbolic of the Republican values, but it would not have been difficult to have her finished off in a far less dramatic way. No need for all the unsavory publicity.

Besides, where did Old Hunter's client come in? To say the least, Sima was another one with government information, having learned so fast about the murder in the Moller Villa Hotel.

For that matter, where did Huang come in? Huang could have agreed to reveal some things about Min and her private parties, but the ex-inspector did not think such a possibility would have led to the killing.

With one question leading to another, Chen soon felt overwhelmed. Things were developing so fast. It was less than a week since he had first heard of the Min case.

That morning he had planned to read *Poets and Murder* through the day before getting the phone call from Old Hunter. Again, he was reminded of the twists and turns encountered by Judge Dee in Van Gulik's novel.

And what he had learned from Judge Liu confirmed one of his earlier assumptions: with powerful people high above involved in the Min case, it was more complicated than he had imagined. In other words, it was just like in the Judge Dee story.

Was it possible that in those cases revolving around Min, crimes had been committed for different reasons? Related yet unrelated, like in the Judge Dee story – in a way still beyond his knowledge. In the Buddhist saying, things as small as a sipping or a pecking are pre-destined and pre-destining, but it is difficult for ordinary people to see.

For that matter, could his picking up Gulik's novel have

also turned out to be such an instance? It was possible to paraphrase the saying as 'things connected and connecting under the sun'.

It was coincidental, or providential, that an email came in at that moment, from Mr Gu, the head of the New World. It was a short one with an attachment.

'The video of the shopping mall's garage for that Friday night. Enjoy.'

Mr Gu had kept his word, as always, delivering without even asking why Chen needed the video.

In the socialism with China's characteristics, people could hardly do anything without connections, though Chen did not want to take Mr Gu just as one of those connections.

Before he downloaded the attached file, Chen took out the video produced at Min's lane, which he had already viewed several times, ready to press 'play' one more time, to make sure that some of its details were etched in his memory before viewing the one recorded at the garage. Then he thought better of it. He put the memory stick from Jin into a laptop, and downloaded the attachment in Mr Gu's email at the desktop computer. When ready to compare the two, he started by watching the scenes from the shopping mall garage, which was equipped with surveillance cameras at various angles, both at the entrance and the exit, with the time recorded in the upper right corner.

The video showed a man in a light-colored jacket striding toward the garage around ten past eleven, but as he drew nearer to the garage entrance, he slowed to a stop before he turned back and walked away in another direction. He was soon out of the camera's view.

It was not until one fifty-five that the video showed the man in the light-colored jacket coming toward the garage again. This time he walked straight into the garage. The video recorded at the exit of the garage then showed a black BMW pulling out five minutes later.

The face of the driver appeared rather blurred, but at that time of the night there could be little doubt that it was none other than the man who had entered wearing the light-colored jacket.

Then Chen retrieved the images in the video as well as the pictures Jin had obtained for him. Comparing them closely, he felt he could be pretty sure about the identity of the man in question.

Still, he stopped the video and wrote down the license number of the black BMW on a piece of paper. There was one thing he needed to do early next morning.

DAY FIVE

Early in the morning, Chen was meeting with Old Hunter at the hot water house on Xinchang Road, which had been repeatedly recommended by the old man.

It was just six thirty. They were the only customers there. The owner had opened the door for them with reluctance.

'You can have as much hot water as you like, you know, and you will have your own special tea leaves, I know,' the owner said with sleepy grouchiness, pointing at the big brick stove. 'The earthen stove cake maker won't come here until seven thirty if you want to wait, but I want to sleep for a couple of hours more.'

Without further ado, the owner withdrew with a limp into the backroom and closed the door after him.

Old Hunter filled a hot water bottle, sat with Chen on the unpainted wooden bench at the unpainted wooden table in the middle of the room, and poured out two cups.

Out across the street, Chen saw another side entrance of People's Park, where, after venturing into the matching corner, the two of them had had their first discussion about the Min case less than a week earlier.

'Under your influence, I too am being a Suzhou opera fan this morning,' Chen said, unfolding a paper fan with a dramatic flourish. 'As you have said so many times, a story has to be told from the beginning. So please be patient for the story that started in the park – we are having our roles reversed today.'

'Finally, you have come to appreciate the art of Suzhou opera, I'm so happy to hear that. Like a loyal Suzhou opera audience, I'm all ears.'

'As we have discussed from the beginning, there're a lot of things so puzzling about the case, related or interrelated. When I try to unravel them as parts of the whole, they appear more inexplicable in confusion. So, how about tackling just one part first? It was hardly conceivable, we both thought, for Min to kill Qing for something like her quitting for another job, and inconceivable too for someone to break into Min's *shikumen* house with Qing as the target that night. No imaginable motive whatsoever for either scenario. On the other hand, if Min instead of Qing was the real target, how could the perpetrator have known about Min sleeping in a drunken stupor that night? Unless he happened to be one of the four guests that night.'

'Hold on, Chief. In that scenario of yours, how could one of the four guests have gotten back into the *shikumen* house without a key? There are no signs of forced entry. None of the four had a key, either. Of course, no one would have admitted so with a murder case under investigation. But if it's one on such intimate terms with Min as to have a key for him to come over any time, why would he have chosen that night?'

Old Hunter, who claimed himself as a veteran Suzhou opera fan, had a hard time stopping himself from raising his questions.

'Come on, you know better than to push. It's not the way to enjoy the opera,' Chen said, taking a deliberate slow sip, imitating Old Hunter's dramatic way of narrating. 'At that stage, it's just a scenario with a lot of guesswork. But remember the Starbucks in the New World? The café is not far from Min's lane on Madang Road. After our meeting in the café, I took a walk in the area, where I noticed one thing. It's a narrow side street, with a number of the old buildings not yet demolished, so a visitor to the neighborhood would have a hard time finding a parking spot for his car. Some of them would have to go to the public garages near Huaihai Road and the New World.'

'They had their own chauffeurs and cars to pick them up after the dinner party with Min, I remember reading about it in their statements.'

'But not necessarily that night, not necessarily every one of them. As it happens, my new office secretary, a very capable young girl named Jin, did a lot of research for the office. The Min case being such a sensational one for the moment, she went to Min's neighborhood committee for something like a background checkup. With the area being close to the New World, several surveillance cameras were installed along the street, and at both entrances of the lane too.'

'What did she find?'

'Something very intriguing. But like in Suzhou opera, let me hold on to it for a little while more. Suffice it to say that it led to another clue.'

'What's that?'

'Here is a car license number. Can you check the identity of the car owner?'

'That should not be too difficult. I still have some old connections.'

'Once you've found it, let me know. The name of the car owner. The model of the car. We can then act in light of the information. That's about all I can tell you for the moment, but a breakthrough is close, I promise you.'

'You have surely learned the art of Suzhou opera, Chief Inspector Chen.'

After parting with Old Hunter outside the hot water house, Chen walked on along West Nanjing Road, surrounded by the oppressive mass of light- and deep-gray concrete high rises where he heard a sparrow twittering. A tiny sound that was rare in the increasingly mega metropolitan city.

And the morning was coming to consciousness, with the smells of stale beer from a cheap-looking bar, a workman spray-washing the windows from outside. The city presented an amazing mixture of the old and new. An elderly drunkard, stripped to his waist, was loitering there and beating at his own chest, his ribs visible like a washboard.

'The Cultural Revolution is coming again!'

It was then that a WeChat message from Jin appeared on his phone screen: 'With Z, to H's with the key, for some—'

After the unfinished *some*, an emoji of a young girl crying in horror.

It was not at all like Jin's usual messages.

Too short. Too fragmented. Too hasty. Not even finished.

And the emoji also appeared too exaggerated for a young, cool girl like Jin.

A black Maserati came out of nowhere, honked rudely, shot by like crazy, and left behind a trail of fumes and dust.

He must have been moving too close to the traffic while brooding hard over the message.

But what could that message of hers possibly mean?

She was with someone, going to somebody else's place, but not in a position to compose the text message properly.

Not enough time for such a short message?

For fear of being detected by somebody in her company – detected by somebody named Z?

But who the devil was Z?

Presumably, somebody Chen also knew, or she would not have used just the capital letter, and for that matter, was H somebody connected with Z as well?

And the two letters that should have made sense in the context of what had happened during the last several days.

What about the dangling phrase 'with the key'?

H being not at home?

Z having the key to his place?

But Chen found his mind rapidly turning into a pail of starch paste stuck and hardened with so many question marks.

He looked up to see a white-haired man flying a dragon-shaped kite in a small garden-like public area across the street, reeling out the thread with a tremulous hand, grinning, jumping like an excited child. It seemed as if the kite had been the one and only thing that really mattered in the entire world – like the moment another old man bit into a soft, warm rice ball on a long-ago cold morning.

There was an angry glare of kite tearing through the late morning light, which struck him like a flash of lightning.

Z stood for Zheng, the one who had attended Min's private kitchen dinner party that night on behalf of Huang; and H, for Huang, the antique businessman who had been killed just a couple of days earlier in Yangpu District.

Zheng wasn't related to Huang as an actual nephew, but was a capable assistant in the antique business for the old man. As such, he was aware of Huang's early morning routine, so he could have ambushed Huang on that street corner.

The ex-inspector came to an abrupt stop in front of a street peddler hawking stinky tofu in a large wok on a portable gas tank, busy frying the pieces into a golden color, and ladling them into a white plastic container.

Chen had told Jin about his talk with Huang, though he failed to recall what details he might have mentioned to her. In her 'research' for the office, she could have come across Zheng's name in one way or another.

And she could have somehow connected Zheng and Huang in her own way, and moved ahead without his knowledge.

If so, it further confirmed his suspicion about what he had gathered from the videos at the lane and at the shopping mall garage.

He shuddered at the thought of what might have happened to Jin.

In his phone he had stored a picture of Huang's business card, which carried Huang's home address. He retrieved the picture and sent it to Detective Xiong with a message:

'Go to the address on the card. Immediately. A matter of life and death! I'm going there too.'

He got to Huang's house in the quickest possible time. It looked more like a European-style villa, in front of which he saw a black BMW parked along the curb. He recognized the car as the one that had driven out of the garage of the Pacific Ocean Shopping Mall that Friday night, after the dinner at Min's *shikumen* house.

So Zheng and Jin must have gone inside.

The front door was locked.

Chen moved around to the back of the house in haste. In the back yard, rank with tall weeds, he saw a cedar deck adjoining a white-painted French window door.

He got up onto the deck and tugged at the handle of the door, which was supposed to open into a sort of breakfast area. With the door locked from the inside, he could only peep in through the wooden blinds. He saw nothing. But then he heard a female voice inside the house, screaming from the direction of the living room.

He froze. Time stopped. But not a single minute could he

afford to lose. He turned around, picked up a large flowerpot from the deck, and crashed it into the French window. It sounded like the whole world splintering into thousands of pieces, shouting, glaring in the light, as he threw himself in through the opening.

The scene in the living room turned out to be as surreal as a tableau in a Judge Dee novel drawn by Gulik himself, but Chen took in every one of its real details.

Jin lying on her back on the floor, the man recognized as Zheng bent over her, his right knee pressing against her left thigh, and his hand crushing her chin and mouth. Her blouse badly torn, revealing a large part of her bare bosom, and her skirt also pulled partially down. She was raising her right leg and pressing hard against his chest with the sole of her bare foot.

The scene galvanized Chen with horror, regret and insurmountable rage.

He ran several steps and hurled himself at the man on top of Jin.

Jerking at the noise of the shattering window, Zheng released his grip, jumped up and bumped his head hard against a large willow-patterned vase behind him. It wobbled, and in spite of his efforts to balance himself, he lurched with Jin struggling underneath him and pulling his leg left in desperation, so he fell under the falling vase. It crashed down on Zheng's head with full force and knocked him out. Chen sprang over and finished the job by hitting him on the neck with the back side of his right hand, which had been badly cut by the sharp broken pieces of the vase, leaving a bloody trail on Zheng's neck and face.

All the details unfolded before his eyes in a slow-motion movie scene of absurdity, unbelievably, until it stopped with a sudden blackout.

Jin was the one that remained unhurt, except for her badly torn shirt and a couple of bruises visible above her collarbone. Neither of them had anything to do with the overturned vase, possibly a Ming dynasty antique, treasured by the late Huang, a silver-haired, Daoist-costumed old man who looked fondly out of a mahogany-framed portrait on the wall.

It was then that the siren of a police car came piercing through the gray smog.

Detective Xiong came bursting into the living room of Huang's mansion, looking flabbergasted at the scene.

Chen was the only one standing up, still reeling, with his hand bleeding, pointing at the broken pieces of a tall Ming dynasty vase by way of explanation, before he took off his jacket and put it around Jin's shoulders. She was making an effort to sit up, pushing her elbow against the floor. Having lost her shoes in the struggle, she tried to reach out to them underneath the coffee table.

Zheng remained lying unconscious on the floor. A large chunk of the vase could be seen glittering near his temple, which registered a thin streak of blood.

'The vase knocked him out. It fell cracking down on his head. Zheng is the killer of Huang and Qing, and he just attempted to kill Jin,' Chen said, still gasping. 'I've called for an ambulance. Probably nothing but a concussion. I've checked his breathing. Quite even. The Ming dynasty vase must have been worth a huge fortune. It was a piece so invaluable to Huang. A providential revenge for the old man.'

Detective Xiong was still at a loss for words, staring hard at Chen, and then at Jin. It took more than a minute for the confounded detective to recollect himself.

'But how did you and Jin come to be here, both of you, together with Zheng, Director Chen?'

Jin was tugging at the jacket Chen had put on her.

'You are not hurt, Jin?' Chen said miserably, turning to her without answering Xiong's question.

'I'm fine. You came in the nick of time, Director Chen. But for you, I would have been the one lying unconscious on the floor now.'

'You should have told me earlier, Jin. I could never have forgiven myself—'

'What are you two talking about?' Xiong snapped. 'So you have been investigating the Min case in secret all along, Chief Inspector Chen!'

'No, it's just an unbelievable chain of coincidences, Detective

Xiong, but I should have seen it coming earlier, much earlier, it's my fault.'

'Please be so kind as to enlighten me, Sherlock Holmes of China.'

'Well, to make a long story short, I happened to have a talk with Huang as I had to sell some antique books left by my father. I had to pay for my mother's nursing home, you know. Nothing to do with the case. Huang was well connected in the antique business. So we met for breakfast in an old restaurant a few days ago. He gave me suggestions and introduced me to an auction house. Of course we talked about some other things. And we found we had one thing in common – to our surprise – a passion for Shanghai street food.'

It was not exactly true. He had contacted Huang because of the Min case. On the other hand, it was with the very pretext of antique books that he had approached Huang, and it was also true that they had talked a lot about their common passion for street food.

'It must be a very long story indeed,' Detective Xiong interrupted in spite of himself.

'Detective Yu's father, Old Hunter, has a favorite Suzhou opera saying: "You have to tell a Suzhou opera story from the very beginning." Indeed, it's the things of seemingly little relevance that make up a real story. During the breakfast, Huang mentioned, among other things, his partiality for an inexpensive rice ball stuffed with fresh fried dough stick at a side street stall in Yangpu District.'

'Why on earth should Huang have discussed with you about all that?'

'I am just another impossible gourmet like him, as you may know. Birds of a feather,' he said with an apologetic smile, patting at a pillow for Jin, who moved to perch herself on the couch beside him.

'But what's so mouth-watering about a rice ball for a rich old man like Huang? You may easily find such a cheap snack on many street corners in the city of Shanghai.'

'You should have listened to his lecture about the sentimental value of a soft, warm rice ball on a cold morning after the night shift. He used to work at a neighborhood production group in Yangpu District. After the first bite of the rice ball more than thirty years ago, he kept on going to the street stall regularly, regardless of his huge fortune made in the antique business. He did not share this secret with many people, as he believed that "Once such a street corner stall becomes known, the rice ball will no longer be made with the same quality." And he made sure that he would not be recognized as a Big Buck there. Not that he was unwilling to pay a bit more.'

Detective Xiong kept shaking his head, opening his mouth yet without saying anything.

'Now back to the Min case. I happen to have a capable secretary in Jin, who manages to keep me updated about the most-talked-about cases in the city with a lot of detailed info from her web surfing. When I first learned about Huang's death, it did not even occur to me that it could have any bearing on the Min case. As far as Huang's case was concerned, I did not think it a case of robbery gone wrong. Why? At such an early hour, and in such a poor section of Yangpu District, no one would have carried much money. I suspected that the murder had been committed by someone knowledgeable about Huang's wealth, and possibly about his peculiar passion for the rice ball too, but it was not my case. I had to be responsible for the work at my new office, like the office statement about the Judge Jiao scandal, you know. So it was just a thought flashing through the mind. I did not discuss it with you, nor with anybody else.

'Then at the Moller Villa Hotel, we discussed Wanxia's case. Not as an inspector any more, but as a former colleague of hers, I felt really obliged to do something for Wanxia.'

'Your colleague was hurt or killed, Director Chen?' Jin cut in.

'It's another long story, which I will tell you later,' Chen said, turning to Detective Xiong again. 'Like you, I also believed that her death was related to the Min case. In fact, it was your talk about the hotel surveillance facilities that prompted me to talk to Jin about some possible scenarios. Mind you, neither Jin nor I was doing any investigation into the case.

'So it's to Jin's credit. She followed the Min case as part
of the office responsibility. She went to the neighborhood
committee for the background checkup, such as the list of
people at her dinner table that night, and then the video
of Min's guests leaving the lane—'

'But Director Chen—' Jin said, sitting up in haste.

'It's truly to your credit, Jin. No question about it. You've
been working so hard in the office, and I, on leave at home
most of the time. And the video you obtained there confirmed
the guests had their chauffeurs pick them up around eleven,
except Zheng, who left for his car parked in the garage of the
Pacific Ocean Shopping Mall. And about an hour later,
the camera registered several people entering the lane
through the back entrance, quite possibly the lane residents,
with one man lagging behind by himself, who struck me a bit
like Zheng, in a white shirt with a jacket draped over his arm.
With the poor light and the angle of the camera, I was not too
sure about it. It could have been another lane resident coming
back late with the others.'

'So you were not sure,' Detective Xiong said.

'As luck would have it, a friend of mine happened to have
access to the surveillance system at the garage of the Pacific
Ocean Shopping Mall. The video there showed the man in
question reaching the garage around eleven ten, but instead of
getting in, he turned and walked away. The next time he
appeared on the garage camera again was about one fifty-five.
This time, he walked straight into the garage without looking
back, and about five minutes later, a black BMW drove out. I
copied the license number. Earlier this morning, I got the
confirmation that Zheng's car was a black BMW, and the license
number matched too. I was just about to call you about all this
when I got a message from Jin.

'Here it is, Jin's message,' Chen said, showing the phone
to Xiong. 'It's cryptic. And I had to read it several times before
it hit me that she was going with Zheng to Huang's place. Jin
has been doing a lot of research for the office, as I've told
you. So it was logical for her to contact Zheng. But why should
she have chosen to go in the company of Zheng? I got panic-
stricken about the possibility of Zheng leading her into a deadly

trap. That's why I texted you for support. And I too hurried over here.'

Zheng's body began stirring a little on the floor. Detective Xiong moved over to squat down at his side and touch his pulse before he said, 'I think he's fine. Please go on, Director Chen.'

'At the same time, something else came flashing across my mind. As Huang's assistant, Zheng was the one knowledgeable about Huang's passion for the rice ball in Yangpu District, and capable of ambushing the old man there that early morning—'

'Hold on, Director Chen. What could possibly have been his motive for attacking Huang?'

'I believe he will have to tell you. For all I could guess, he was paranoid that Huang might talk to me about his infatuation with Min.'

'What? Zheng had never seen Min before that dinner party.'

'He had not seen Min in person before, but a lot of her pictures are online. Huang had not talked to me that much about Zheng, just mentioning that Zheng had jumped at the opportunity, and saying, "He's so impressed by the stories about her beauty and grace." After his leaving with the other guests at Min's dinner party, he could not have helped turning back and sneaking into the *shikumen* house again—'

'But in accordance with your theory, how could he have sneaked back in with the door locked?'

'Min was wasted that night, and he helped her into the bedroom, remember?'

'Yes.'

'He could have taken her keys in the bedroom without her knowledge. It's just my guess, I have to say.'

'Min could have told us about the loss of her keys, but she never said anything about it.'

'It was too chaotic the next morning for her to instantly become aware of it. Besides, it's not unusual that keys are misplaced somewhere for a day or two before being recovered, but by then she was already put into the secret detention place.'

'So you think he had planned it all along despite being a first-timer to her *shikumen* house?'

'No, it came to him on the spur of the moment, I mean the

key part, when he laid her down on the bed. They were alone in the room, but he did not have the time to do anything else with her as other guests were waiting outside. Then he caught sight of the keys—'

'Cut it here, Director Chen. You mean Zheng sneaked back into the *shikumen* house with the key to attack Min, and he ended up killing Qing? It does not make any sense. He murdered Qing because Min had been so upset with her?'

'He sneaked back into the *shikumen* house without knowing Qing was still there. He killed Qing for some reason still not yet known to us, but more often than not, what a murderer thinks is not known to us.'

'It's so beyond me.'

'For a possible scenario, he could have been so freaked out when Qing caught him in the act of attacking Min. Anyway, he will make his confession about what really happened that night. I don't think he went to the *shikumen* house because of Qing, the way the murderer went to the Moller Villa Hotel because of Wanxia.'

'Murder in the hotel?' Jin chipped in again, looking up at him in confusion.

'Anyway, I got here just a few minutes earlier than you, Detective Xiong,' Chen went on without responding to her question. 'I heard Jin screaming inside, so I broke in through the French window door. In panic, Zheng jumped up and knocked over the Ming dynasty vase, which fell crashing hard on his head. It was then you came in and you saw the rest.'

'But for Director Chen's arrival in time,' Jin said, with tears in her eyes, 'what could have happened to me there, I shiver to imagine.'

'What the devil made Zheng bring you to Huang's place, Jin?' Detective Xiong said, still with a dubious edge to his voice.

'He told me that he had some intimate pictures of Huang with Min – nude pictures. I thought this could turn out to be some clues—'

'Hold on, Jin. You mean Huang was killed because he was a secret lover of Min's?'

'I don't know. To tell the truth, I did not have my wits about me when he suggested, out of the blue, that we go and get hold of the pictures at Huang's house.'

'But how could Zheng have learned about such a secret? Even if it were true, how could he have taken you into Huang's house?'

'He said he had worked closely with the old man, with a key duplicated in secret.'

'So he took the key . . .' Chen too cut in, nodding, yet without finishing the sentence.

'I, too, had doubts about it, but he practically dragged me into his car. That's when I managed to send out a message to Director Chen. Zheng was driving in the front, keeping me under watch through the rear-view mirror. My hands trembling, I had to do it quick – without being detected. Luckily, Chen got it and came to the rescue here.'

It sounded plausible enough, Chen reflected, that statement of hers. She surely had her wits about her. Detective Xiong could not have done anything about it.

Once again, Detective Xiong was turning to Chen with even more questions in his eyes. He shook his head instead.

In the short spell of silence that ensued in the room, a faint moan was heard escaping through Zheng's lips, though he still lay on the floor, barely moving. He opened his eyes, blinking in disbelief.

It was at this juncture that another siren came tearing through the air to a sudden stop in front of the door.

Probably the ambulance Chen had called for.

To their surprise, two Internal Security officers came bursting upon the scene. They must have hurried over in extreme haste, both panting with flushed faces. One rather tall, one really short, the pairing of the two could have added a comical touch to the uncanny scene.

'Oh, we've got Zheng here, the suspect in the Min case,' Xiong said to the two officers in haste. 'Possibly in the Huang case, too. He was caught in the act of attacking Jin.'

'But why is Inspector Chen – oh sorry, Director Chen here?' the tall one asked, seemingly more and more stiff, like a weather-beaten bamboo pole.

'His secretary Jin was attacked by Zheng,' Xiong said. 'Director Chen got the message from her and rushed over to the rescue.'

'Yes, Director Chen saved my life. But for him—'

'It sounds like a long, long story indeed, but we don't have the time for it right now, I'm afraid,' the short one cut in, with more authority in his voice. 'We've got to take it over from here, Detective Xiong.'

'We have to question Zheng first,' Detective Xiong said with a long face, his hairline receding further. 'If he was truly involved in the Min case as well as the Huang case, then—'

'Don't bother, Detective Xiong. We'll do all the questioning, and—'

'Sorry, whatever you're going to do,' Chen said, cutting in too, 'I think I'd better accompany Jin home.'

With the arrival of Internal Security at the scene, it was a matter of course for them to take over. The ex-inspector was in no position to say anything about it. It would not do him any good to be seen as one actively engaged in the investigation – in the midst of his own political trouble.

'It was a horrible experience for her,' Chen went on. 'She was just doing some research for the office. Neither she nor I know anything about your investigation.'

'Of course, you should take her home now, Director Chen,' the tall Internal Security officer readily agreed. 'Sorry for your bad scare, Jin.'

'Thank you, Director Chen,' the short one echoed. 'You surely have helped.'

'Yes,' Detective Xiong said, nodding, without saying a word more.

As Chen and Jin got into a taxi, he felt worse about her dreadful experience, for which he could not but hold himself responsible.

He had not mentioned anything specific for her to do regarding the investigation, but it was also a fact that he had made no effort to stop her when she'd reported to him, again and again, about the 'research' for the office – for him. There had been a tacit understanding between the two of them. She had gone through all this because of him, which he had to admit to himself.

For the first two or three minutes, he could hardly look her in the eye, nor did he know what to say.

Not just because it was difficult for them to talk about the murder case in a taxi, with the driver stealing looks back to them in curiosity. She still appeared to be terribly shocked, and with a couple of her shirt buttons torn off, the bruise more pronounced above her collarbone under his gaze. The two of them were now sitting close to each other on the back seat.

She turned out to be more resilient, however, than he had imagined, meeting his concerned look with a light smile, saying in a low voice, 'Don't look so miserable, Director Chen. I'm just fine.' Then she leaned slightly over – almost nestling against him – and started whispering into his ear, off and on, about what had happened before his arrival at Huang's, as the taxi labored through the entangled traffic with constant jerks.

It turned out to be pretty much as she had depicted to both Chen and Xiong – except for some minor details she knew better than to give out in Xiong's company.

Aware of Chen having his hands tied, she'd tried to take the initiative herself. That morning, she'd visited Zheng. He appeared nervous, even panic-stricken, though she declared her visit as just part of the routine office research. After she raised no more than two or three questions regarding Min's private kitchen dinner party, he asked her whether she worked for Chief Inspector Chen. She said yes, and out of the blue he made an offer to show her intimate pictures of Huang with Min as possible clues for the investigation. The pictures were still kept in Huang's residence, Zheng said, but no one could tell what would happen to them when his nieces or nephews moved in. She had read blog posts about the relationship between Huang and Min, and it sounded not that unimaginable. So he dragged her into his car, and she decided to send the message to Chen. The moment they got into Huang's house with the key, he turned abruptly to attack her. It was at that critical moment that Chen came bursting in upon the scene.

'I'm so sorry for having dragged you into all this, Jin.'

'Nothing really happened. It's not your fault, Director Chen. Don't be that hard on yourself,' she said in a comforting tone. 'But for you, what could have happened?'

'But you could have told me earlier about the visit to Zheng.'

'As a secretary to the legendary Chief Inspector Chen, I have to learn to take the initiative myself.'

The taxi was slowing down and coming into view of her apartment building. The driver turned back to her with a simple question, 'Here?'

Chen got out, holding the door for her as she stepped out, turning to him with a smile, 'Would you like to come in for a cup of tea with me?'

He was surprised at the invitation, tongue-tied. Before he could answer, however, a text message came in with a dull ding. It was from Party Secretary Li of the Shanghai Police Bureau.

'Go back home immediately, Director Chen. A bureau car is waiting there for you in front of your apartment building. An all-inclusive vacation arranged for you in the Yellow Mountains – in recognition of your excellent work . . .'

'Another vacation out of the blue!' he said, murmuring to himself, without the time to read the message closely.

'Another vacation,' she repeated after him, leaning over to take a look at the message.

A cicada started screeching, unexpectedly, for the time of the year. It was early May, though fairly warm.

The vacation in the Yellow Mountains must have been arranged in extreme haste while they were on their way to Jin's home. 'In recognition of your excellent work.' The message did not specify what he had done, possibly in implicit recognition of his help in the investigation of the Min case. As for the abruptness of the vacation, it was said to be because of an unexpected vacancy in the most luxurious mountain hotel. A high-ranking Party official could not make it there at the last minute for a special package already prepared for him.

'Would you like to come in for a cup of tea,' she said again. 'Your hand is still bleeding a little. It needs to be taken care of.'

'No, I have to head back home right now – a car is waiting for me there for the vacation.'

'Then don't worry about it, Director Chen,' she said, turning back to him again on the doorstep. 'Remember to put a bandage on your hand the moment you get back home, and then enjoy your vacation in the mountains. I'll keep WeChatting you about things here in the office.'

A leaf was seen swirling down like a yellow-winged butterfly over her slim shoulder. The scene reminded him of an image in Xuanji's poem. He was filled with an ominous feeling.

DAY SIX

C hen rubbed his eyes, unbelievably, in the morning light streaming into the spacious hotel room. It was almost ten, but considering the late hour he had arrived at the Cloud Sea Hotel at the mid-mountain range the previous night, and the fact he was officially 'on vacation', sleeping in later than usual seemed to be more than justifiable.

He made himself a cup of tea. Still disoriented, he moved out to the balcony, taking a slow sip at the tender green tea named Monkey Prize, and looking out toward the breath-taking scene of the verdant mountains mantled in the white clouds.

It seemed as if he had been transported in a dream to the Yellow Mountains, the collective name for a range of more than seventy peaks in the south of Anhui Province. A celebrated resort for tourists for more than a thousand years, and an everlasting inspiration for poets and painters, the attractions of the mountains appeared to be manifold – pines, clouds, rocks and peaks, each with its peculiar charms and legends. With newly built highways, it was an easy drive here from Shanghai, about four hours, so the mountains appeared to be overwhelmed with tourists moving and hiking around those fabulous peaks.

For an all-inclusive vacation, just like so many other things, it had been pushed on to Chen, who had to take it at the shortest notice. But why the sudden vacation for him? It was a question he had raised with a couple of people above him.

The reason officially given was, invariably, that Director Chen would benefit from a vacation in the mountains, with the fresh air and pleasant scenes and excellent service there, logically serving as a much-needed part of his convalescent leave. It was difficult for an ordinary tourist to book a hotel in the mid-mountain area because of the government regulation about the limited number of hotels built there. Much more so for a luxurious hotel suite connected to the celebrated mountain spring. But for a 'distinguished guest' like Chen, it was all understandable.

In reality, however, it was nothing but the hasty removal of a potential trouble-maker – at least temporarily – from the situation developing fast in the city of Shanghai. With the case given back to Internal Security, damage control had turned into the top priority for the Party authorities.

And the vacation could also move him further out of sight, and further out of mind – and then into oblivion. There were so many things happening in China today, no one seemed to have a long memory about anything or anybody. Like the Judge Jiao scandal, the topic had already disappeared from the Internet. Eventually, nobody would be concerned about the disappearance of the ex-inspector or the ex-director.

That's why things had been happening to him in such a speedy sequence.

After his parting with Jin, he had returned home to find a uniformed chauffeur waiting for him there with a white Lexus. He was practically thrust into the luxurious car, which immediately set out, driving all the way from Shanghai to the Yellow Mountains in Anhui Province. All he'd managed to do was to make a phone call to his mother, assuring her that he was fine, then to Old Hunter, promising that they would have tea again after the vacation, and he'd sent a message to Jin through WeChat, typing it out in the bureau car as it was curving up the mountain path, precariously, to a five-star hotel named Cloud Sea which loomed against the dark night in the mid-mountain range.

Now for his first morning in the mountains, the scene which was unfolding out before him appeared to be unbelievably enchanting.

He was no stranger to some of the incredible perks of a 'prominent Party official', but such a vacation still turned out to be beyond his expectations. With the hotel halfway up in the mountains, it had a distinct advantage over those scattered in the base area, providing easy access to the peaks around and a panoramic view of the encircling hills as well.

And he was beginning to feel like a distinguished guest, with his glance sweeping around to a rock plateau about the size of a basketball court in front of the hotel. Standing on the rock, the tourists were said to be able to enjoy the miraculous experience of touching the waves of white clouds with their fingers, feeling at once lost and at one with the elements at the altitude.

Further beyond, he could see over across the plateau the famous pine tree on the cliff, commonly called 'blossoming-brush-in-dream', with a number of stories about it. One version he remembered concerned Jiang Lang, a Yuan dynasty poet who, after a prolonged period of writer's block, visited the mountains and dreamed of his brush pen bursting into blossom at night. Waking up, Jiang dashed off a brilliant essay before he walked out – to his astonishment – to the very sight of a pine tree standing out on the cliff exactly like the one in his dream.

Could that be a sign for Chen to start writing at the end of his cop career? Maybe one's memory could select its contents subconsciously, and that's how he happened to be remembering that particular version.

Yet he felt like anything but a writer on vacation for the moment. Stepping back into the room, he took out his cellphone again.

As Jin had promised, there were several WeChat messages from Shanghai:

'This morning, Director Ma of the City Government Office came down to our office the moment I got in. He spoke highly of your contribution to the successful conclusion of the Min case. "Now it's over, Director Chen doesn't have to worry about it. Not about anything in Shanghai. Not at all. Tell him to just enjoy himself in the mountains." He also wants me to keep him informed of anything you may do or say during your vacation.'

It was Saturday, but perhaps no surprise that both Jin and Ma were in the office on the eventful day. No surprise, either, that Director Ma wanted her to keep him informed of any possible move made by the ex-inspector, but Chen wondered whether she would ever choose to do so, after her having worked together with him in the last few days.

A white cloud was drifting on, seemingly careless, over a

distant peak, which was called the Lotus Flower Peak, as described in the hotel brochure. He failed to see any remote resemblance in the angular shape of the peak.

Then he scrolled down to the next WeChat message in his phone.

'Kong, the editor-in-chief of *Wenhui Daily*, called into the office. According to him, with news of your help in the investigation of the Min case being spread online, the serialization of your Judge Dee novella will turn into a huge success. He's anxious to start tomorrow, perhaps with your selection of Xuanji's poems – along with something you may want to say, like a prologue to the Tang dynasty murder story. And that's what Kong said to me in his own words. "Make hay while the sun shines. It is a Judge Dee story told by a legendary Chinese inspector in today's China, with far more historical accuracy and literary value, far more than the one penned by Van Gulik."'

Kong's suggestion was no surprise, either. A seasoned Party official/editor, he was aware of the political mire Chen might have landed himself in. But for the moment, it was politically correct for the newspaper to carry such a serialization. Besides, everything was possible in China; no one could tell whether Chen would stage a comeback. Last but not the least, the Judge Dee novella could be a plus for the newspaper with the relentless hits it had suffered from the new media.

The next message was a short one.

'I forgot to mention that Kong offered to pay the advance to you right now. Alternatively, he could have it sent directly to your mother's nursing home. He said you had talked to him about it.'

He might have mentioned it in passing to Kong, though perhaps more as a pretext. It was also true, however, that he was having a hard time continuing to pay the nursing home fee. So he was left with no choice but to start writing. Anyway, it might well be something worth doing, alone in the mountains. Then he read the next message.

'Someone nicknamed Old Hunter also called, saying you gave him my cell number. The message from him is cryptic. "The client is satisfied with the prospect of her being released soon. Apparently a truce between the high above. Zhangzhang is thrilled with the twenty percent bonus, promising not to say a single word about it to anyone. He also pledges he will keep his word to you."'

What could that mean? The unexpected conclusion of Zheng's pleading guilty in the private kitchen murder might have led to a compromise between the two rival factions in the Forbidden City. A temporary truce, so to speak. With the news of Zheng being caught as the murderer coming out in the official media as well, any further pressure for Min to 'talk' could backfire. Hence the prospect of her release soon. And the extra twenty percent from the mysterious client Sima as the bonus in return for their having done the job, and then for their not talking about it to anybody. As for the role Chen had played in it, no one could really tell, but the conclusion was enough to convince Sima that Chen had delivered.

As for Min, she would not get away unscathed, what with enough spicy, salacious material about her private life leaked and heaped online, and with irreparable damage done to the myth of the Republican Lady. What was worse, the knowledge about her being on a governmental black list would have scared away future customers to her private kitchen dinner.

But Chen did not feel exactly sorry for her. Like in an ancient Chinese fable, not one egg would have remained unbroken with the whole nest overturned. Much worse could have happened to her.

He made himself another cup of tea, in spite of the queasiness in his stomach. He turned to look up across the plateau again, and beyond the famous pine he thought he recognized the Heaven Gate Peak in the cloudy distance.

Master Liu regrets that Mount Peng is too far away,
And I, thousands of times farther from the mountains.

These lines from Li Shangyin, a contemporary of Judge Dee's, contained a nostalgic reference to an ancient Chinese legend. Master Liu, a young man in the Han dynasty, ventured to Mount Peng, where he had a wonderful time with a beautiful woman. Upon returning to his home village, however, he found it already changed beyond recognition – with hundreds of years passed – and he failed to find his way back to the mountains. The Tang couplet was often read as a regret over an irrecoverable loss. It was said that Li Shangyin's best poems were composed, paradoxically, at the lowest point of his life.

Perhaps Chen too was at one of the lowest points of his life, except that not a single line came to him. So many things had happened in just one day. He was kept too busy even to think about it.

Gazing at the celebrated peak, he was struck by the desolation of its rising so abruptly from the valleys. Wondering at its formation since time immemorial, he thought of another ancient Chinese proverb: 'One day in the mountains, a thousand years in the world of red dust.' Then why worry so much in the fleeing time?

Shaking his head, he caught himself resorting to clichés again, so pathetically, as it was criticized in the well-known essay 'Politics and the English Language' by George Orwell.

With the battle fought as best he could, there was nothing else left for him to do. No point brooding too much, he concluded. It was his last case. In fact, it already was not his case.

In spite of the two cups of strong tea, he found himself feeling drowsier than before, but it was still too early for him to take a nap.

In a tourist resort, do as a tourist would do, he told himself another paraphrased cliché.

He decided to take a walk out in the mountains. He was supposed to be on vacation here, with a vacationist role to play for the benefit of those watching out for him in the dark.

So he walked out like a tourist.

It does not rain but it pours.

After Director Ma's visit to the office, Jin got two more unexpected phone calls. Both fairly early in the morning.

One from someone nicknamed Old Hunter, at least so he introduced himself. The other from Kong, the Party boss and editor-in-chief of *Wenhui Daily*. Neither seemed to carry any urgent message, but she did not want to take anything for granted, not on a day like this.

She typed a couple of messages to Chen about these, and sent them out.

Then suddenly a spurt of seemingly routine phone calls and messages swarmed into the office, most of them directly or indirectly related to the latest developments in the Min case, and she tried her best to answer them.

Afterwards, she checked several websites, where speculations and theories had begun popping up about the conclusion of the Min case, though not in any detail yet.

About ten, Detective Xiong came striding into her office, carrying a small bamboo basket of fruit in his hand.

Xiong had not been on too friendly terms with Chen, as she had witnessed just the day before. It was understandable. The Min case had been first assigned to the homicide squad headed by Xiong. Even after being taken over by Internal Security, Detective Xiong was still the one supposed to cooperate on behalf of the Shanghai Police Bureau.

Detective Xiong started by expressing his gratefulness to Chen and Jin.

'You two are just like the legendary team of Chief Inspector Chen and Detective Yu. You surely made a difference to the conclusion of the investigation.'

It sounded quite flattering to her, though a bit embarrassing too, when Xiong added, nodding emphatically, 'Indeed an inseparable team.'

What was he really driving at? But Detective Xiong was moving on, ready to brief her about what had happened since.

It turned out to be a long, comprehensive briefing, with lots of details not known to her before, and lots of explanations and discussions not expected from him.

Obviously, Detective Xiong did not have to go out of his way to make such a detailed account – not to her. And for that matter, not to Chen either.

Did Xiong believe that he owed it to Chen? But for the latter, the conclusion would not have been conceivable. And as an ex-inspector, Chen would have surely liked to know as much as possible, even though he had categorically declared the distance he wanted to keep from the investigation.

Supposing it was awkward for the detective to approach the ex-inspector directly, it then seemed a reasonable move for Detective Xiong to come to her in the office while Chen stayed far away in the mountains.

Still, why all the details and explanations?

The case was already concluded, and she was not an assistant to a chief inspector, unless . . .

Unless Detective Xiong, too, had his reservations about the 'conclusion', the way he had just described it to her.

If so, was it possible that he wanted Chen to probe deeper into it, without saying it in so many words?

After Detective Xiong left, she started pacing about in the office. Presently, her glance fell on a big envelope sent to Chen earlier that morning. It was marked 'extremely urgent'. A number of mails to Chen often appeared so marked, and as a rule, she had them forwarded to Chen by the in-city express carrier – delivered the same day. For today, however, Chen was too far away in the Yellow Mountains.

She also noted that the mail came from the Central Party Discipline Committee of CPC in Beijing.

Moving back to the computer, she started checking the schedule of the long-distance bus to the Yellow Mountains. There was one leaving at half past eleven near the west end of the People's Square, with the bus stop just about a five-minute walk away. It took four hours or so to reach the foot of the Yellow Mountains, she double-checked.

She had no idea as to what could be so urgent in the envelope from Beijing. But as the office secretary, she thought she was justified in making an effort to deliver it as fast as possible, particularly at the critical juncture.

At least it appeared justifiable to herself.

Not exactly like a tourist, Chen reflected, as he absentmindedly stepped out of the hotel.

The hotel manager had recommended a personally guided program for a distinguished guest like Chen, but he wanted to walk just by himself.

The mountain trail was steep, slippery, even treacherous, winding between clumps of larches and ferns, and he had to move very cautiously, at times almost stepping in and out of the gathering clouds. He soon realized he was inappropriately dressed for this activity. In the windless heat, he began sweating profusely, his steps slowing, and his shirt clinging to his body in discomfort.

He tried to rationalize his weariness – because of the physical effect of the changed altitude, or because of his changed attitude toward what had been happening around him, or because of the fact that he was no longer young?

There was no point laboring up and down the mountain trails, climbing from one peak to another – he was quite ready to give up. No mood for it. Nor the energy.

Like a tourist done with hiking, he turned onto a relatively even road for a change, strolling along with more leisured steps, and thought about how to start the first chapter of the Judge Dee novella in a more suspenseful fashion. He had to start writing while in the mountains.

Sometimes, he thought more clearly while walking at an unhurried pace, but in spite of his efforts, his thoughts remained in confusion. It took him just two or three minutes to learn that this was a shopping street, which provided too many distractions. He could not concentrate there.

The street was lined with an impressive array of boutique stores of mountain products, some of them quite antique-like. It saddened him to think of Huang again. He still held himself responsible – to some extent – for the death of the old man.

He had barely moved down a short block, however, when he failed to resist the temptation of a rustic-looking grocery store with a red-painted door and a thatch-decorated roof. He stepped in and browsed among the local products, such as dried bamboo shoots in bundles, pickled fish, Jinhua ham, and some others he could not describe or name. Like a tourist, he chose a bunch of dried bamboo shoots as well as a tiny glass jar of hot fermented tofu, a special Anhui product which he knew his mother liked. Then from a small local gift shop with a bamboo-bead curtain at the door, he purchased a bamboo owl for Old Hunter, a possible companion for his birds at home. At a dainty store with its glass counter displaying an impressive array of ink sticks made of the fabulous local pine smoke, he succumbed again. On the white store wall, he noted a wooden plaque allegedly left behind by a Qing dynasty emperor, praising the premium quality of the locally made sticks. He was particularly impressed with a large ink stick embossed with a golden dragon. Despite the rediscovered 'emperor complex' in today's China, the dragon was no longer used as a decoration exclusively for the emperors. He picked up several glass-and-brocade boxes of ink sticks shaped into turtles, tigers and dragons, with the fronts inscribed with gold characters. All of them were supposedly inspirational for men of letters, though he doubted whether he would ever use the ink stick for writing. *He was not Judge Dee, / nor meant to be . . .* But perhaps one small box of ink sticks could be a souvenir for Jin, a sort of decoration for her desk in the office. He then wondered whether he would ever go to work with her there.

It was around four thirty when he got back to the hotel. Passing by the front desk, he lifted up his purchases in plastic bags like a satisfied tourist.

'A young lady named Jin is waiting for you in the lobby,' the front desk manager said with a smile.

'Jin?'

'Yes, she says she's from Shanghai.'

He pivoted around to the sight of her sitting on a sofa facing the front desk, sipping from a cup of orange juice and listening to music with earpods. A shaft of late afternoon light was streaming in through the large window behind her, streaking her black hair slightly brunette.

From the very beginning, he'd known how capable she was, and then how understanding and caring, and then how surprising.

'What a surprise, Jin. Sorry, I was taking a walk out in the mountains.'

'I have to say sorry, Director Chen, for the unannounced visit. I tried to reach you, on both the hotel phone and your cellphone. No success. I was worried.' She stood up, a bulging satchel flung from her shoulder like a young student.

'Don't be worried about my disappearance. The signal must have been bad in the mountains.'

'A mail marked "extremely urgent" for you, Director Chen,' she said, smiling, producing a large envelope out of the satchel.

'A number of my mails are so marked,' he said, taking the large envelope from her hand without tearing it open. 'You did not have to hurry all the way to the mountains here. Not that I do not appreciate it.'

'It's from the Central Party Discipline Committee of CPC in Beijing. So it's my responsibility, I believe, to deliver it to you as fast as possible,' she said with a knowing smile. 'That's what a secretary's for, right?'

'But it's not easy for you to come all the way from Shanghai.'

'I checked the bus schedule online. A special bus all the way to the terminal at the foot of the mountains, and then a cable car to the hotel. It's easy. I've never been to the mountains before. And I hope, with your approval, I could have the ticket reimbursed as a legitimate business trip.'

'That won't be a problem.'

But that was not the real reason she had hurried over here, he knew. The lobby suddenly became noisy with tourists moving in and out, talking in loud excitement about the wonders of the mountains.

'Believe it or not, I have a grand suite here, the top floor of the hotel, with a super view of the mountains, and a full-stocked minibar as well, all included in the package. Let's go up, Jin. Much more comfortable there.'

The moment they stepped into the suite, she kicked off her shoes and moved barefoot on the soft carpet of the living room like a dancer.

'My poor feet! The cable car broke down this afternoon. So I had to hike all the way up to the hotel. My high heels were killing me.'

'Sorry to hear that, Jin.'

'Nothing for you to say sorry about. I left the office in a hurry, and I forgot to change my shoes for the mountains.'

He leaned down to fetch a pair of hotel slippers for her. She pulled them on, touching at a blister on her bare sole. He felt a touch of awkwardness, standing by her side as if being pulled by invisible strings.

'What a grand suite! It really becomes a high-ranking Party official like you,' she said, her glance sweeping around the lavish living room. 'Almost fit for an emperor.'

'Don't say that. The words "Emperor Yuan" have recently become politically sensitive on websites in China,' he said, raising a finger to his mouth cynically. 'I'm just enjoying a break pushed on to me.'

'I know. The emperor who tried to restore the monarchy system at the beginning of the twentieth century, but without success. And people know what it means in the politics of today's China. Oh, but so many things in the office this morning. I too need a break.' She perched herself on the sofa, taking down the satchel from her shoulder and tucking one foot underneath her.

'Yes, it may be a good idea for you to take a break and look around a bit. It's your first visit to the Yellow Mountains, isn't it? The view here is fantastic. Let's sit out on the balcony.'

She followed him to the balcony, where she noted a wine glass standing alone on a cedar table. He asked her to seat herself there before he turned back into the room. Looking through the balcony window, she could see him leaning over the hotel phone, talking to someone. It was a short talk, and he came back with another glass and a bottle of wine.

He poured out a glass for her, and then one for himself. They touched their glasses, the panoramic view of the mountain ranges unfolding before them like a silk scroll of traditional Chinese landscape painting.

'Look, the celebrated pine blossoming into a pen in the dream,' she exclaimed like a young student. 'I've seen a post-card of it.'

'Yes, after the original tree died, another tree must have been replanted there, and then still another, always on the same spot. The tourists must be so pleased at the sight of it, believing what they see is the original, the magical, the eternal, and they keep posing for pictures or videos with the celebrated pine in the background.'

'For a tourist attraction, people have ways of reviving a

legend, but it is meaningful as long as you believe in it,' she said, echoing his cynical comment.

'Anyway, it may also serve as a sign, if only psychologically, for me to start writing, with the relentless push from Kong for the Judge Dee story.'

'So true!' She was amused at the familiar self-deprecation in his smile. Instead of looking annoyed at her unannounced visit, he seemed to be quite pleased with her company on the balcony.

'Now, before you tell me about things in the office, first, is everything OK with yourself? I'm so sorry about what happened yesterday.'

'I'm fine.' She reached across the table, abruptly, to take up his hand for a closer look. 'It's almost healed, but you still should not touch water.'

They would be in full view – holding hands like lovers – if people happened to look up to the balcony. Perhaps more like a Party official vacationing with his 'little secretary', or 'sextary' in the new WeChat slang, which was said to have been invented by a well-known scholar in his updated new entries for a popular English–Chinese dictionary.

Such pictures were not uncommon on the Internet. Like those in the Judge Jiao scandal, she recalled, blushing in spite of herself. She'd gone to Chen's apartment for the first time because of the office statement for the scandal. It was just about a week ago, yet she felt like she'd known him much longer, though he was still an enigmatic Party-member boss to her at the same time. And she his secretary. That was all there was to it.

'I went to the office this morning as usual, as you may have read in my messages sent to you from there. Oh, I forgot to mention one thing in those text messages. Director Ma promised me a great future in the city government.'

'As long as you do what he wants you to do, I bet.'

'But he doesn't know what *I* want to do? Now apart from the things I told you in the messages, I checked and double-checked the news this morning. Only some very brief, vague mention of the conclusion of the Min case in the official media. Also, Judge Liu called in and he told me that Internal Security had contacted him about the latest development, and it may take some time for them to come up with ideas about how to spin it.

'And then it's Judge Liu's turn to have his show about how great the judicial system works out in the socialism with China's characteristics. Primetime appearance on TV. Another eloquent demonstration of our judicial system under the leadership of the great, glorious Party, and blah-blah-blah,' she said, imitating a well-known anchorwoman on TV. 'But Judge Liu also said to me that he would definitely touch on the excellent work done by our office.'

'Well, what else could an office like ours possibly do?'

She noted the increasingly satirical tone of his question, and she chose not to push.

'Not a single word yet about the release of Min, I presume.' Chen went on without waiting for her response, 'With Zheng in custody, her release should only be a matter of time. In a couple of days, possibly, but with her image so demonized, she would not be able to have those private kitchen dinners any more. Few would want to be associated with the negative coverage.'

'I don't know that much about her in spite of the research done for the office. By the way, just before I left the office, someone surnamed Gu called, leaving a message for you.'

'What message – something to do with our office work?'

'Not really. He said he was going to visit your mother today. He knew you were away on vacation in the mountains, but said you don't have to worry about anything back in Shanghai. He would take good care of her, calling your mother his auntie.'

'He's just impossible. It's all because of my translating a business proposal into English for him years ago, and he keeps saying that he got the first investment loan for the New World because of the English proposal.'

'That Mr Gu! The head of the New World. I've heard such a lot about him.'

'No mention of my Yellow Mountain vacation in any newspapers?'

'No, not yet.'

'Mr Gu learned about my vacation really fast – through his

connections, I believe. I may not have told you, he's actually the one that provided me with the video of the garage, showing Zheng's movements that night.'

So the ex-inspector had done his investigations without her knowledge. That was why he had rushed out to Huang's residence the moment he got her message sent from Zheng's car.

But she was far from being upset. It was a risky gamble for him. He did not know her so well as to tell her everything, and he might not have wanted to drag her through the mire. With all the conspiracies behind the scenes, the less one was exposed to the dire situation, the better.

At least he was sharing it with her now.

'There are so many things connected to one another in this world,' she said, taking a small sip at the wine before she produced another envelope – a smaller one. 'Something else I got just a couple of minutes before leaving the office. The galley page of tomorrow's *Wenhui Daily*. In the literature section it carries an announcement of your forthcoming novella about Judge Dee and the most sensational real murder case in the Tang dynasty. There's also an editor's note.'

Chen shook it out.

> Readers have long waited for something new from Inspector Chen – now Director Chen – who has written and translated a lot in spite of his busy workload. Now *Wenhui* is going to have something new and surprising from him. Instead of a poem, this time we are going to carry the serialization of a Judge Dee novella about the most sensational real murder case in the Tang dynasty. For ages, Western critics have been saying that Chinese writers could not write crime novels, with the exception of the *gong'an* genre, but even in that particular genre, it's a Westerner that did so much better in his Judge Dee stories than Chinese crime writers. So Inspector Chen's going to prove something different for us.

'It's probably written by Kong himself,' she said. 'Indeed, so many things happening at the same time.'

*   *   *

'Room service!'

The doorbell rang insistently.

Chen rose to open the door. A hotel attendant pushed in a cart with several covered platters. With Chen's approval, he placed them on the table in the balcony.

'I've ordered the room service for you,' he said to her after the attendant left with the food cart. 'It's a generous vacation package here. All expenses covered. So why not? In your hurry to take the bus over here for the urgent office business, you may not have had your lunch.'

The deck table turned into a dining table with an impressive array of the mountain specials. Chen lifted the covers and introduced each of them.

'The hotel brochure describes the wok-fried rock frogs as a must-have mountain special. Because of its constant jumping among the rocks, a rock frog's legs are supposed to be particularly sinewy and tasteful. Fermented tofu is another highly recommended local special, like stinking tofu elsewhere, but with a hairy cover on the surface. As for the stinking bass steamed with dried mountain bamboo shoots, it's also a celebrated Anhui delicacy, but I've never had it before. You don't have to touch it if you don't like the smell. And I don't think I need to say anything about white rice porridge with a thousand-year-old egg, salted duck, mountain mushroom, organic cold tofu mixed with chopped green scallions—'

'You should have been sitting at that private kitchen dinner table, Director Chen.'

'So you were saying,' he said, after placing a piece of the frog leg onto her plate, 'so many things happening all at once.'

'Yes. Detective Xiong also visited the office this morning, briefing me on the latest developments,' she said, moistening her lips with the tip of her tongue and taking a sip at the wine. 'About the latest he had just learned from Internal Security.'

'Really!'

'According to Internal Security, Zheng has made a full confession. He killed Qing in the *shikumen* house that night, though he still calls himself an accidental murderer in this case. Done on a moment of impulse.'

Chewing on a frog leg, she ladled a small bowl of porridge for herself and finished it in three or four spoonfuls.

She then went on with a detailed account of what had happened in the *shikumen* house, the way Zheng had told Internal Security.

Long before that fatal dinner, Zheng had heard a lot from Huang about the private kitchen parties at Min's *shikumen* house. Huang, a lone old man, was pleased to find an enthusiastic listener in Zheng, a division of labor that suited both of them. Zheng was not a gourmet, but Huang's constant raving about Min as a consummate Republican Lady prompted him to search the Internet, which instilled into him a passion he had never known before. It soon developed into an obsession. He following her blog posts and collected the clippings about her. Far from being wealthy or powerful enough to be placed even on her waiting list, he knew better than to try to approach her. 'It's like admiring the moon in the night sky; it is more than enough to feel the streaming softness of the moonlight.'

But Zheng could not help blabbing to others about his infatuation. And to Huang, too. Any crumb of information from the old man about her came to him like another hopeful straw. When Huang decided not to go to her place that Friday night, he let Zheng fill the unexpected opening. It was an extraordinary opportunity for Zheng to cultivate some connections there for himself.

Sitting at the same table with her was more than Zheng had dreamed of. He was flabbergasted, not so much with the unheard-of delicacies, as with her unimaginable charm and gracefulness, as if he too had been transported to the Republican period in her company.

To his surprise, she started downing Maotai like water after making that unexpected toast to the maid. The scene broke his heart. He became so upset with the ungrateful maid, even though he hardly knew anything about her.

Shortly afterward, it became obvious that Min could barely sit still at the table, her hand trembling, spilling a spoon of chicken soup over Zheng's lap. Looking at each other in embarrassment, the guests suggested that she should go to bed. Zheng, the youngest among them, offered to help her back to the bedroom.

Before he put her down on the bed, she began throwing up, making a mess of her mandarin dress. Trying to remove the soiled dress, he found himself incapable of taking his eyes away from her half-naked body – until he heard footsteps hurrying over to the bedroom. Seized by an inexplicable impulse at the sight of a bunch of keys on the nightstand, he pocketed them without thinking before the maid stepped into the room.

He had no choice but to leave. The maid dutifully saw him out of the *shikumen* house. Outside, he saw Kong of *Wenhui Daily* waiting for his car at the lane entrance. He exchanged a few words with him and headed to the garage of the Pacific Ocean Shopping Mall.

It took him just about five minutes to reach the entrance of the garage, but he slowed down to a sudden stop without going in. A black Lincoln Town Car was pulling out, looming like a nocturnal monster against the surrounding darkness. He stared hard at it in confusion, but among all the entangling thoughts, one was intensely clear. He had to see Min again that night.

And for that night only, he would be able to have the chance of his lifetime – with her still wasted, unable to wake up anytime soon, with the keys in his pocket. He could sneak back into the *shikumen* house under the cover of night. It was an opportunity he could not afford to lose.

Afterward, he would put back the keys on the nightstand, as if nothing had happened.

But he was cautious enough to walk around the lane a couple of times first. Huang had told him, he recollected, that the maid usually left shortly after the dinner. So he waited about half an hour before he re-entered the lane through its back entrance.

He got into the *shikumen* house without having met any problem. A night light was flickering in the shadowy courtyard, but he saw and heard nobody moving inside the house. He headed directly to her bedroom. She was lying in bed like before, sleeping half naked in a drunken stupor. Assuming that only two of them were there in the entire *shikumen* house, he started to remove her remaining clothing before he pounced on her, like in a dream.

But he must have made some noise. Out of nowhere, Qing appeared at the bedroom door like an apparition, staring aghast at the scene of his body pressing against Min's. Instantly, Qing turned to run away, too horrified even to shout out for help.

He jumped down, chased her across the dining room and into the kitchen with only a night light on, where he caught up with her. Panic-stricken, she grabbed a heavy food processor from the kitchen counter, making a desperate attempt to fend him off. He wrenched it out of her hand and struck it hard at her head with all his might, lightning-quick in the semi-darkness.

Swaying, she fell to the floor as he let the processor drop, still panting and unbelieving. It was not until one or two minutes later that he realized what had happened. He looked around in a daze. The house was wrapped in a shroud of silence.

But he decided not to call for help. She would have spoken out if brought round. He leaned over her unconscious body and checked for her breath. Unable to feel any, he turned on the light in the kitchen. Her lips now looked bluer, colder. It was probably too late, anyway.

Checking around, he collected himself enough to clean any possible fingerprints from the objects he had touched.

Then he moved back into the bedroom, where he found Min still sleeping heavily, undisturbed. And there he also cleaned up thoroughly before he put back the keys on the nightstand.

Remembering there might be some people still moving in the lane, he waited for another half hour, sitting beside Min's bed, gazing at her sleeping naked there, trying to keep the image etched in his memory, without doing anything else. Then, as he finally sneaked out of the *shikumen* house, he made sure to leave the front door properly locked.

Walking toward the garage in the surrounding darkness, he

saw some neon lights along Huaihai Road still changing their lonely projections, which struck him like will-o'-the-wisps in a deserted graveyard.

It was a fairly long account narrated by Jin, and Chen listened in absorption, hardly making any interruption, except to warm another bowl of rice porridge and a plate of fried rock frogs in the microwave for her. Most of the mountain specials remained barely touched on the table.

'I must have been too carried away by the *shikumen* murder case,' she said, a grain of rice stuck in the corner of her mouth, and she touched it with a pink napkin.

What Zheng had said was probably true, at least for quite a large part, Chen reflected, nodding.

Zheng had had no idea that Min could have been so drunk that night, and that he would have the opportunity to carry her into the bedroom, where he obtained the keys without being detected. He left with the other guests, but the keys in his pocket made him come back to the *shikumen* house with the devilish plan. As for Qing's stumbling upon the scene of his attacking the unconscious Republican Lady, it was too much of a shock for both of them.

'Perhaps not that unpremeditated, according to Internal Security,' Jin added reflectively. 'Their search at his home yielded an incredible number of pictures and clippings of Min.'

'What about Huang's murder then?' he said, changing the subject abruptly.

'Just as you reconstructed yesterday. Zheng learned from Huang that you two had talked about things concerning that night, and that you were going to see Huang again for some antique business. Zheng became paranoid about it.'

'But I had no plan to see Huang again anytime soon. Antique consultation was nothing but a pretext on my part, as you may have guessed.'

'Well, that's what Huang had said to him after his meeting with you in the Old Half Place. Zheng could not stand the uncertainty. Since he knew about Huang's passion for the rice balls, he followed Huang out the next morning – all the way to the street corner stall. With no one else there in the area at that early hour, he crept up from behind and struck at the old man's head with a hammer he carried with him. Huang fell with just one violent stroke.'

'He carried a hammer with him?'

'Yes, Internal Security has recovered the hammer at his home. He did not even have the time to get rid of it. The blood stain on the hammer proved to be Huang's.'

'But why so paranoid about my visit to Huang? It's true that Huang told me about Zheng being impressed with Min, after having heard stories from the old man and seeing pictures of her online. That's one of the reasons why Huang let him go to the dinner party that night. But so many people would have jumped at the opportunity. Zheng's going there did not appear suspicious to me. Definitely not when Huang told me about it.'

'There's something else about things between Huang and Zheng,' she said, picking up a piece of the celebrated stinking fish meat, smelling it, and putting it back on her small plate with an apologetic smile. 'At first, Zheng's job for Huang was that of an errand boy. Huang had him go to several Anhui villages for antique-hunting, with the minimum pay plus the expenses and a smart phone. Zheng would send pictures of those he saw as potentially valuable to Huang, who would decide whether to purchase them or not. The arrangement worked well. Huang was too old, and too rich, to make trips to those poor, backward villages. A farmer in Anhui before coming to Shanghai, Zheng was able to approach those uneducated farmers for incredible bargains. A bronze three-foot urn of the Zhou dynasty purchased for fifty yuan from a poor villager, for instance, was later auctioned for two million yuan. After several domestic trips, Zheng was sent abroad as well. In Italy, he obtained several precious pieces from a retired woman, whose great-grandfather came to China as a soldier during the Boxer Uprising in the late Qing dynasty. These brought in even more incredible profits back in Shanghai. And it did not take long for Zheng, now an indispensable right-hand man to Huang, to become aware of how much the antique collector had made from these deals. A shrewd and experienced businessman, Huang raised Zheng's pay, but not in proportion to the profits made, and he never shared with Zheng any secrets of the trade. Zheng could not help feeling resentful toward him.

'Huang had no children. Though not a real nephew, Zheng still hoped that Huang would leave him some of the valuable antiques obtained through his efforts. Huang kept saying, however, that he would donate all his collections to a museum in his name. So Zheng managed to get hold of Huang's desk drawer key, which he reproduced in secret, and an examination of Huang's will confirmed that the old man meant what he said. That was another reason for Zheng to plan something. After all, nobody else knew more about the value of Huang's collection than Zheng, and about where the old man kept his most treasured pieces. The murder in the *shikumen* house triggered the killing.'

'No, all these I did not know. Greed plus fear – the two of them combined to make the murderous motive for him,' he said, nodding.

'From their own perspective, people always see themselves as justified to want more, and always worry too much about what they may lose.'

'Well said, Jin. With the murderer caught, I pray Huang may rest in peace. Perhaps I may be able to do something for the museum Huang had planned to create in his name. But what has Detective Xiong said about the murder in the hotel?'

'I've read about the murder in the Moller Villa Hotel online, but those bits and pieces are not that reliable, a lot of guesswork, you know, and you have never told me anything about it, Director Chen.'

'Things happened too fast over the last two or three days, Jin. I did not know whether it was really related to the Min case. And I did not know what to tell or not tell you, honestly, with Internal Security prowling in the background.'

'I understand,' she said, without pushing further. 'According to Detective Xiong, Zheng told Internal Security that he became less and less sure about Min's total unawareness that night. She was drunk, but she could have recalled something, and that would spell the end for him. So he sneaked into the hotel to put her out of the way.'

'No, that does not add up. And hardly a credible motive either. Besides, how could Zheng have found out about Min's staying in that hotel without inside information? He's not a man with government connections like . . .'

He did not finish up saying the name of Sima, the mysterious client who had informed Old Hunter of the hotel where Min was being kept in secret.

'That's a good point, Director Chen. It beats me too, but I know little about the murder case in the hotel.'

'And the hotel is so well guarded. Impossible for a novice like Zheng to sneak in without being detected, let alone to commit such an elaborate crime all by himself.'

'Well, that's the confession Zheng made to Internal Security, at least so Detective Xiong said. And that's about all I've learned from him.'

It was a longer briefing than he had anticipated. And possibly even longer if he had raised the questions he wanted to – especially those about the murder in the hotel.

But Jin had hardly known any details about the hotel murder case, or the background of it. To discuss it with her in detail, he also had to answer a lot of questions, and he did not know how to. And too much knowledge might not be to her benefit. The ex-inspector decided not to push further.

He produced a cigarette, shook his head apologetically, and put it back.

'Go ahead if you want,' she said.

'No, but thank you – for everything.'

A short spell of silence ensued in the room.

When she looked up again, the dusk was falling over the mountains.

'Oh it's late, Director Chen. I have to go back. There's still a bus leaving for Shanghai, before six thirty, I think.'

'But the cable car broke down this afternoon – you have just told me about it, haven't you? I don't think you can make it to the bus terminal in time. And it may not be safe for you to walk down the mountain trail alone in the failing light.'

'It won't be a problem—'

'Let me make the call,' he said, cutting her off like the real boss he was, as he produced his cellphone, starting to search for a number.

'What are you looking for?' she said in confusion.

'The number of the general manager of the hotel here. It is fully booked, but he may somehow have a room for me. It gets dark quickly in the mountains. The steps and trails can be quite slippery.'

'But no need to bother,' she said on a moment of impulse, much to her own surprise. 'It's such a large suite, I mean the guest room is probably better than a standard room.'

But he was already speaking on the phone.

'General Manager Gang, this is Chen Cao staying at the grand suite of your hotel.'

'Oh, Director Chen. Anything can I do for you today?'

'I ran across a friend in the mountains this afternoon. Can you arrange a room for her? Just for one night. It's too late for her to go down by herself.'

'The hotel is fully booked, but for that friend of yours, let me try my best. I'll call you back in a couple of minutes, Director Chen.'

In less than two minutes, Gang called back, saying the hotel was fully occupied, with only one room left for the hotel staff to stay overnight in some unexpected circumstances. A room not good enough for a hotel guest, not adequately furnished, but clean, convenient, on the same floor.

Chen accepted the arrangement and thanked the hotel manager profusely.

'It may not be a fancy room,' he said, turning toward her with a smile, 'but I think I can stay there for the night. This is the only suite directly connected to the celebrated mountain spring through a special pipe. Ordinary tourists have to stand in long lines waiting three or four hours for their turn to enjoy the spring water bath in a large pool. A really special treatment, supposedly beneficial to your health, though you don't have to believe that it's as miraculous as described in the hotel brochure.'

'But how can you make such a suggestion, my director?' she said, pulling on her shoes. 'Of course I'll go to the staff room. Period. The general manager will not be able to fall asleep, I bet, if a high-ranking Party official like you actually stays overnight in a hotel staff member room.'

Left alone in the suite, Chen tore open the large envelope Jin had carried over from Shanghai. Inside was a letter from Comrade Zhao, his 'political patron', the ex-Party Secretary of the Central Party Discipline Committee of CPC, who still had influence within the Forbidden City.

> Chen:
>   Glad to learn about your excellent work at the new office. Come to Beijing for a three-week seminar at the Central Party School after your vacation in the mountains. We are talking about a judicial system reform office at the central government level in Beijing. You're one of those on the shortlist for the position. I have recommended you as a man capable of taking things into consideration in the larger picture for China.
>   Zhao

For a personal letter written in such an official language, a number of interpretations were possible. It could have been read as a positive sign, indicating some room still available for him in the Party system. The proposed new office position, if really meant for him, meant an advance – at least in terms of the Party cadre rank. At the same time, it was possibly a bad sign too, which would put him further out of the city of Shanghai. And out of police work, too.

Besides, how could Comrade Zhao – staying far away in Beijing – have learned so fast about his 'excellent work' in Shanghai and his vacation in the mountains?

He popped open a can of Starbucks coffee. Taking a small sip, he started pacing about in the room, and going over in his mind what Jin had just told him about the case.

In a nutshell, the Min case was concluded – concluded in a way acceptable to the people high above – like Comrade Zhao, and possibly to the rival factions at the top, too.

As a result, the ex-inspector now had to shut up regarding all the misgivings he had about the conclusion of the case.

Detective Xiong might have shared some of his misgivings. Particularly those about the murder at the Moller Villa Hotel, which could have prompted him to visit Jin in person. After all, Wanxia had worked under him in the homicide squad, and Detective Xiong felt responsible for her.

Chen too could not bring himself to take Zheng as the murderer at the hotel, but the ex-inspector was in no position to prove otherwise.

For the moment, he was 'exiled' in the mountains, and then to a seminar in Beijing, possibly under closer surveillance, and further away from the city of Shanghai.

Perhaps he could try to spread his misgivings about the conclusion of the Min case – with the help of Jin – through WeChat and other social media platforms. But his theory about the murder in the hotel was just another possible scenario, not necessarily any more convincing than the official one, which was at least backed up by the 'confession' made by Zheng. For the real murderer in the hotel, there must have been a specific reason, which the ex-inspector thought he could only guess without saying out loud.

Furthermore, what was the point dragging Jin further into trouble? She had done so much for him, and that possibly at her expense. Director Ma of the city government would no longer see her as one of the people the Party authorities could trust. A young, vivacious girl, she should have a promising future.

But what about Wanxia in the Moller Villa Hotel? A young, vivacious girl, who should also have had a promising future.

With his glance sweeping over the mountains silhouetted against the growing dusk, he seemed to hear the murmuring of a cascade, somewhere not too far away, in a rustle of the pines from the depth of the valley. And he glimpsed a faint flickering light in the distance.

What could that possibly be?

Against the woods and hills, the tiny light gleamed for a second and was gone.

Thousands of years before, someone else – possibly Judge Dee – had stood here, looking at the night-enveloped mountains under the deep glitter of the stars.

The same mountains, the same moonlight, and the same wind.

The same question, perhaps.

But what question?

Taking a deep breath, Chen tried to dispel the confusion of these ideas. He was not a high-ranking official like Judge Dee, who was able to make a real difference in the cruel, complicated Tang politics.

From the very beginning, different factions within the Forbidden City had tried to weigh in on the Min case from their respective angles, and he was in no position to do something about it even now, with a fairly clear picture in his mind.

Min had been connected with *someone* at the top. With Qing murdered in the *shikumen* house, his rival must have taken it as an opportunity to launch the attack. That accounted for the appearance of the mysterious client Sima, who tried to clear Min's name by enlisting the help of Old Hunter's agency with an incredible offer. But the power struggle in the Forbidden City must have escalated rapidly. The possibility that Min could have talked under the increasing pressure of *shuanggui* had thrown *someone* into a panic. In order to forestall it, she was to be silenced once and for all in the hotel, but the murderer had no idea that instead of Min, it was Wanxia who took the night meal.

As for Zheng, it made no difference for him to make such a 'confession' to Internal Security, saying whatever they wanted him to say. He had killed both Qing and Huang; it mattered not for him to add one more to the confession.

It did not take long for Chen to find his mind worn out with all those plausible and not-that-plausible speculations. He decided to take a mountain spring bath in the suite, a privilege for a distinguished guest. Hopefully its 'miraculous effect', as promised in the hotel brochure, could wash away the worries and revive him a bit.

But he was discomforted at the color of the brownish water flowing into the tub, possibly discolored with some mineral deposit, but more probably, he reflected with a wry smile, with some rust from the pipe. Instead of immersing himself for a long and luxurious bath, he got out of the tub in less than ten minutes and wrapped himself in a white terry robe.

He lay stretching out on the sofa, ready to close his eyes for a while.

Then came a light knocking on the door, tentatively, in the enveloping silence of the night.

He jumped up and opened the door to the sight of her standing barefoot in a white terry robe – like his double in the mountain hotel.

It struck him with a sense of déjà vu as he took in the details of her framed in the doorway, her shoulder-length hair still wet under the soft light.

'Come on in, Jin.'

'You're not sleeping, Director Chen?' she said, her eyes dreamy-looking, as if focusing on something distant.

'No. Are you?'

Both the question and the answer seemed to be redundant.

'I saw the light from under your door, so I thought . . .' she said in embarrassment, touching at her slightly wet hair. 'The shower in my bathroom broke down after just one minute—'

'Of course you can use my bathroom, which is connected to the mountain spring, as I've told you.'

'Thank you,' she said, smiling with a sudden twinkle in her eyes before stepping past him.

Watching her disappearing into the bathroom, he was in no mood to lie back on the sofa.

He felt restless, listening to the water gurgling in the bathroom. It was hard for him not to let his mind wander under such a starry night.

She seemed to have never let him go, not even in the night-covered mountains. But he soon ridded himself of the thought. For a young, bright, attractive, hard-working girl like her, she had been simply doing an extraordinary job as a secretary to the office.

And for a trouble-plagued, middle-aged man like him, he could hardly take care of himself at the moment, much less a young girl of great expectations.

He rose, moved to the window, and stood there with his hands resting on the sill. He pushed open the window a little, hoping that the fresh night air could help to cool him down.

The moonlight streaming fair, soft on the peaks, the night air was sweet. In the distance, the mountain ridges looked like undulating waves in 'Dover Beach' by Matthew Arnold.

Thousands of years earlier, Judge Dee could have looked out at a night scene just like this, writing a poem, or contemplating a difficult case, in the middle of his own troubles in the fierce Tang power struggle around the throne—

Something buzzing in his robe pocket brought him back to the present. He took out the phone. It was a WeChat message from Kong.

'Some of Xuanji's love poems will come out in the newspaper tomorrow, like a prologue to the serialization of your novella. So excited about it. *Shanghai Daily* is interested in the English version.'

It was just another cunning push from Kong, but Chen did not feel obliged to immediately respond to the message.

And then came another message, in which Kong enclosed several links to poetry readings in English, saying they were from *Shanghai Daily*. Absentmindedly, Chen clicked one of the links.

He was then lost in the reading of a poem by a British actor with a deep, singularly sad voice. What a coincidence! It happened to be one of his favorite poems, also about such a starry night, with the poet looking out of the window, thinking not just about the present, but the past too . . .

'*The sea of faith was once—*'

He did not even hear the door of the bathroom opening, and her moving light-footedly across to him – not until she came to stand beside him by the window.

And he turned off the recording of the reading.

She remained standing by his side, her terry robe brushing against his. She seemed not to be in a hurry to move back to her own room.

Neither of them said a word for a minute or two.

'Still dwelling on the conclusion of the case, my director?'

'No point dwelling on speculations,' he said, aware of her wet hair touching his shoulder before changing the subject. 'Thank you for introducing me to WeChat.'

'Why?'

'I was just looking out, and listening to the reading of a poem through WeChat. It's so convenient.'

'What poem?'

'"Dover Beach" by Matthew Arnold.' He fast-moved the cursor toward the ending of the poem.

> *For the world, which seems*
> *To lie before us like a land of dreams,*
> *So various, so beautiful, so new,*
> *Hath really neither joy, nor love, nor light,*
> *Nor certitude, nor peace, nor help for pain—*

'Hold on. I think I've read a collection of English poetry translations you have done, including that poem. "*And we are here as on a darkling plain, / Swept with confused alarms of struggle and flight, / Where ignorant armies clash by night.*" That's the very ending of the poem, right? I love that poem.'

'Right. And it's one of the saddest love poems, as if the world without joy, love, light, peace, or help for pain, provided the only justification for two people to be true to each other. The only thing that comes with a sort of certitude.' He added like in afterthought, 'I was thinking of Xuanji, the heroine in the Judge Dee story—'

'For Xuanji in your Judge Dee story, did she ever stand at the window in the company of someone really caring for her, looking out together to the night with certitude? I've read some more material about the ill-starred Tang poetess, but I don't know. And for that matter, I doubt it about Min too.'

He felt her leaning against his shoulder, her wet hair touching his face, and her hand touching his, lightly—

All of a sudden, a furious flapping sound against the window startled them apart. Looking out, he thought he discerned something black hovering close to the pane. Possibly a night bird that had lost its way back home, flustering against the lit window, he supposed. But at such a height? He pushed open the window.

To his astonishment, it turned out to be a black-painted drone – the size of a large black raven.

It was perhaps just an uncanny coincidence in the dark night, but as an ex-cop, he did not believe it.

'Following us all the way here?' She was echoing his thoughts, her hand grasping his in panic.

'You're worrying too much, Jin. Wealthy people fly drones like kites.'

'Even up in the mountains?'

He did not have to answer. It was a rhetorical question, he knew.

He was suddenly consumed with rage. Even in the mountains, he still would not be let alone . . .

And he was not alone.

Outside the window, the mountains seemed to be nearly lost in darkness, though some peaks and ridges remained dimly visible at a distance.

'I think I have to go to Beijing for a seminar,' he said to the inquiring look in her eyes. 'A seminar for Party cadres.'

'What does that mean?'

'Your guess is as good as mine.'

'But I don't know how to guess.'

'Perhaps, out of sight, out of mind . . .' He did not finish the sentence. 'But for now, I can still enjoy the spring bath here. At least for a week or so, and hopefully I can finish the Judge Dee novella before leaving for Beijing. You'll be the first reader of the manuscript, Jin, I promise you. Your history major will surely make a difference. You have been so helpful.'

'You should have watched those Judge Dee TV movies. They don't care about the accuracy of historical detail.' She went on, abruptly switching to another subject, 'But do you think that the arrangement of the seminar in Beijing is a bit strange? You're still on convalescent leave.'

'What those people in Beijing have in mind, you may never be able to figure out.'

'A preparatory step for you to move to a higher position?'

'It's open to interpretation, but I don't think so.'

'Can you tell whether you will come back to the office?'

'No, I can't.'

She grasped his hand tighter.

'And you don't even know whether our office will still be there – if and when you come back.'

'The office was set up just about a month ago, you know, as I was removed from my position in the Shanghai Police Bureau. Indeed, "*History has many cunning passages, contrived corridors / And issues . . .*" Sorry, I'm being Eliotic again.'

'One thing I still remember of those history lessons I took in college. All history is the present history. People always read and interpret history from their own perspective at the present moment. So why worry about what other people have said.'

'Yes, the moment we speak, the present is already turning into the past.'

'So what we have is only the present moment, which is fleeting. And what will happen tomorrow? No one knows,' she said, not releasing his hand. 'But for tonight, I'm here – with you.'

He was taken by surprise. If he had not thought about her as the one for him, it was mainly because of his own trouble. No point dragging down a lovely young girl with him, he had told himself, subconsciously if not consciously. The thought that she should have a bright future for herself had banished other thoughts coming to his mind.

But the conspiracies of the circumstances, as if joined link by link in a long, invisible 'red rope' in an ancient Chinese tale, were bringing them together at this moment, standing by the hotel window that looked out to the mountains being lost in the dark.

She was turning to him, grasping him in her arms, and gazing with an unmistakable message in her eyes – perhaps the same message as on the day she first stepped into his apartment . . .

A message that was now defying the black evil iron drone buzzing, hovering outside the window here.

He found himself not afraid of fighting back. Now he had another reason to fight, not just for himself.

Smiling, he touched her wet hair.

They embraced each other.

Afterwards, he said quietly to her, 'We have the mountains to ourselves.'

She whispered a throaty agreement, curling up against him before she fell asleep in his arms.

He was wondering at the sensation of being above and beyond the earth, perhaps due to the elevation of the hotel, which stood over one thousand feet above sea level. Looking up, he was surprised with a vision of the white clouds surging through the window, pressing against her sweat-covered back, her black hair flowing in the soft moonlight. Her body felt soft, almost insubstantial, like the clouds after the rain in the mountains.

It reminded him of a celebrated rhapsody composed by Song Yu, a poet in the second century BC, about the liaison of King Chu Xiang and the Wu Mountain Goddess. Clinging to the king, the Goddess promised she would come back to him in the clouds and rain. It turned into a breath-taking metaphor for sexual love in classical Chinese literature.

Their feet brushed. Touching her arched sole, he felt something, a grain of sand stuck between her toes. Possibly from the mineral deposit in the spring bath water.

Drowsiness was beginning to take over, peacefully, like the night covering the mountains.

But he was startled by a hoarse, long-drawn-out sound across the valley.

As he was blinking in the night light of the room, the sound was repeated several times in the distance. So disoriented was he, he had a feeling that the sound came, eerily, from another world.

The disorientation was intensified by the sight of her sleeping, nestling against him.

Deep, deep in the mountains, as Li Bai had written lyrically in the Tang dynasty, the realities of the world seemed to be so far away. The sound was probably just a white owl's call, not too unusual in the area. Turning over, he reached for his watch. It was almost midnight. An owl's hoot was supposed to be ominous, according to the traditional folklore, especially when heard deep in the morning. He felt uneasy. Rubbing his eyes, he made an effort to shake off the feeling.

There was no reason to suspect that it would turn out to be a bad day – with her beside him.

He finally sank into sleep.

DAY SEVEN

For Chen, it was the first dreamless night for months.

He woke up feeling refreshed, recharged, when he realized and reached out.

No one was lying beside him in the bed.

On the nightstand, there was nothing but a note staring at him in the glaring morning light: 'I have to hurry back to the office on the first Yellow Mountain bus to Shanghai. As your secretary, I have to take care of things there. Don't worry about it. Enjoy your well-deserved vacation in the mountains. Thanks for everything, Director Chen.'

So she had spent the night with him here.

He was not exactly disappointed with her leaving like that, though the note came almost like an anti-climax. After such a night in the mountains, it appeared as if nothing had happened there.

On second thoughts, it might have been just as well. They were high in the mountains under the cover of night, disoriented at such an altitude of the Cloud Sea Hotel, but they had to come down, one way or another.

She was probably on the morning bus back to Shanghai right now.

For a girl of the younger generation, a night in the mountains might not have meant a lot.

And he was too old – at least too old-fashioned – for her, not to mention all the troubles he had landed himself in.

At the moment, a complication in his personal life was the last thing he wanted. Still, it had happened. Whether it would happen again, he did not know. But he was grateful.

> *Not expecting miracle again,*
> *But glad to have been staying*
> *Beside you with the rain*
> *And the cloud unfolding,*

Against the night mountain,
And grateful for its happening.

Not exactly his own lines, he brooded in self-satire, but inspired by Louis MacNeice's poem titled 'The Sunlight on the Garden' which was written in the days after his wife left him.

The personal aside, it was also a disappointing ending to the investigation for the ex-inspector.

Nothing to his credit, which was the least of his worries. Nothing he could do about Min's damaged life. While he did not have too much sympathy for the Republican Lady, that was not to justify the Party system intent on crushing her for its political interest. Nothing he could do about Wanxia's death, either. What Comrade Zhao had said in terms of taking into consideration the larger picture for China was another reminder to him. In the 'larger picture for China', Wanxia's death had to be conveniently explained as the work of a diabolical murderer who was to be executed anyway for the other crimes he had committed. But Chen could no longer bring himself to toe the line. In spite of the one-of-us tone of Comrade Zhao's letter, he now refused to see himself as 'one of the system'. It was a point of no return for him, he knew.

For years, he had kept telling himself that things in China could not change overnight, and that he should be content like others, as he was doing all he could to facilitate the change. It was for the country, and for himself too – whether as an ex-inspector or the director of the Judicial System Reform Office. Self-realization would be more likely, as he had read long ago, in something larger than oneself. But whatever had to be done, he was determined it should not be done at the expense of law and justice.

A long-distance phone call came in, to his surprise, from a TV producer surnamed Bi in Beijing. After a brief introduction, Bi brought up his proposal:

'Your Judge Dee novella is an excellent one. Professor Zhong highly recommended it to me, and told me about the exciting storyline. Tell you what. I immediately made up my mind.

'It has all the makings of a huge box office success. Murder, beauty, love, fox spirit, sex, conspiracies high up. What's more, we don't have to worry about censorship. It's a Tang dynasty story.

'And you yourself can write the screenplay. Or work with someone else. What do you say, Director Chen? I've already talked to a couple of investors. All of them are really interested in the project. One suggests that you shall serve as a deputy producer for the TV series.'

'Really!' That was about all he could manage in response on the phone.

'We will be sending you the contract tomorrow, Director Chen. We're looking forward to a long-term working relationship with you.'

Things were developing so fast. People already took him as a writer or even scriptwriter more than anything else. The ex-inspector shook his head at his blurred reflection in the window looking out to the mountains.

In the meantime, the newspaper would begin to serialize the novella next week. He had to give the first five to ten pages to Kong, plus something like a prologue to start with. He was not at all sure what the novella would actually turn out to be like.

Having just gone through the latest investigation, he knew it would be a story quite different from Gulik's, almost a subversion of it. Nevertheless, it might work.

There could be quite a few days left for him in the mountains. In Comrade Zhao's letter, the ex-inspector was told to come to Beijing for the seminar after the mountain vacation, yet without a specific date.

So it meant that he might be able to complete the novella, he contemplated, while vacationing.

Publication and loyalty aside, it would serve as a test of the feasibility of his starting a new career. And also as a way for him to get off the hook as a full-time writer for the moment. At the same time, it might remain as a cover for him if he were to go on writing as a cop.

And according to Kong, *Shanghai Daily*, the English newspaper of the city, was interested in the English version of the novella. So they would like to have Xuanji's poems translated into English first, as a test of the reaction of the non-Chinese readers.

> *The verdant trees stretching long*
> *along the desolate bank, a tower*
> *distantly dissolving into the faint mist,*
> *the petals falling over an angler's shoulder,*
> *with the reflections spreading*
> *on the water of the autumn river . . .*

Xuanji had dreamed of something like a recluse's life in a poem of hers, but in vain; with luck, he could probably spend a week like that, writing undisturbed in the mountains covered in the verdant trees.

Then came another familiar ringing from his silver-colored phone. A WeChat message from Jin, he guessed. Instead of a message, it presented a selfie of Jin, sitting against the bus window, pressing a finger against her lips. He refrained from reading too much into the meaning of her pose.

Putting down the phone, he wondered whether he could add a note at the end of the story, saying, 'The juxtaposition of the past and the present. Written in the midst of the investigation into the Min case.'

Failing that, something like Gulik's postscript at the end of *Poets and Murder*, mentioning his reservations about the Xuanji case in a subtle parallel to 'a present case' he'd just looked into. Some close-reading readers should be able to pick up the clues.

So he was ready to start the Judge Dee novella in earnest.

ACKNOWLEDGMENTS

Thanks to Glen Barclay, whose email inspired me with the original idea for a book about Inspector Chen in contemporary China in comparison with Judge Dee in ancient China.